MOON PROMISE

THE WILD PACK
BOOK 1

CARMEN FOX

Moon Promise
Copyright © 2018 by Carmen Fox All rights reserved.
Website: www.carmen-fox.com
First Print Edition: 2018

Edited by Dylan Quinn

ISBN: 978-1-911573-06-7

Proofread by Sharon Gibson and Kallysten

Cover Design by Ana Grigoriu

Formatting: Streetlight Graphics

First published by Smart Heart Publishing 2018

Nana

WYWH

Acknowledgments

Books are written in isolation, but many wonderful people did many wonderful things to get Moon Promise from my desk into your hands. Dylan, Ana, Shaz, Kally, Carole—I thank you all.

My gratitude also belongs to you, my reader. You take my worlds and enrich them with your enthusiasm and kindness.

Garry Rodgers has helped me tremendously with his extensive knowledge of all things dead. Garry, you've been amazing. Any mistakes I made are entirely my own.

I also want to thank my mother for her unwavering support. Without her, my life would be a mess.

ONE

SINGING AT A VOLUME THAT might pierce most human eardrums, I tapped my fingers to the track on the radio. My white Ford Fusion Saloon, a recent purchase, smoothly ascended State Highway 119. At the apex of the hill, the sun exploded into my vision and blinded me for a second.

The long bed truck came out of nowhere.

My fingers clenched around the steering wheel as I flashed through my options. A pickup to my left. Shoulder to my right.

No way out.

I slammed on the brakes until my teeth fused together. The tires screeched. My Ford came to a halt two feet from the truck some idiot had abandoned in the middle of the lane.

Damn, that had been close. If my car and its brake system hadn't been brand-new, or if I'd traveled another ten inches, I'd have been a footnote in history. I took a deep breath of *eau de singed rubber* and rolled my shoulders to shake off the stiffness that had seized my body. If my reactions hadn't been lightning fast—

A violent jerk propelled me forward, knocking my head and

spine out of alignment. The seat belt cut painfully into my chest. Then, a loud bang.

Maybe I'd blacked out, maybe not. My neck felt like it had been snapped in half, yet it wasn't the pain that had woken me to my predicament, but a siren that blared without mercy. That, and the smoke billowing around me.

I rattled the door, swung it open, and clambered, almost fell, out of my vehicle, coughing, gasping for air.

A hand helped me up.

"Are you all right?" A guy, maybe in his early twenties, led me toward the shoulder.

I ran my hand across the base of my skull. The area was tight and sore, as if I'd been craning my neck for hours watching a one-sided tennis match.

"Can you hear me?" the guy asked. His baseball cap largely obscured his face, but his voice rang with concern.

Through my dark sunglasses, permanent shadows bathed the road and cars. Even though my car wasn't on fire, both airbags had deployed and its nose had accordioned into the rear of the truck. My trunk hadn't fared any better, seeing how a big-ass SUV had smacked the hell out of it.

The siren continued droning.

Not a siren. The noise came from my car's horn and ran roughshod over my nerves. Why hadn't anyone taken a sledgehammer to it yet?

"Hey, lady." The guy scratched his arm, which had a warm brown tone that made his white T-shirt seem luminescent.

"Yeah. I'm fine." I rubbed my neck again. "Is anyone hurt?"

"I don't know, but I don't think so. The jeep's driver and her sister are on the phone, and I have no idea where the owner of the truck is. What a great place to break down, right?" He shaded his face with a hand against his forehead. "Can I call anyone for you?"

I lifted my sunglasses onto my head. "What's your name?"

"Mark. That's my car." He pointed at a banged-up saloon that stood some distance behind the SUV. At least, he'd managed to brake in time. "Well, my dad's."

"I'm Kensi." I withdrew my phone from my jacket pocket.

"You want me to do anything for you?"

"If you don't mind, you could call the police and maybe take some pictures for my insurance." I found the number I was looking for and pressed dial. "Thanks."

Mark nodded and headed away with his cell in his hand.

"Hello." Jonah and I had never met in person, only conversed by email in the past, but his voice was as I'd imagined: smooth and authoritative.

When I explained my situation, he went into alpha mode. To me, he was all comfort and warmth, while he barked orders in the background. His no-nonsense efficiency earned him some brownie points. I could almost forgive the methods he'd used to lure me from a breezy Chicago to his hometown in Colorado in the middle of an unprecedented heat wave.

Once Jonah had assured me help was on the way, I hung up, rearranged my beige culottes, then made sure my white blouse was tucked in and inspected my jacket. Its three-quarter sleeves were creased from my drive, even though the shop where I'd bought it had promised a crinkle-free design.

Given the temperatures, I was overdressed, but I wanted Jonah's first impression of me to be a positive one. Yet no one else out here seemed concerned with their appearance. The woman leaning against the SUV proudly showed off her wild straw-like hair and sunburned chest. She sipped water from a bottle, while another woman, maybe her sister or her mother, whispered to her.

Then the second woman marched over to me.

"Look at my sister's car." She gesticulated wildly around her, but her movements were too fast for my still dazed brain. "You crazy?"

"Why? What did I do?" I sent a pointed glance at the truck. Where was its driver anyway?

In the other lanes, cars crept past our conjoined vehicles, while their drivers threw us curious glances.

"Instead of arguing, we should be exchanging insurance details." I gave her a soothing smile. "I know it looks bad, but at least no one's hurt, right?"

"My sister is. The cops are on their way, and we'll see what they have to say." The woman's shoulders heaved. "You're going to pay for this."

Her ire didn't match the extent of the damage to her car. Its bumper had come loose and the front was dented, but otherwise her vehicle was in an okay state. More likely, she or her sister were looking for a payday.

"It wasn't her fault." Mark pushed himself between us, even though he was shorter and younger than me. "Kensi managed to brake in time. The tire marks on the road prove that." He wiggled his phone, which hopefully contained the corresponding proof. "It's you who drove into *her*."

"Shut up." The woman stalked back toward her sister, but not without shooting me another nasty glance.

"Don't worry." Mark patted my arm. "I know exactly what happened."

That made one of us, because my memory was still playing still frames rather than one cohesive movie. Maybe the woman was right, and there was something I could have done. Damn. Thinking was tough today. The heat pressed down on me, the area now heavy with fumes and light on oxygen. Suddenly, the world went blurry and swayed before my eyes.

"Whoa, hang on." Mark grabbed my arm.

I inhaled ultra-hot air through my mouth and exhaled through my nostrils, surprised—and slightly disappointed—I wasn't spewing flames.

"I'm okay. Come on, give me a hand." With Mark's help, I ripped open the back door of my car.

I reached inside and caught sight of myself in the side-view mirror. Normally my skin held olive overtones, not sun-tanned but not Hispanic or Indian either. Yet right now, no one was going to mistake me for anything but Caucasian. My cheeks and forehead, basically my entire face, had paled to a sickly gray.

I retrieved my tote and my laptop bag, and shut the door just as the police and two ambulance crews arrived on the scene. At long last, someone killed the sound of the car's horn.

Luckily, the cops didn't seem too impressed with the SUV-driver's account. Mark and I explained what happened, and then I showed the officers my papers. The paramedic insisted I go to the hospital, but I was hardier than she assumed and declined. I hadn't even sustained any cuts—just a few bruises on my chest that were nobody's business.

Once the paramedics were done with me, I dragged my suitcase and laptop bag to the shoulder and sat in the dry grass. Mark sent his pictures of the accident to my email account, then joined me. I was glad for his company. The stiffness in my neck had gotten worse. To straighten my back, I leaned back onto my hands, while he told me about his little brother, who had to be the funniest five-year-old on the planet, if the tales were true.

Maybe the sun dulled my thoughts or the effects of the crash still lingered, but either way, the world slowed and became quiet. I'd never before been involved in an accident, and the bureaucracy that was bound to follow made my stomach heavy. Worse, sooner or later, I'd have to tell my dad what happened. Would he be pissed that I hadn't called him the minute it happened, or proud because I was handling the situation without running to him? Damn. This adulting malarkey was tough.

Mark nudged me. "Are they here for you?"

Two guys, broad-shouldered and with determined expressions, came unerringly toward us.

"I think so." I pushed off the ground and straightened without letting the pain show on my face.

The shorter of the two had a moustache and oversized sunglasses, and his gait looked as if the other one had kicked him in the balls.

The second dude seemed to be the one in charge. He towered over me by a couple of inches, yet his neck didn't have the "kink of humility" that tall men frequently acquired; that constant bow of their heads that tried to convince the rest of us their size was merely an illusion. No, this guy made excuses for nothing.

"Christ. What happened?" He stood in front of me and viewed the damage with an appreciative whistle.

Intricate tattoos spilled from his short sleeves and ran across his curving biceps. The long summer days had washed his skin a dark bronze. Between his fine ass, a pool and a cocktail, my dream vacation could become a reality. Maybe my stay in Marlontown wouldn't be as dreary as I'd feared.

"It's kind of self-explanatory." Mark pointed at the truck in front. "That guy seems to have broken down. Kensi stopped, and the jeep behind her didn't." He swiveled his gaze to the SUV, which was being raised onto the tow truck.

"Ouch." The tall guy shook my hand. "Anyway, nice to meet you, Princess Kensington. I'm Drake."

A tingle ran across my skin, sharp and painful, and the tiny hairs on my arms stood up. I tamped down my unease. If Jonah was the Wild Pack's alpha, Drake had to be his protector. He certainly possessed the alpha gene. His display of power was a natural reaction to meeting a rival werewolf for the first time. Nothing for me to do than ride it out.

"Princess?" Mark's mouth goldfished. As a human, he'd be unaware of Drake's show of dominance or the complicated hierarchies of the werewolf world.

The prickle stopped as abruptly as it had flared, and I furtively rubbed the taut skin on my arms.

"Don't pay any attention to that princess stuff." I pointed my chin at his jeans pocket. "You have my details?"

He slowly closed his lips and nodded.

"And I have yours." I took his hand and squeezed it. "Expect the largest gift basket this side of the Atlantic coming your way."

He glanced at the ground and gave the road a tap with the toes of his sneaker. "You don't have to do that."

"Of course I do. You've been fantastic." I stiffly hugged him.

"Okay then. If you no longer need me, I'd better go." He raised a hand in a salute and headed back toward his car.

The papers were full of kids his age joining gangs and making trouble. Why did they never write about guys like him?

"Are you ready to leave?" Drake asked.

"I guess. What about my car? I probably need a police report for the insurance, and—"

"Buck's going to take care of everything." He pointed his chin at his friend. "Just give him the details."

Buck eyed Drake and then shook my hand. "Such an honor to meet you, Princess Kensington. Honest."

"You too."

The next days would bring more declarations like this. Even though America's free packs had cast off royal rule decades ago, nobility and titles still carried a certain fascination.

I searched my bag for the necessary documents and handed them over.

"Come on. Let's get you to Jonah's." Drake reached for my suitcase.

"I got it." I gripped the handle before he could, and then slipped the laptop bag's strap around my shoulder. "Just point the way."

Male werewolves had a tendency to get overly "helpful" around women. Better to nip the sexism in the bud before it had a chance to flourish.

Drake frowned, and the tingle across my sun-beaten skin

returned, more intense than before. It had been a while since I'd been in the presence of a powerful werewolf—at least one I didn't call 'daddy'—yet I couldn't shake the idea that Drake's dominance at this moment was calculated rather than instinctive.

"As you wish." Drake turned on his heels and headed to a dirty brown pickup that harked back to the era of the dinosaurs.

The coquettish looks the SUV sisters shot at his fine figure bounced off him like he was Teflon Man.

Weathering the assault of his dominating pheromones without any outward sign of discomfort, I deposited my suitcase in the open bed, flung my laptop bag on the back seat, and then climbed in through the passenger door. The heat inside hit me with the force of a frying pan, and the truck's trim didn't half singe off my skin when my shin bumped against it.

Drake started the engine, which came to life with a glug and a stutter before settling into a steady hum. The scent of peppermint clung to his skin and his clothes, a splash of freshness amid the relentless heat. He set off at a steady speed and threaded his truck into the flow of traffic without difficulty. His pheromones had faded fast once again, without giving me any indication either way as to whether the whole thing had been a test for dominance.

If so, he had to wonder why I hadn't displayed my own power.

Even driving, he held his head with the knowledge that he had the alpha gene, and everyone had better watch out. His close haircut masked a high forehead, rumored to be a sign of intelligence—or of a receding hairline. Still, all in all, Drake was at most a seven or an eight, because his gruff expression had shaved off a couple of points.

"Sorry about the inconvenience," I said. "Is Jonah pissed at me?"

"Certainly not." Drake's regular voice was without bumps or edges, and not as deep as his physical size suggested.

All things considered, I was in no particular hurry to meet the Wild Pack's alpha. Not by accident had it been a long time since

I'd come face to face with other werewolves. Six years ago, the power plays within my father's Boroughs Pack had sent me fleeing to Chicago, Illinois, home of The Bean, the Sears Tower and the jibarito sandwich. Would Marlontown wolves be different, or was I headed into more of the same drama?

Since I wasn't the one driving, I filled up on my first proper view of the Rocky Mountains in the distance. "Majestic" was one word for them. "Freakin' awesome" two better ones. The Rockies weren't triangular like the Matterhorn my father and I had once visited, but consisted of a huge mountain range complete with craggy, flat and pointy peaks. If I had the time, I'd look at them all day long.

"Your first name is Kensington?" Drake angled his left elbow against his windowsill and placed his other hand in his lap.

"Yes."

"It's an unusual name."

"Maybe. Like the Wild Pack chooses names pertaining to animals, my father's Boroughs Pack picks districts from across the world. Kensington is a borough in London, England."

"But you're German?"

"Yes. I came over to the US to study and work, and now live in Chicago."

"Your English is very good."

Aww. As if it wasn't hot enough already in the truck.

"Thanks." I grinned. "So's yours."

Drake acknowledged my joke with a nod, but didn't look at me. "And you're a private eye?"

"Yup. You lose it, I find it. I'm a true where-wolf. With a 'h.' Geddit?" I checked his face.

Finally, a hint of a grin.

"I got it." He flung a short-lived glance at me. "Very clever."

I finally relaxed into my seat. Humor was an international ice breaker, but just because something cracked *me* up didn't always mean others shared my opinion.

"So glad this is over." I flicked a finger against the air vents that weren't blowing cool air my way. "The other car's driver made it sound like the whole thing was my fault."

Drake hmm-ed.

"It wasn't." My voice left no room for doubt. "Guess she needed someone to blame."

"I'm not surprised. That's what humans do."

"It's what everyone does."

"You live among them, don't you?" He bit on his mint with a crunch and swallowed. "Humans, I mean. You didn't find a pack to live with when you came over, but chose a human environment, right?"

"Yes. So?"

"Then you might have become blind to their idiosyncrasies." He shot me a sideways glance. "Not your fault, of course."

If it hadn't been lava-level hot in here, I'd have crossed my arms. "Idiosyncrasies like what?"

"Werewolves would have made sure you're okay first, whoever was at fault. Blame would be the last thing we'd focus on. Our kind sticks together."

"I thought you lived in Marlontown, not Pleasantville circa 1950s."

Drake ripped the steering wheel to the side to overtake a car, and the jolt aggravated my sore back.

I leaned forward into his peripheral vision and gave him a prolonged look. "Not all werewolves are alike, and neither are all humans. Look at Mark, the kid from the accident. He wouldn't leave my side for more than a few minutes. He took photos of the cars for the insurance and stuck up for me when the other driver made the collision sound like Waterloo."

"I'm not saying humans are bad, but on balance, they are quicker to overreact and get violent."

I made a show of my disapproval by shifting in my seat and mumbling words like "twenty-first century" and "tolerance." Living among humans was my choice. Werewolves could learn from their social interactions.

"Oh no, don't hold back on me, Princess Kensington." Drake's fingers had tightened around the steering wheel, and the needle of his speedometer was creeping up. "If you've got something to say, say it."

"At one time, the free packs and the royal packs were at war. A violent war."

"That was a long time ago, and it was hardly a war."

"Maybe not on a global scale, but werewolves died at the hands of other werewolves. Same way as humans have over the centuries." I turned my head away from him. "And not for nothing, but it was barely forty years ago that your own pack was warring among itself."

One way or another, my father had found himself right in the middle of their skirmishes, even helped Jonah become the Wild Pack's alpha. Some argued the bond the two forged back then had become the foundation on which peace between all packs was built.

"That was different." Drake pushed a button on his dashboard, and a rocky tune filled the interior. "Maybe you shouldn't talk about stuff you know nothing about."

I'd clearly hit an old wound.

Still, werewolves could be as mean and petty as humans. Growing up hadn't been a picnic. The taunts, the shoving, and the swirlies only lost their hold over me once I was old enough to understand who I was: the alpha's daughter. The heir apparent to the crown. And I'd emerged stronger for all their efforts to keep me down.

One day, I was going to rule my father's pack, and the boys who'd tormented me—men now—had better watch out.

Drake was stewing in his perceived righteousness, and I was too hot to care. To my left, green fields stretched far and wide, veritable oceans of tall plants with large leaves.

"Sunflower fields?" I tapped the window with my knuckle.

"Yeah." Drake took a deep breath, then dropped his shoulders and lowered the volume of the radio a fraction. "You're about a month too early to see them in their full glory."

"I've read about these fields, but never seen them in bloom."

"Right."

And that was it. Once again, we'd run out of conversation. Jeez, I was facing a difficult few days if Drake was representative of Jonah's pack.

We bypassed any further signs of civilization and, after another ten minutes' silence, drove up a steep path, past alfalfa fields with tractors and neat windrows. I was used to tall city blocks and the exhaust-clogged roads in Chicago, and of course to the densely wooded mountains of my home town. These large areas of green didn't do it for me.

If anything, the wide-open setting only intensified my unease. I'd been summoned to find a missing girl in a town of strangers. What was I going to find once I started digging into this ostensible paradise?

Two

"You must be Princess Kensington." The blond guy who'd opened the door for us shook my hand emphatically. "I'm Leo."

I pushed my sunglasses up onto my head. "Hi, Leo."

A flicker of dominance brushed my skin and vanished in an instant. If this wasn't the alpha, and Drake was Jonah's protector, what the hell was Leo's role in this pack?

"Come on in. Jonah can't wait to meet you." Leo reached for my laptop bag.

I didn't mind my suitcase boiling in the truck's bed, but my computer contained important files I couldn't afford to lose to heat-related damage.

"I'm good." I pulled in my stomach and slipped past his outstretched arm, keeping my laptop carrier firmly pressed under my arm. In an instant, a mellow stream from the AC cooled my body.

"Oops," I mumbled as the corner of my bag dug into Leo's side. "Sorry."

He winced and withdrew his helping hand.

There I was being rude again, but until I'd assessed how this pack treated their female members, I'd stick to my game plan and refuse any male help.

"You can leave your stuff over there, if you like." Leo pointed to the area next to the door.

"Okay." I did as he asked.

Leo was tall, a healthy specimen with fair skin vibrant with red undertones. A kink in his nose turned what could have been a pretty face into a handsome one. Who knew they produced eye candy of his and Drake's caliber in a far-away place like Marlontown?

"Right." I tugged my jacket straight. "I'm ready."

Leo flashed a five-hundred Watt beam. "Follow me."

Drake was coming up behind us, then climbed a wood staircase to the upper level, without even a nod to acknowledge me.

Good riddance. Leo was going to be better company, for sure.

The inside of the building was more spectacular than the outside had suggested. Recessed lights created subtle patterns on the travertine floor. It was my luck that the framed mirrors on the walls showed every wrinkle and every unflattering pose. The drive and crash had taken their toll on my appearance, and the shadows under my eyes knocked my confidence.

"I hope you weren't seriously injured." Leo rolled up his shirtsleeves, revealing strong forearms. His gray slacks were a little tight, although I didn't mind, since they clung to a pair of nice legs.

"No, I'm resilient. Buck stayed behind to deal with the car and the insurance." I straightened my jacket and smoothed my dark hair back into its bun in one of the mirrors. The best I could do for now.

"Buck's a good guy, although entirely without aspirations."

A diplomatic way of saying that Buck wasn't strong enough to climb the ranks to a position of note, especially not in a free pack. Free packs valued physical strength more than any natural birthright to lead.

The end of the corridor opened into a space of undefined purpose. Heaps of sunlight pooled around an oval dark-wood table in the middle of the room, which was ringed by six chairs.

A slim guy, older than me but younger than my dad, shot to his feet and walked toward me, hand outstretched. "Kensington. It's so good to meet you."

The prickle chasing across my skin intensified to remove all doubt: he was the alpha, and a formidable one to boot. He'd be expecting my own dominance to greet him right now, but all I had for him was a smile.

"Hello." I measured my breath for a steady voice. "You're Jonah, the alpha?"

As if the pheromones that signaled his power hadn't already answered that question.

"Yes. Yes, I am." He gripped my hand with both of his. "Please excuse my rudeness. Is Kensington okay, or do you prefer Princess Kensington?"

The tingle sharpened into the full-on assault of a thousand bee stings.

"Please call me Kensi." My voice didn't tremble yet, but his authority battered my insides and physically weakened my legs.

Sheer doggedness drove me to stretch my spine, make myself taller, my demeanor fiercer. Dominance was about more than pheromones. It was also a game that relied on appearance, posture, and a well-timed look to throw my opponents out of their comfort zone.

His mouth moved. His eyelids lifted by a fraction

Leo, who had installed himself a few feet away, tensed his shoulders. Had I been wrong about Drake being Jonah's protector?

"Kensi it is." Jonah patted my back and in doing so, sneakily herded me toward the table and to a seat on the long side of the oval.

Not one word about my lack of dominance.

No way he'd know the truth. To my knowledge, only my father's closest advisers had been told of my "troubles." *Their* word choice.

Being of a more realistic mindset, I had no use for euphemisms. I was a dud—as in *dudn't* shift, *dudn't* run, *dudn't* intimidate. Even though my dominance, that ability to induce fear and awe in my fellow werewolves, had so far eluded me, hiding my shortcomings from others only became an issue when my status was being challenged, usually around alphas and protectors.

It wasn't like I hadn't tried to squeeze the wolf out of me. For months, I'd meditated for an hour at the crack of dawn, and had even experimented with mind-expanding drugs in the hope that I could dream myself into my alternate shape, but nothing had worked.

"*The wolf is in you, Schatz,*" Dad would say. "*Somewhere. Hidden deep. Waiting to explode.*"

"So, you're finally here." Jonah tugged his pant legs up and sat in his chair at the end of the table.

"Yes, it's been an adventure."

He added another dollop of power to his dominance, which was beginning to piss me off. My misgivings must have shown on my face, because Leo stepped closer, yet without interfering. He, too, had to wonder why I wasn't repaying his alpha's assault in kind.

"Anything wrong?" Jonah asked.

"Not at all." I forced the sweetest of smiles onto my lips. "I'd assumed Drake was your protector, but—"

"I have two."

"Two?"

What kind of alpha needed two protectors?

"Politics." Jonah's face twisted for a fraction into a pained grimace. "Still, it has many advantages as you can imagine."

That made total sense. In fact, my future reign might benefit from a similar situation. Two protectors would strengthen my position, assuming I could find two powerful werewolves I could trust enough not to depose me down the line.

"You're considering it for yourself, aren't you?" Jonah chuckled, and finally relaxed his aura. "I can see it in your face."

"Maybe." I let my gaze drift across the two desks by the back windows, and massaged my hands. My fingers ached because I hadn't rolled them into fists, even though failing to do so had gone against the alpha's unspoken command.

Jonah smoothed his russet hair, which was cut neat but not styled, before picking up a white pot with an elegant spout. "Coffee?"

"Yes, please."

Jonah poured steaming coffee into a large cup and handed it to me. He wasn't pretty or even handsome in a Hollywood sense, but with his charisma and physicality—tall, packed with sinewy strength, and sporting a determined jaw—he was every woman's dream hunk.

I also knew he was single.

It was tradition and indeed encouraged for royal alphas-to-be like me to take a mate before ascending to the throne. No doubt this thought had crossed my father's mind when he'd dispatched me to this place. Jonah would make quite the trophy. Besides, a strong alpha by my side would quieten all those doubting whispers about my ability to lead.

Still, I had no intention of ensnaring Jonah or any of his males with my womanly wiles. *Sorry, Dad.* To me, being single was a mission statement.

"Have you spoken to your father yet about the accident?" Jonah asked.

"No. I'll call him tonight. He's got more important things to worry about."

"How is he?"

"He's well."

"Good. I knew the rumors weren't true. Strong as an ox, your dad. Always has been." Jonah tipped back his head for a laugh I was warming to. "I can't believe I finally get to meet you. *Aldwych*, I keep saying to him, *you must come visit me and bring your daughter. I bet she's a firecracker.*"

Jonah seemed like a good man, and his affable manner was effective. The tension in my neck lessened as I assumed a less rigid posture.

"My father asked me to convey his apologies for not accompanying me." I wrapped my hands around my mug and allowed myself a sentimental smile. "His priority is for me to do my job, and he feared an official visit by an alpha king would get in the way."

"He's a wise man." Jonah leaned forward and studied me, his pale fingers moving against the tabletop in alternation. "And yet he agreed to let you pursue a career before you accept the royal title. Not as a manager of a company or in some other leadership role, but as a private investigator."

I snapped my gaze up to his face. There it was. That doubt.

Damn. I'd really wanted to like him, too.

"Of course," I said in a way others would say "duh." "What better way to prepare me for what lies ahead than letting me forge my own path? Every day I hone my mind and find new solutions. Brawn isn't the only qualification a good alpha should have."

My dig at the violent ways of the free packs couldn't have been lost on Jonah, but his features barely stirred.

"Not the only one, but one of them, surely." He squinted. "If you cannot show strength, how do you expect the men under your command to respect you?"

Now he was openly questioning my ability to lead?

"The same way the *women* under me will respect me. Believe me, I'm fully aware that some people like to push their physical advantage, and I'll make sure they get what's coming to them. Everyone will." I sipped my coffee slowly, very slowly, even though my blood was raging underneath. "Take my word for it."

"Meaning?"

I licked the coffee taste off my upper lip. "Let me put it this way. I initially turned down your job with a clear, unequivocal 'no.' Next thing I know, you ask my dad to intervene. Now I'm here."

"I hope going over your head won't be a problem." Spoken like a true grade-A chauvinist superior son of a bitch.

I leaned my head to the side and raised my eyebrows.

His pupils dilated, his mouth froze in a half-smirk.

"One day, I will succeed my father to the throne, and let me assure you, I have a long memory." My voice rolled in my throat. For a few precious seconds, I was all wolf. "You might not understand that when a woman says no, when *I* say no, I mean no, but if you ever hope to deal with me again, you'd do well to learn fast."

Leo, who'd repositioned himself a few paces away, stepped toward us. My words had been close enough to a threat to give him cause to smack me all the way to Sunday, but what choice had his boss given me? Attacking my alpha credentials could not go unpunished, as Jonah knew.

Jonah raised a hand to stop his protector. Weirdly, the onslaught of dominance I'd invited didn't come.

Instead, Jonah's lips curved into a smile, while his head moved slowly up and down.

"You're right. I understand I didn't make the best first impression, and I'll work hard to convince you I'm worthy of your trust." He snapped his fingers, and Leo scurried to hand him a file. "And I'm not half as sexist as you think I am, I promise."

Was this a win? It was tough to tell sometimes. After dealing with Drake, I'd kind of hoped for a smooth ride, but werewolves weren't that accommodating. One-upmanship always got in the way of a nice conversation.

My personality didn't necessarily help, either. While I didn't seek out confrontation, once cajoled into one, I made sure I came out on top. This time, though, I would have to live with the uncertainty, because I had the distinct feeling this whole thing had been a test. A battle of wills Jonah had devised to see how I stacked up as a future alpha and ally.

God. Werewolf politics sucked.

"Right then." I added a hint of sass to my voice and straightened. "Now, I was told you've *misplaced* a werewolf."

"Her name is Raven." Jonah slid the file across the table. "She disappeared four months ago. One of my young ones, only twenty-three years old. The police refuse to investigate, since there's no evidence of a crime and she was an adult…at least in human years. They believe she ran away, but werewolves don't run away."

"No, they don't."

"This matter must be dealt with by the next full moon."

I frowned. "That's less than three weeks from now."

"I followed the Society Strangler case. What the police couldn't get done in a year, you handled in a week." The charming smile that accompanied his words didn't make up for him siccing my father on me or putting me through the wringer. "I have the greatest confidence in you."

"Why the full moon?"

"Many fear a crime has been committed, and since pack members obey pack law, Raven's disappearance is being blamed on the humans. My people want retribution. To diffuse the tension, I promised an answer to this mystery by the next Moon Festival, but our efforts so far have failed." His concentrated look reflected the gravity of his words. "You understand now why I had to involve your father to get you here so quickly. I'm running out of time."

"Right."

Drake's dislike of humans finally gained some context. Cut off from urban melting pots, tolerance had become a rare commodity in this place, and humans—somehow—had become the focus of the pack's prejudices. They weren't entirely alone in their views. My father's pack lacked the will to be fully inclusive, but at least they tried to get along with their human neighbors.

"Okay. Then… Actually, I don't know what to do next." Jonah chuckled and once more adjusted the collar of his crisp, white shirt. "I've never hired a detective before."

Either this guy was a master of manipulation, or deep down, he was genuinely disturbed at having lost one of his own.

What was I thinking? Of course he was upset—which made me a total ass for acting like a spoiled brat. Raven's wellbeing was his responsibility.

My dad had a close relationship with the whole pack. He was the first non-parent to hold a baby, attended every funeral, dispensed hugs and shoulder slaps as needed, and he never merely went through the motions. Their happiness was important to him. Their grief was his grief.

Jonah, too, would have mourned Raven's disappearance, and not only was he stuck in this emotional limbo of not knowing what happened to her, he also had to deal with a pack looking for someone to blame.

"It's all good." I softened my voice and interlaced my fingers at the edge of the table. "Your e-mail set out the terms, which I've already agreed to. I'll do my best to find her in time. I promise."

"I appreciate that."

"All I need from you is to show me where to hang my hat, so to speak, and I'll get started. Do you have a local cab company I could use? Since I no longer have a car."

"We don't have cabs out here, but I have something better. I've asked my protector to accompany you during your stay. My pack tends to be suspicious of outsiders, and having him around will make your life easier."

I fixed Leo with a hopeful stare. *Please let it be you.*

Jonah pointed a thumb toward a door on his right. "Would you get Drake, Leo?"

"Of course." Leo sauntered out, hands clasped behind his back.

"Drake gets on well with every member of my pack. Well, you've met him. It's tough not to like him, isn't it?"

And yet, I'd managed without great difficulty.

"He'll be such an asset to your investigation." Once more, his hands flew up to his shirt.

He wasn't wearing a tie, but I'd bet my new apartment he wasn't used to tailored clothing at all. That meant he'd made an effort for me and probably got Leo to dress up, too.

Damn it, I was warming to him, despite his underhanded way of getting me here.

The prospect of having to share more breathing space with Drake aside, I hadn't driven all the way across the America just because Jonah had requested my help. I, too, benefitted from my presence here. What Jonah didn't know was that my father didn't have to work all that hard to get me here.

When Jonah called, Dad could have ordered me to take this job. He was my alpha, after all. Instead, he'd used all the arguments in his arsenal to get me here voluntarily. Make allies. Earn favors. Learn about your mother. As usual, I eventually saw his wisdom.

Maybe my mother's relatives knew why I hadn't yet been able to shift. Either way, Jonah's gratitude would help me down the line. No alpha could lead without outside support, and the Wild Pack was one of the largest packs in the U.S.

Steps resonated from the door to my left, and Leo emerged, followed by Drake.

"As I said, consider Drake your personal protector during your stay." Jonah grinned, proud of his generosity, no doubt.

Drake's mouth tightened. "If you're sure you don't need me."

"Leo and I will do fine." Jonah shot Drake a look as fleeting as it was stern.

Clearly Drake didn't like the idea of following the new kid around any more than me.

"I appreciate your kindness. Really." I waved Jonah off. "Maybe I should have mentioned it before, but it's better if I work alone. People are less likely to open up when confronted by two investigators."

Jonah's eyes twitched.

Not again. Didn't he know how tired I was? The crash still haunted my bones, and his constant challenges were draining me to the point where I wanted to curl up and submit.

Pricks clawed up my arms in the thousands and cascaded down my spine, as if my body was frozen in a swarm of fire ants.

I rolled my toes into a foot fist, flexed my thigh and ass muscles against the onslaught, while keeping my shoulders relaxed and my breathing even. Yet how long I'd be able to last was anyone's guess.

Get a grip. I'd last as long as it took. I had to. Sweat collected on my back and under my arms, the price I paid for my *whatever* expression. I might not be able to counter Jonah's dominance, but I wasn't going to duck or break either. Not in front of him. Not in front of anyone.

Jonah leaned forward. "I insist. You need transportation, and more importantly, you don't know my pack. Many remember the troubled history from when we declared our independence from the royal packs, so let's play it safe." He slapped his palms together and rose to his feet as if powering out his dominance was no big deal. "Now, if you have any questions, call. Otherwise, Drake will see to your needs."

"I don't—"

"I said, Drake will see to your needs."

Just like that, the discussion was over, at least for him. Once again, he'd steamrollered right over my objections.

If I weren't so useless, I'd have forced him to reconsider his ridiculous demands. What did I need a babysitter for? But I had nothing with which to counter Jonah. Not an ounce of what I needed to assert my authority.

"Fine." I gave a shrug; aloof on the outside, yet a welcome relief for my aching arms.

The assault stopped, and Jonah looked at me with wide-eyed innocence.

Rather than give him a piece of my mind, I left his hand unshaken and marched my ass out of the room, without waiting for his official dismissal.

"You may go." Jonah's voice trailed after me, leading the way of the mother of all dominance displays.

The force of his power nearly made me stumble, but I kept my poise until I was outside his range. It had been years since I'd treated an alpha with such insubordination. Back then, my father had grounded me for a month, but Dad wasn't here, and Jonah wasn't *my* alpha.

Oh, I'd find Jonah's missing werewolf *despite* the babysitter, and then I'd watch him eat crow.

THREE

BEHIND ME, IN JONAH'S OFFICE, the three men whispered, and a moment later, steps followed me through the entrance hall.

Drake crossed the space with a languidness that was at odds with his powerful frame. How likely was it that anyone would open up to someone who looked and acted like him? Besides, airing dirty laundry in front of a protector who could make your life miserable? This investigation was doomed before it began.

I picked up my laptop bag.

Drake's bare arm grazed mine in passing.

My skin tautened then burst into flames. Not literally, but *fucking hell*. A second later, it was over. I flipped him off with a look, ambled outside after him, and slid my shades down to cover my eyes. Jonah's power play had already left my flesh raw, but it seemed the Wild Pack wasn't done with me yet. This new assault was all about Drake getting his own alpha on. Making sure *he* was the one calling the shots for as long as we worked together. Clearly, he hadn't met me.

Bring it on, slugger.

Bring.

It.

On.

Drake had parked his pickup to my left, shaded by three massive pine trees. Farther away, farm buildings peppered endless fields, and at the flattest part of my vista, the outlines of Marlontown and its two sister towns, Denville and Robson's Creek, appeared.

I climbed into the furnace on four wheels and reached through the headrests to place my bag on the backseat again. Drake was already reversing by the time I'd strapped myself in.

With Raven's file clasped between my hands and my lap, I leaned back and stared out of the window at the "Triangle," as the locals called the trio of towns.

The road from Jonah's house was unpaved and almost deserted. All around us stretched open fields, while a relentless sun left us with nowhere to hide. I only had eyes for the long stretches of woods that encircled us. Forests were magical places of peace and freedom. The smell of moist earth and leaves, the crackle of wind between the canopies... The woods were where I belonged. They were in my blood.

I was born in Germany's Black Forest, but a forest right here in Marlontown, Colorado was where my dad had met my mother, whose sketchy past was rooted deep within this place.

I tightened my grip on the folder in my lap and inhaled a lungful of hot air. Looking for traces of my mother would have to wait until the morning. Today, Raven would get my full attention.

The road smoothed as we approached the town. We drove past a mildly busy row of cafés and shops, where people walked without hurry, chatted, laughed. Whether they were human or werewolf was impossible to tell. Maybe both. A red-bricked structure had been erected in the center—a type of building with a large arch that spanned the road. A terracotta clock mounted on its tower read four o'clock.

"Is this Marlontown?" I waved a hand to encompass our urban surroundings.

Drake pushed a peppermint into his mouth. "Yeah."

Not that it mattered either way. The three towns were so close together you were never more than an hour away from anywhere you might want to go. That was another nugget the Internet had shared with me, amid anecdotes of sunflowers, cherry pie and the annual outdoor movie festival. A different world from Chicago, or even my ancestral home in Wildbach, Germany.

I closed my eyes, tried to blank the heat that tightened my skin and made every breath I took painful. The air conditioning in this truck was atrocious. It blew cool air every which way but in my direction.

I rattled the narrow slits to adjust the stuck vent on my side of the truck. "Would you mind if I opened a window?"

"Won't do you any good."

This guy had a problem with me, even though getting him to follow me around town hadn't been *my* idea. Maybe if we teamed up, we'd get Jonah to change his mind.

"Do you like living here?" I asked to thaw the ice.

"Where else would I live?"

"No, I didn't mean..." Damn it. Had my question been ambiguous? Most of the time, my English was fine, even accent-free according to my friends, but occasionally, I messed up.

I licked my lips. Straightened. "I meant, what kind of place is this? Does it have everything you need or want?"

Great, now my pronunciation was slipping.

"We're not starving." Drake faced the road in front without wavering. "We have shops, you know."

Now my question sounded stupid, mainly because *he*'d made it sound stupid.

Jerk.

"You know exactly what I was asking. What do you do for fun? That kind of thing." I shook my head and muttered, "Seriously."

"There are lots of outdoor facilities. Plenty of woods to run in, but I thought you were here for work, not for leisure."

I was all out of small talk and had little desire to strike up another conversation. Not the way Drake sat there, with his lips pressed together so tight, he'd spit diamonds the moment he opened his mouth. Letting him shadow me while I worked? Hell, I'd ditch his ass the moment I got the chance.

I retrieved my cell from my jacket's inside pocket and checked my email.

No fewer than twenty requests for my services waited in my inbox. A handful of potential clients offered to compensate me handsomely for my time, multiple times better than this gig, while others were looking for pro bono services. The price of success. Since my work on the Society Strangler's case had become national knowledge, everyone and their dog wanted to hire me, usually for peanuts. Jonah himself hadn't reached deeply into his coffers either.

The truck slowed, and Drake killed the engine outside an adorable one-family house. Bright blue, it stood at the corner of a quiet intersection, with a covered porch that ran across its width and a looked-after lawn in the front.

I exited before he could open the door and studied the neighborhood, my fingers hooked inside the slim belt that held up my culottes. "Nice."

"It's nothing special."

That dude would come down on the opposite side of whatever I said. Why hadn't Jonah forced Leo's company on me? He'd seemed nice enough, even made me feel welcome.

Drake and his coat of silence, meanwhile, headed for the driveway.

I followed, lugging my suitcase with me.

Drake turned and retrieved a set of keys from his jeans pocket. "Did you want to settle in or get started right away?"

"It's been a long journey." I dropped the suitcase and blew air up against my forehead. "Mind if we get started in the morning? Say, ten o'clock?"

"No problem. I assume you don't need the bag you left in my truck?"

I whipped my head around and squinted toward the truck. "Shoot, my laptop. Good call. Would you mind getting it for me?"

"As you wish, *princess*." He spread the *princess* across his tongue like a piece of moldy bread.

That dude needed an attitude adjustment STAT.

"Christ, I've had it up to here with you." I sliced my hand through the air past my nose. "Have I hurt you in any way? Have I damaged your fragile ego? What is it about me that bothers you? The sooner you tell me, the sooner you can get over it."

"Don't speak to me that way." Drake's voice lowered. "I'm a pack protector and have *earned* my rank."

"Doesn't make you superior."

"That's exactly what it does. So while you're here, you will respect me and you will respect my alpha, is that understood?"

Okay, so his dislike of me had a reason, and I'd brought it on myself. Dissing Jonah the way I did had pissed off his protector big time. My bad. But did Drake seriously think his little outburst would shake my confidence? Puh-lease.

As if I hadn't gotten enough of that crap at home. From stealing my toys in Kindergarten to tripping me up during gym class—every day, some wolf would sling a test at me, hoping I'd crumble. Over the years, their taunts had hardened my shell and turned my resolve into steel.

I stepped closer until Drake and I stood almost toe-to-toe. Since I didn't wear heels, my nose only came level with his bottom lip. Jonah was an alpha, and challenging him to a stare-out was a big fat no, but this yahoo?

This was no longer about my stupid laptop. This was about boundaries, and he had to learn his.

I tipped my head back and tensed my muscles against what was no doubt about to hit me.

The hairs on Drake's jaw zoomed into focus. His breath warmed my face. His eyes, like liquid mercury, could do real damage to a weaker woman's willpower.

Shit. There it was. The stings and pricks. The dominance to prove his point—and he wasn't taking prisoners. I latched onto his gaze, focused on the play of silver against the black of his irises.

About ten percent of all wolves possessed alpha pheromones, and those who did were destined to become protectors or leaders. My father was part of that elite group, as was his father before him. As for my mother, Dad always joked she'd been the real boss all along.

But Drake… Man, that dude knew what he was doing. His dominance scraped my skin like sandpaper, sliced into my muscles to weaken them fiber by fiber.

"That all you got?" I gave him a slow-motion smile.

His dominance exploded to full force, driving invisible spikes into my guts. I breathed through the pain, even managed a sarcastic lift of my eyebrows. Jonah might have come close to beating me. This asshole wouldn't.

Drake's control over his body bordered on the surreal. Not a muscle in his face moved. His eyelids remained still. Even the breeze obeyed and left his short hair alone.

My smile held, but sweat collected in the small of my back. One of us would have to give in soon. *Please, don't let it be me.*

Drake's eyes darkened, and the burn ate deep into my body.

Come on, man. Give it up already.

His chest moved once, twice, then a little faster.

I clenched my muscles, focused on the pain. Drew strength from it.

He flared his nostrils.

Gotcha.

He spun on his heels and strolled to his truck as if he hadn't just established himself as the biggest jerk this side of the Milky Way.

The ache ebbed away. My lungs expanded. I rubbed my neck, still stiff. Were we done? Had I proven myself?

Drake retrieved my laptop bag and slammed the truck door shut. His determined gait looked like he was gearing up for a rematch.

No way.

With one hand pressed against my waist, I cocked my hip and slid my sunglasses down for an evaluating peek over the rim. My earlier rating might have been a little hasty. His even strides were powered by nice legs. His biceps and shoulders flexed as he worked off his frustration. I licked my lips and trailed my gaze across his body. He was a nine and a half, all day long.

He frowned, switched the bag to the left arm, and resumed his walk, less certain now.

I turned and, hips swaying, carried my suitcase up the steps, where I dropped the weight at my feet.

Drake came up behind me and unlocked the door.

I took my bag and keys off him and intensified my smile. "You may go now."

Then I went inside, suitcase in one hand, bag slung over my shoulder, and gave the door a gentle shove with my ass. *Take that.*

"Fucking hell," he mumbled before it fell into the lock.

Like Dad said: Werewolves relied on their pheromones too damn much.

I plodded across the hall's stone floor and leaned my bag against the wall, letting the AC cool my overheating body. Outside, the pickup's engine powered to life and gave a painful squeal. Drake strangled his truck, probably because he couldn't strangle me.

I slid down the wall and buried my face in my hand. Not one part of my body didn't hurt. Why did I have to prove myself to them in the first place? I had come to help them. Didn't that mean anything?

Instead of giving a departing roar, the engine belched and stopped. The truck door slammed.

Hell. What now?

Out on the porch, Drake shuffled toward the door, no louder than the rustle of leaves. In most aspects, I was a blight on my species, but my hearing was as acute as any wolf's. A scraping sound. A curse. Then silence.

Was he gone? I wasn't capable of going another round with him. There was a reason I preferred human company.

I snuck back to the door to peek through the spyhole.

Two raps on the door.

I bounded back. Dammit. Was his plan to give me a heart attack?

I opened the door and batted my eyes. "Yes?"

"We should establish ground rules." He'd crossed his arms but so far kept his dominance holstered.

"For what?"

"Working together."

"Jonah was clear on how this worked." I enunciated, hoping my accent didn't stand out, as it tended to when I got agitated. "I tell you what I need, and you provide."

His jaw tensed.

I rested my arm against the doorframe and assumed a more relaxed stance. "Fine. Neither of us is happy with the situation, but this is what Jonah wants. Still, I see no reason why we can't work together as equals. Final offer."

"Works for me." He half turned away and took a single step.

"Hallelujah." My fingers clamped tightly around the wooden frame.

Maybe Drake wasn't the bully I thought he was. I hadn't been on my best behavior toward his alpha. In the end, it had been Drake who'd sought open dialog with me. Not many men would have, and even fewer werewolves.

He pivoted back and ran his gaze down across my length and up again. "You showed strength against Jonah and stood your ground against me without going dominant."

"My father made sure I exhaust other options first. Different cultures, different habits, you know." After all these years, my lies still flowed smoothly off my tongue.

"Ah, okay. Impressive."

If only he knew what it had cost me. How close I'd come to buckling both times.

"Thank you." I bowed my head without dropping my gaze.

A gust of wind moved the branches of the large maple tree out front, and dancing sunlight lit up Drake's face. His features were made of stone, smooth and flawless, and entirely unreadable.

Fine, so maybe he was a ten.

The air steadied, and the brightness fled. Who was this man who could go from cold to hot without blinking an eye? Who was he really?

Drake lowered his arms and curled his thumbs into his front pockets. "Truce then."

"No more pissing contests?" I kept my voice light.

"We'll see." He laughed, then rolled his weight onto his heels and back. "I'll be back in the morning."

"Okay. See ya."

With his gait light, he returned to his pickup. This time, the engine purred as the truck glided away from the curb and sped off.

I closed the door and angled my face up for an extra helping of cooled air.

Drake was a complex guy. Since he was a male of significant dominance, subjugating himself to Jonah was his choice, in the same way I'd never even consider challenging my dad for leadership, even if I could. Trust, love… Something stopped Drake from making his claim for the top spot.

Sharing the rank of protector with Leo, on the other hand— what a crock. How could he stand that, yet get so rattled by little old me? He was an onion, with layers as yet unexplored. An enigma.

And hell, how I loved myself a good mystery.

Four

MY TEMPORARY HOME WAS JUST as charming on the inside. I left my tote by the curved staircase and dropped my other bag on the gray three-seater sofa, squashing one of the many throw pillows in the process. The open floorplan and double French doors leading to the neat-as-a-pin backyard let in sufficient sun, and I didn't have to turn on the ceiling lights. I grabbed a couple of yoghurts from the well-stocked fridge and returned to the living room to study the file Jonah had given me.

My everyday life played out in the human world, far away from my kind, but nothing could make me forget werewolf rules.

Werewolves lived in packs. End of story. Outside an alpha's reach, wolves had no incentive to keep our existence secret. Once in a while, a young, idealistic werewolf proclaimed we should live openly in peace and harmony with our human cousins. Lovely sentiment, but not practical given people's suspicions of things they didn't understand. Without an alpha to stop these well-meaning hippies, our kind would be toast.

The file gave no indication that Raven had a rebellious streak.

She was about my height with longish brown hair. Her entire life, she'd lived with her mother and father in Marlontown. Her grades had been excellent. After high school, she got a job in her father's bakery, which to me reeked of unfulfilled potential. Then again, I'd always been more ambitious than the average female werewolf.

I pushed the file aside and yawned. A bunch of facts wouldn't tell me where to look for Raven. To figure that out, I'd first have to get to know her. So I plugged my laptop into the wall, changed into my PJs, and then set to work with my notebook by my side.

Raven's public social media accounts told an interesting story. At first glance, she was one of those people who never gave much away. She'd certainly been careful enough not to share photos or status updates.

Her posts, however, finally offered a glimpse into the kind of person she was.

Once I'd taken ample notes and created a plan of attack, I shut down the computer and reached for my cell. I owed my father a phone call. Better he'd hear about the accident and the welcome I'd received from the Wild Pack from me.

For once, he answered the phone himself.

"Hi Dad. How are you?"

"Nice to hear from you, Schatz. We're doing great. How was your first day?"

His voice at once squeezed my heart and soothed my mind.

"So-so. First, I totaled my car, then—"

"Oh no. Are you all right?"

I rolled my eyes, even if only to convince myself his concern didn't give me all kinds of fluffy feelings. "I'm good, but I'm now carless. That makes my secret mission more of a challenge."

"You thrive on challenge. But were you hurt? What happened?"

I gave a condensed version of the crash, elaborated on Mark, before smoothly moving on to my real gripes. "Jonah assigned me a baby-sitter. Can you believe that?"

"I'm sure he has his reasons. Remember why you're there."

"Find the missing woman. Turn the Wild Pack into an ally. Track down Mom's relatives."

"Do you have a plan yet?"

"On Mom? An online search gave me nothing. Not even a place to start, but I tracked down a historical book collection. It's in the local library, and the librarian is meeting with me in the morning before they officially open."

"Keep me apprised. What about your case?"

"I've done some initial research." I picked up my notes and pulled my legs up onto the sofa. "The missing woman's called Raven. The file Jonah gave me mentioned she was musically gifted. What it failed to say was that, after high school, she'd applied only to universities as far flung as England."

"And that's important?"

"I don't know. At least it's an indication she has adventurous spirit—or is a woman who's unhappy at home. Most colleges accepted her, and yet she doesn't attend any of them." At least not according to the information Jonah had provided.

"Maybe she wanted to take a year off first?"

"Maybe. I sent an email to a research assistant I occasionally use and asked her to check with the colleges in question, plus any other places that might be of interest to a violinist. If Raven has run off to get the education she deserves, my work will be done."

"You think she's run off without telling her parents?" My father didn't sound convinced.

"She wouldn't have, if she had the world's best dad, but alas, that position's already taken by you."

He laughed his big, rattling laugh. "And don't you forget it."

Had Raven's desire for an education been strong enough to drive her to leave the pack's protection? Jonah and Leo had struck me as approachable, welcoming ports in any storm.

"Raven's social media accounts also featured environmental

news, which tells me she has a social conscience. The list of organizations she's following online includes a couple of local ones."

I underlined the relevant words in my notebook. If she'd met people that Jonah didn't know of, they were worth talking to.

"What's wrong, *Schatz*?"

"Nothing. Except I couldn't find one word about friends or boyfriends. If Raven was lonely, maybe even depressed, could she have…"

"Taken her own life?"

"I'm going to call the morgues and hospitals in the area tomorrow, but I hope for the best."

"That's a depressing thought. Are you going to be okay? Not just with the case, but handling Jonah and his dominance? You've been away from us for a while, so it might be a little hard on you at first."

I rubbed my arm, where the ghost of a prickle still lingered. "I'm good. The alpha that could force me into submission hasn't been born yet."

"Okay. Remember to use your entire arsenal."

"I will. Don't worry about me."

"That's my job. Are you nervous about digging into your mother's life?"

"A little. I don't know."

"You don't talk about her. Maybe that's my fault."

I briefly closed my eyes. "I always thought that part of my past, her family, died when she died. Learning about her won't bring her back."

Dad made a non-committal noise. "You're wrong. But this is your journey."

Now it was my turn to let out a weird sound, born of frustration and anxiety. "What if I don't like what I find, or, worse, what if I find nothing?"

"All will be well, Schatz." A phrase so often used by him, it could be considered a family motto.

"I'm sure you're right." Yet I shook my head. "Anyway, I'd better call it a night."

"All right then. Keep your ears stiff, Kensington. You hear me?"

"Loud and clear. You too."

We hung up, and slowly, I lowered my cell. It had been a long day, and nothing more would be accomplished tonight.

I placed my notebook on the table and frowned. One alarming possibility I deliberately hadn't considered was the one Jonah had hinted at: something terrible might have happened to Raven. Even so, why did his people immediately suspect human interference? Had there been precedence? Had the pack drawn the animosity of the humans somehow?

I scribbled one last line into my notebook before turning in for the night. Tomorrow morning, long before I was to meet up with Drake, I was expected by Natalie, the local librarian. Maybe she'd have good news.

Ⅎive

I woke up before eight in a room decorated in a weird nautical theme—anchors on the pillows, little boats stenciled across the wall.

I pulled back the drapes to let in the morning's rays and took in the backyard. Sunshine glimmered off the lawn. The carport had a skylight and had been repurposed as an outdoor seating area. A turquoise-colored patio set sat on a wooden deck, shielded by a large umbrella. I'd assumed they'd put me up in a hotel or, worse, lodge me right there in Jonah's house. That would have definitely impeded my coming and goings.

After my routine of sit-ups, lunges, and squats, I had maybe two hours before Drake would pick me up, but my app assured me the library was only a skip and a jump away.

Expecting another scorcher of a day, I pulled my hair up into a high ponytail to keep it off my neck. A short-sleeved blazer over my strappy top would keep me safe from the sun. My father's best tailor had made the jacket from lightweight material. It boasted two zippered inside pockets and a waist-hugging cut.

At fifteen minutes after eight, I snatched my keys from a

sideboard and stuffed my slim wallet into one of the hidden pockets, where I also kept my charged USB voice recorder on standby. This ingenious device had once helped me obtain a restraining order against an ex, when it had recorded his threats in crystal-clear audio. Bastard thought he could terrorize me, but he stood no chance against the evidence.

Since then I'd made it my practice to carry it with me on all my jobs.

I gently closed the door and slid my shades in front of my eyes. The quiet neighborhood's cheerful landscaping was the result of loving care and many a green thumb, while the tall trees provided sufficient shade against the sun that was breaking through the haze. Once again, Marlontown projected the image of the perfect idyll, and once again, my spidey sense tingled. In my line of work, nothing was ever what it seemed.

After ten minutes of Stepford-like suburbia, it was time to face facts. The app I'd consulted had lied to me about how long it would take to get to my destination.

I hated not having my car with me, and the feeling of helplessness, even nakedness, that went along with it. It had taken me weeks to decide on the perfect set of wheels, and the Ford had been the culmination of my effort. But what I hated more than being without a ride was being late. Natalie had agreed to open the library early for my benefit. The least I could do was show up on time.

The surroundings held less appeal as my pace increased. Of course, walking fast came with its own problems in temperatures such as these—a thin film of perspiration on my forehead and my back.

The information I was about to uncover had better be worth it. Did Natalie's books contain details about my ancestors? Maybe pictures of grand-parents or great-great uncles? If Dad had been a tad more specific about what he was hoping I'd find here, I could have prepared targeted questions for the librarian.

A brown sedan rolled up beside me.

"Hey, Princess Kensington." Buck, Drake's partner-in-grump from yesterday, had his windows down and beckoned me.

Once again, his oversized sunglasses sat on his nose, obscuring his eyes.

I headed to the passenger side. "Hi Buck. You can call me Kensi."

He beamed. "Great. Can I give you a lift?"

I scanned the streets, but had to admit defeat. Wherever this fabled library was, I wasn't going to get there on time by the power of my own feet. Who knew my savior would come with a brown Nissan and a huge moustache?

"I appreciate that." I climbed in and fastened the seat belt. "I need to get to the library by, well, pretty much now."

"In Denville? No worries. I'll have you there in no time." Buck zoomed off at Mach-10, forcing me to support myself on the dashboard.

"I appreciate your taking care of my car." I leaned against the bend in the road so my shoulder didn't bump against his.

"No problem. I filled out everything as far as I could and collected a copy of the police report on your behalf." Buck gesticulated wildly, only nudging the steering wheel when it was necessary. "Jonah has all your documents. He'll need a few signatures, and you're golden."

"Again. Thank you."

"What do you need at the library? If you're after stuff to do, I can take you places tonight. We have an awesome bar you're gonna like."

The bar that I was going to like hadn't been built yet. I was more of a stay-at-home, read-a-book kind of person. "Maybe some other time."

"How about tomorrow? There's a great rave in the woods where we can go to hang loose. Just werewolves. Humans not allowed."

Jeez. Why had everyone in Marlontown boarded the werewolves-only train? Sure, there were differences, but differences didn't need to lead to segregation or discrimination. Or maybe Drake had been right, and life among humans had changed me. Was I making an elephant out of a molehill?

"Thanks, but while I'm working, I won't have time for play. Jonah asked me here to do a job. I get the feeling he won't take kindly to my skiving on his dime—or to you leading me astray." I added a coquettish laugh to soften the blow of my rejection.

Buck's sunglasses concealed his eyes, but his frown told its own story. "Yeah, he wouldn't like that. Maybe when you're done."

"Yeah, maybe then."

The sleepy setting perked up almost as soon as we passed the sign into Denville. The endless array of colorful houses gave way to cafés, restaurants and boutiques. Trees and bushes added occasional splashes of green.

In front of us, a young man pushed a black stroller with a fully extended hood across the road. Buck slowed, and the man raised a grateful hand.

"Pretty town," I said.

"That it is." Buck aimed a finger at the Victorian-style buildings we passed. "Most of us live in Marlontown, but we consider the whole Triangle our home."

"By 'us' you mean werewolves?"

"Yeah. Since the humans arrived, much has changed. Not sure why we need three coffee shops for every street, or shops that sell swanky fashion when most of us still live off our land, but that's the way the world rolls nowadays."

"I read that Marlontown didn't have its own school until thirty or forty years ago."

"We schooled our kids at home."

Simpler times they were, no doubt. Maybe it took a special

frame of mind to yearn for the good old days before inside toilets and running water.

"Right, we're here." Buck pointed at a huge silver-black statue of a wolf that stood outside a glass-fronted building, and slowed to a stop. "Here's my number, in case you need another ride."

He handed me a small sheet that contained many phone numbers. Jonah, Drake, Leo, and others I hadn't met, were also listed.

"It's the call sheet for the Moon Festival group," he said. "As in, we're the ones who organize the Moon Festival. Maybe you'll come this month?"

My last Moon Festival at my father's court had ended with me drinking too much wine and not getting enough sleep. Maybe the Wild Pack's Moon Festivals were the same, maybe they were a more somber affair, but was Buck the person I'd want to accompany to such an important event? He'd been helpful, sure, but he lacked excitement. Leo had a pleasant disposition, too, but he at least carried himself with the confidence of a protector.

"We'll see how long I'll be in town." I gripped the door handle. "Thanks, though. You really helped me out."

He grinned and tipped his non-existent hat. "Any time. Any time."

I got out and watched him drive off. Despite the early hour, the market at the far end of the street was in full swing. A floral scent wafted across, mixed with the earthy smell of vegetables. Two ladies with bulging shopping bags strolled toward me. One pointed at me then held her hand up to her mouth to whisper to her friend. Had she recognized me from the papers? Or was the presence of a stranger that big a deal?

I smiled politely and made my way past the wolf statue, which I took for a monument to the triple town's werewolf-dominated past. Inside the library, a woman, around my age, sat behind an oversized desk. Her auburn hair was short and suited her flawless light-brown skin. She was typing on her computer with her right hand and held up the left to indicate I should wait.

"…D two." She leaned into her computer screen with a squint, and eventually straightened. "Hello, Miss von Berg?"

I smiled. "Yes."

Two prior emails had explained to her where I was from and what I was after, including my father's Nordic origins. But if she'd expected a typical German blonde with a Scandinavian face, she kept her surprise well hidden.

She rolled her wheelchair around the desk and shook my hand. "I'm Natalie Daniels. Call me Nat. This town isn't large enough to bother with last names." She let out a melodic laugh.

It was a rare laugh. A laugh that came not just as a noise from a throat, but also as a feeling from a pair of inquisitive eyes and a big heart. A laugh that blew away my reservations and shyness and instantly connected with me.

"In that case, please call me Kensi." I beamed back.

"What a lovely name." Nat beckoned me to follow and rolled through a door into the deserted main library. A selection of books covered two of the tables.

The library's layout was wheelchair-friendly both in terms of the sparse furniture and the height of the shelves, which came up to my chest. Overall, the surprisingly small space appeared as loved and cared for as the impressive landscaping that had greeted me in Marlontown.

"I hope I'm not late," I said.

I was, by three minutes, but Americans tended to be less anal about that than Germans.

"Not at all. And you don't need to whisper." Nat gestured for me to sit. "One lady comes in every day to read, but I'm not expecting her or anybody else until this afternoon."

"I like libraries. They remind me of my childhood." I shook my head. "Not that they're only for children."

"No, you're right. We live in a rushed world and people simply don't make the time to kick back with a good read. Anyway, let's get started." She pulled one of the books toward her. "You said you're interested in a woman called Maaren Kamlo, right?"

I nodded.

"I had some downtime yesterday, so I took the liberty of checking our historicals for you."

"I appreciate that."

"Although the name Maaren Kamlo isn't mentioned specifically, the Kamlos were also known in their circles as Lovel, meaning *lover*. As luck would have it, I did find an entry for Maarah Lovel, which is close enough for me to think I got the right name."

My heart banged against my ribcage. Just once, and just long enough to make me notice it. This was real. My mother, once flesh and blood, had over the years become a feeling for me, a vague notion of warmth and love. Now the time had come to breathe life back into her, but was I ready?

Nat opened the oversized volume at a marked location and traced her index finger down the page.

"Here." She angled the book so I could read.

Maarah Lovel, born on February fourteenth, no year given. Finding out my mother had been known by another name messed with my head. Maaren Kamlo was something that caused my body to respond. Maarah Lovel, on the other hand, read like a stranger.

I sat back and kept my disappointment to myself. "You said in their circles the Kamlo name was also known as Lovel. I don't understand. What circles?"

"Oh. I thought you knew. Maarah was Roma."

"A gypsy?" I touched my mouth.

"Gypsy" was most likely an offensive term, although I didn't know enough about this ethnicity to understand why the word was supposed to be off-limits. Hell, I didn't even know werewolf travelers existed, although clearly there was no reason why they shouldn't. My kind might have taken its first steps on the American continent, but since then, we'd spread all around the globe and now lived in every country under the sun.

"Maarah's tribe was part of the Roms, a group of Eastern Europeans that arrived in our triangle of towns after 1880." Nat opened another book. "They used to live in the woods around here."

"I see." I scratched my head. "Anything about Maaren in particular?"

"As far as I can tell, Maarah walked away from her clan. She became an outsider when she left to marry a man who wasn't part of their culture. Maybe he refused to pay a bride price. Whatever the reason, a woman leaving in disgrace was a big deal, as you would imagine from a patriarchal society."

I gave a demonstrative sigh. "Is there any other kind of society?"

She closed the book. "I hear you. The glass ceiling's alive and kicking in the twenty-first century. Anyway, we have more books on the history of the Roma who lived locally, but they've been checked out by our local history buff. In fact, he might be able to tell you more. There's little he doesn't know about this place." Her cheeks turned a healthy pink.

Damn. My palms were moist, my mouth dry. Even though I'd prepared myself for the search, I hadn't prepared myself for what I was going to find. And now that my past was within reach, I needed to learn more. I needed to know *everything*.

"Could you tell me how to get in touch with this historian?" I fingered the page that held the only reference to my mother. "This is important to me."

"I can't give you his details. He's a private person, you know. But I could give him a call right now, if you like."

"That would be great."

Nat pushed away from the table. "I'll be back in a sec. In the meantime, you might want to read this."

While she was gone, I studied the article she'd placed before me. According to the author, the Lovel family used to be a big deal in their community. Whoever penned the book referred to Maaren's father—my grandfather—as a *king*.

Without a recognized royal status, no werewolf would today be called a king. Then again, things were different when my mother, then in her thirties, met Dad. In werewolf terms, she'd been a young woman who should have looked forward to another fifteen decades or so by my father's side. Instead, she got ten years.

I took a long, labored breath.

No point crying over the past. Dad did enough of that for both of us.

Why did my mother's departure cause such an uproar, though? Dad had plenty of money, so he could have surely afforded the going bride price, from a couple of camels to a case-full of dollars. Besides, what better catch for a traveler's daughter than a bona-fide future king?

Natalie returned to the table and gave me a thumbs-up. "I managed to get ahold of our expert. He's agreed to meet you here in twenty minutes. You're going to like him."

"What's the time now?" I had to be at home by ten, and it would be considered bad form to ditch Drake on my first day.

Nat glanced past my shoulder. "It's nine."

"Thanks." That gave me time to greet the historian, arrange a more appropriate time to pepper him with questions, and then jog back to the house to meet Drake with a nothing-to-see-here face.

"All we can do now is wait, so how about a bottle of water?" Nat closed the books and arranged them on top of each other.

"That would be fantastic. You've been so nice to me. Can I help you?"

"Oh no. Let me work for my pay check." She placed two of the volumes on her lap and wheeled over to a wall shelf to my right, in which she arranged both books.

What an amazing woman, and a prime example of why human

company was preferable. She'd never heard of me, and therefore she had no expectations of how I should be. She simply accepted who I was. No stupid games or challenges.

If only the wolf world were that unassuming.

My mother had broken with her family and gone off to join another pack, and here I was, caterwauling about my fate. Despite moving from one male-dominated world to another, Mom had left her mark on our society, both as the alpha's mate and as a beloved queen. Her human side had dispensed wisdom, her wolf had been fierce. How could I expect anything less of myself?

As alpha-in-waiting, I was supposed to be strong, and I needed to be to turn the plans I'd been making for the past twenty-eight years of my life into reality. Once I took the throne, things were going to change drastically for my pack. The era of men was over. The poor bastards just didn't know it yet.

I got out my phone and looked at the picture I'd taken of my parents' wedding photo. The dark-haired woman next to my father usually seemed a virtual stranger, but at this moment, I felt close to her.

Natalie returned with a plastic bottle tucked between her knees.

"You're an angel." I gulped the ice-cold water.

"Not if I have my way." She tipped back her head and laughed. Her shoulders shook as she wheeled herself back to the desk in the foyer.

I returned my attention to the photo and my parents' smiles. Long-ago smiles I never got to witness.

Dad got misty-eyed talking about my mother now. He'd kept her things and flew into a rage if anyone dared speak her name with anything other than reverence. He'd mated for love, even took the antiquated Moon Promise with her, which bound them together for eternity.

A promise to love one another beyond death.

How idiotic was that?

Humans didn't live half as long as us, but even in their society, happily-ever-afters were a notion exiled to Hollywood movies. Love simply didn't last, not at a time when unplanned pregnancies, the Internet, and a generous amount of alcohol were the accepted ways of finding a partner.

If my father had shown an ounce of common sense, he never would have taken the Moon Promise. The magic created that night had ensured the love they'd felt at that moment would never falter. If he'd simply married her during the day, like most werewolf couples did nowadays, he would have gotten over her death by now. Maybe he would have even chosen another mate, rather than wasting the rest of his life pining for a woman he'd never see again.

This amount of grief didn't leave room for a daughter.

The sound of voices pulled me from my dark thoughts. I placed my phone on the table and leaned forward for a better view of the door.

Nat rolled into the room, face flushed, and gave a flirty laugh.

Behind her—

Uh-oh. Busted.

Drake's frame pushed through the door. So much man in such a small space left me breathless. He had a wolf's natural grace, but even so, there was a confidence in him that disarmed me. Despite his height, he didn't stoop or bend his neck, not even now as he talked to Natalie.

In fact, he was acting as if he hadn't yet noticed me.

But the tightening of my skin told the truth. It built slowly, from a prickle to the flutter of a hundred lashes. I surged to my feet, unsteady. A new wave of pain flooded me and, despite my efforts, made me flinch.

"Kensi." Natalie gestured at him. "This is Drake. He knows the history of this place like no one else."

Drake's silver eyes fixated on me like tractor beams, while his dominance pulled and pinched at my body. My thighs trembled, and my knees were ready to call it a day.

A flicker swept across his expression.

He'd seen something in my face. Something that tugged on his lips.

Maybe it was too early, or I was out of practice. The alpha's onslaught yesterday hadn't left me half as shaken.

But I did have one advantage. This was a human library. My wheelhouse.

I put out my hand. "Nice to meet you."

With a tiny delay, he shook it.

My gaze refused to leave his frown, but my voice sounded cheerful enough. "Nat speaks *very* highly of you. I expected some kind of superhero."

Drake's dominance wavered.

"We're old friends." Nat patted his back, which in terms of their height difference manifested as a slap on the ass.

Why hadn't I seen it earlier? Nat had blushed when she spoke of him. Were they seeing each other? Had they had a fling in the past?

I gave the smile of a woman who'd stumbled on a naughty secret. "I can see that."

Drake rolled back his pheromones, giving me room to breathe again.

"I didn't mean it like that." Nat wagged a finger at me. "You're a bad girl. I knew I liked you." She snorted a laugh. "Anyway, I'd better leave you two to it. See you later." She patted him again.

I waited until she was out of earshot. "You make a cute couple."

My voice was sharper than I'd intended. What did I care if the two of them had a flirtatious relationship? I was neither her nor his keeper.

"Why are you here?" His tone quivered, and he yanked back a chair. "Jonah made it clear that I'm supposed to accompany you."

I sat back down. "Yeah, while I'm on the job. This isn't the job. This here is private."

He lowered himself into the chair next to me and leaned in. "No, he didn't say while you're on the job. For the duration of your stay."

"That's not going to happen. I understand why you feel you need to be my protector around other wolves, but this…" I gestured around me. "This is my world."

He scoffed. "If you consider the human world your world, you're deluded."

"Watch it!"

"I like humans. I do. But they know jack about our urge to run free as wolves. About the thrill of the hunt, the joy of clamping our teeth around a young buck's throat."

So they knew as much as me.

I crossed my arms. "Who cares? There's more to life than that."

"Yes, all things they can't comprehend: a loyalty humans only dream of; love that lasts a lifetime and beyond; a code of honor and unity. We may share a world with them, but we are not of their world."

"You're wrong," I mumbled.

What gave him the right to trample over everything I clung to? To dismiss the life I'd built as a grand delusion?

"No more lone excursions, princess."

Males didn't dictate my life, especially not bullies like him. But the tightness in my throat stopped me from saying any of it.

If only to shut him up, I nodded. No doubt, I'd pay for this concession later.

Drake relaxed the frown on his face and withdrew the last of his dominance. "Nat said you're interested in the Roma tribe that used to live in these parts. How come?"

I sat up. "Used to? You mean they don't anymore?"

"You haven't answered my question."

"You haven't answered mine."

His mouth quirked. "I asked first."

"What are you, five?"

"Do you want answers or not? Up to you." He got to his feet. "Anyway, it's nearly ten. I told Raven's parents we'd be by this morning."

"What? Why? This is my investigation." I stood and glared at him across the table. "If you've taken over as PI, be my guest. I'll be glad to go home."

"I just assumed." He exhaled loudly through his nose. "Hell, you're difficult. Why must you fight back on everything? Do you want to meet with them or not?"

"Since you've already made the appointment, what choice do I have?" I flicked my wrist, as if dealing with jerks like him should earn me double the pay. "Give me a minute."

I stalked to the bathroom, which was clearly marked with a humorous sign of a woman holding her knees in an *I-can't-hold-it* pose. Of course, a visit to Raven's parents would have been my first stop anyway, but this was *my* show. The sooner Drake got that, the higher my chances of success.

I splashed cold water over my face before performing an acrobatic act to dry it under the automatic dryer.

Nat's information had deepened the mystery of my mother's origins. Fate was playing a crummy game with me by placing at least a few of the answers in Drake's hands. But my mother was dead, while Raven hopefully wasn't, so I had to get my priorities straight.

I exited the bathroom and collided with Drake outside the door.

"Jeez, give me some space, will ya?" I glared.

He cocked his head and raised his eyebrows. Once again, his gaze connected with my mouth.

My cheeks warmed and my breathing sped up.

Dammit.

His sly smile deserved a good kick.

Instead, I shrugged as if Drake was a minor annoyance. Not even a blip on my radar. "Ready to go?"

He held up my phone. "You left this on the table."

I snatched it from his fingers and mumbled my thanks. Having this oaf around had me all discombobulated. Not good when I needed my wits about me to find the missing woman.

We stepped through the door, with me taking the lead. He'd better get used to walking behind me from now on.

"Leaving so soon?" Nat's chirpy voice skipped and bounced across the foyer. "I hope Drake can help you find what you're looking for."

"We'll see." I raised my hand. "I'll be in touch."

"See ya, Nat," Drake said.

Natalie waved at us, and unless I'd completely got her wrong, probably stared at Drake's ass as we walked out.

Six

THE SILENT JOURNEY TO RAVEN'S parents' house
stretched. Maybe my behavior in the library had
crossed a line. Drake tried to be helpful by arranging
the interview, and picking up the phone I'd carelessly left behind
also wasn't the heinous act that deserved a dressing down.

In fact, I'd been pissy since I arrived. What I couldn't overlook
was that these people—Jonah, Leo, Drake—had lost one of their
own, without warning or explanation. The alpha and his protectors
ran the pack under a promise of safety, yet Raven had slipped
through the cracks. Understandable that this was eating at them.

The humility in calling in outside help deserved my respect,
not my petulance.

American flags waved from a handful of porches, angled up in
a proud salute. I'd prepared well for my trip and read whatever I
could on Marlontown. Patriotism aside, this place bulged under
its historic significance. Stories from here had survived across time
and space.

Many centuries ago, before Leif Erikson and Christopher
Columbus, the local woods had birthed the First Ones of our kind,

when a young Native American woman and a male wolf fell in love. Separated by species, they made a pact under the full moon—a pact that had survived to this day as the Moon Promise. The wolf gave her a piece of his animal soul, and the woman shared with him her human soul.

After that fateful night, they'd spend half their lives in human form. They and their offspring would build shelters, hunt food, and live in harmony with nature. Once a month, however, the moon would bring about their change into their animal forms, so they might quench their thirst for freedom and run together without constraints.

Much of our origin story might be romanticized BS to explain our existence. In any case, the moon no longer determined our shifts—certainly not mine, damn it.

"Are you ready to tell me why you're interested in the travelers?" Drake barely held on to the steering wheel, yet his relaxed posture didn't mean he was careless. He was not a guy that would allow himself to be in an accident.

I placed my head against the headrest of my seat and continued to study him from the corner of my eyes. Maybe, for once, I could put on my big-girl pants and act like a decent person rather than an entitled diva.

"My father told me about the travelers," I said by way of apology. "I was simply curious. Who were they? Where are they now? I gotta say, though, Natalie's books threw up more questions than answers."

My evasive answer did the trick—of pissing him off. His hands clasped the steering wheel, as if not slugging me took effort.

Maybe it did. He wasn't the first to feel the call of violence around me.

"So?" I loosened my hair then retied the ponytail.

"So what?"

"So what can you tell me about them?"

"I give you that, princess. You have a talent for using a lot of words to not answer my question."

"What? I told you why I want to know. I'm curious, that's all."

He overtook a car and signaled the driver hello. "Yeah, and I dress up like a fairy every night and prance around the forest."

I looked at him wide-eyed with feigned disbelief. "I would have never guessed that about you."

"I'm a man of mystery." His tone remained cool and matter-of-fact. "Anyway, if you want answers, I want to know why."

I prodded at the blasted air vent, which was currently angled at my knees. "Fine. If you stop calling me princess, I'll tell you what you want to know." I hooked my fingers into the slits and yanked, but all I got were cooler breasts. "You can't tell Jonah, though."

He scratched his jaw. "That's a problem. He's my alpha."

"Yeah, but he doesn't need to know everything. If I asked you not to tell him I own pink bunny slippers, that wouldn't be a problem, right?"

"Do you own pink bunny slippers?"

I lobbed a rare and deliberate smile at him. "Maybe. But you dress up like a fairy so I'm ahead."

Drake chuckled, a sound that ran like a warm shower down my back. "Okay, I get what you're saying. If the reason you're interested in the travelers has nothing to do with Jonah or Raven's disappearance, I won't tell him."

Dad had urged me to keep my search for my past a secret, but unless I confided in Drake, at least to some degree, I'd never find out where I came from. What's more, maybe this town or my mother's origins held the answer to my inability to exude dominance or turn into my wolf shape.

I coughed, shifted from one butt cheek to the other, and finally settled back into my seat. "Okay then. You see, the thing is, there might be a genetic link between the travelers and my family. And Dad doesn't want anyone to know."

"He's embarrassed?" Drake shot me a sideways glance.

"No. What I'm saying is, like any pack we'd love to trace our lineage back to the first werewolves, but what if it goes the other way? What if I find out we come from a line of thieves or pirates or serial killers? That *would* be embarrassing."

"Right."

"You sound disappointed."

"No, I get that, but I don't get why Jonah can't know about it. He and your father are friends."

"Still, it's private. For me, too."

He cocked his head for a second, then gave a nod. "The travelers weren't your ordinary Roma travelers. That was the image they cultivated for the humans, sure. But really, they were werewolves who simply liked their own company. They didn't mix with humans or other werewolves."

I balled a fist. "You're speaking in the past tense."

"That's because the travelers are gone now. All that's left is the old campsite. No one knows for sure what happened to them once they moved on."

"Why did they leave?"

"Many reasons. Some believe they left because of Marlon, our old alpha. Others say they had internal squabbles that led them to break up and move away." Drake's focus lay with the road, but his mind seemed to have wandered into the past.

"Is the town named after your old alpha?"

"No, after his grandfather. Anyway, Marlon wasn't what you'd call tolerant. He had…" Drake coughed. "Issues."

"The travelers must have been used to getting the cold shoulder."

Drake's thumb caressed the curve of his steering wheel, a sensual motion entirely wasted on a truck, before he tightened his grip. "Around forty years ago, Marlon ordered his people to attack the travelers. To kill the males and the children."

"What about the women?"

"They were to be eliminated too, you know, after they'd served their purpose." He lowered his voice. "Traveler women might not have been good enough to marry in Marlon's opinion, but there's nothing wrong with a bit of brutal fun, right?"

Drake's words clamped around my chest like a vise. If my mother hadn't got away, that could have been her fate. On second thought, maybe her precarious situation was exactly why my dad had sided with Jonah against Marlon.

All the more reason for her father to approve of her relationship with Dad. Why hadn't he?

"Killing the travelers was what Marlon wanted to do, but he didn't succeed, did he?" I opened and closed my fist a few times. "Your people stopped him, right?"

"It wasn't so easy. You obey your alpha. End of story." He shrugged away my rebuke with his eyebrows, but the tightness in his jaw remained. "But yes, eventually, people did stand up. It was a dark period, and when the dust settled, Jonah became our alpha, with your father's help, I'm told. If those two hadn't banded together, who knows what would have happened. Still, too many people got hurt in that conflict."

Drake sounded forlorn, trapped in a past he could no longer access. He couldn't have been more than a cub back then, but it was possible his family suffered under Marlon's rule. Was his past, whatever it was, the driving force behind his interest in history?

I reached out, nearly touching his arm, but ran my hand through my hair instead. "I assume your pack is more enlightened now?"

He moved in his seat, neglecting the accelerator, before wrenching his attention back to the task of driving. "All in all, yes, but the regime change has been an adjustment, for some more than others. Marlon ruled with an iron fist and kept us isolated not only from travelers, but from humans, which is how he held on to our land. Jonah's more inclusive, but mingling with humans had the unfortunate result that he had to sell our territory bit by bit to make ends meet."

"That's a sign of the times though, isn't it? Werewolf numbers have been stable for centuries, unlike humans, who plant their roots anywhere they go. They multiply and take over. It's nature."

"Maybe."

Drake pulled into a road of smoky-blue single-family houses, each with a wide drive. "This is where Raven's parents live. Birdie and Pike." He parked in the shade of two large trees that at least stood a chance at preventing the truck from melting. Rather than get out, he laid his hands in his lap. "Listen. They haven't moved on since their daughter disappeared."

"Meaning what?"

"Meaning they're hurting. But they're not bad people. Life hasn't been kind to them, so tread lightly."

I pointed a thumb at my chest. "You and I haven't met, but I have empathy coming out of my ass."

He rubbed his palm across his face. "Jesus. Maybe we should—"

"Calm down. I'll be good." I chuckled. "And please, don't tell them I'm a princess."

"You *are* a princess."

"Not today. Today I'm a private investigator. Okay?" I shooed him out of the truck. "Let's go."

We got out and headed to the front door.

"Does Raven have brothers or sisters?" I asked. "The file didn't say."

"Had. A brother. We went to school together. He was hit by a car when he was eighteen."

"I see." This family had indeed been through a lot. "Sorry."

Drake leaned forward and pressed the doorbell. "It happens. It's all kinds of fucked up, but it happens."

"Yeah."

A middle-aged woman with an eighties-style perm opened. "Drake."

She only stood as high as his chin, but she drew him into a determined hug that forced him to bend low. Their private gesture held a degree of tenderness, and I took a few steps back to give them space.

"Hi, Birdie." Drake gave a muffled chuckle.

"It's so good to see you. It's been too long."

He slithered out of her embrace with skill and gentle charm. "I'm sorry."

"No, don't be." She waved him off. "Life gets busy. I understand."

Drake moved aside and gestured at me. "This is Princess Kensington. She's here to ask you some questions about Raven."

She brushed past his bulk with the vigor of a running back.

I stretched out my hand to create a buffer zone. Unlike her, I wasn't a hugger.

She took my hand and curtseyed.

It had been years since anyone had done that. Humans weren't aware of my royal lineage, and wolves from free packs didn't know the protocol or deliberately ignored my status in defiance of the crown.

"Pleasure to meet you," I pitched my voice to sound polite yet warm, like my dad had taught me.

"Come in, please." Birdie smoothed her pleated skirt. "A real princess in our house. This is exciting. Pike!" she shouted. "Look who's here."

I gave Drake an annoyed glance and he returned an innocent smile. Hadn't I told him to leave the title alone? Sooner or later, he'd pay for that, but first, I'd have to ride out the interview.

Pike ambled into the hall and bowed before retreating through the door to the living room, where TV noises clanged loud enough for the neighbors to hear.

So far, so painless.

"Sorry about that, your highness." Birdie led Drake and me into the living room and prodded her husband with a stern glance.

He got the hint and switched off the television.

Birdie sat down beside her husband and gestured to two wingback chairs.

We sat, and all eyes turned to me.

"Right," I said. "You know why I'm here?"

"You're here to help find Raven." She fingered a blue rectangular pendant on her necklace. "It's good one of our own is still taking the matter seriously. The humans simply gave up. Said she ran off."

"I'll do everything I can to locate her, that I promise."

Birdie's sad gaze flitted from me to Drake and her face broke into a smile. "Drake, it is so good to see you. So good." She nudged her husband. "Isn't it good to see him?"

Pike nodded slightly.

"Why, Drake and our Ralph were two peas in a pod. Inseparable." Birdie lifted a flowered teapot from the coffee table and served tea in delicate china cups. She then recalled at length the antics the two boys had got up to in their youth.

I set down my tea. "Excuse my skepticism, but it's hard to imagine Drake as a gangly teenager."

She chuckled. "Oh, he was as gangly as they come. Look here." She opened a photo album. She didn't even have to get up to get it. It sat right beside her, this link to her past.

She angled it for me to see.

There he was, skinny and without the tats, among a group of boys. Even then, Drake oozed dark intensity. The slightly sloping smile hadn't changed. If I'd met him at that young age, before I grew jaded and distant, I could have so easily fallen for him.

"This is Ralph?" I pointed to a guy, roughly the same age as Drake, but who had already filled out well for his age.

"Yes. And Dirk, Leo, and look, here's Raven and Sable, right at the end there." Birdie glanced up, her cheeks flushed. "Sable was our Raven's best friend." Her head jerked back. "Is, I mean. She *is* Raven's best friend. They stayed close even after Sable moved away."

I placed my hand on her arm. "That's a lovely necklace Raven's wearing."

Birdie touched her own. "Pike gave them to us on the day of Raven's first solo performance. She's a gifted musician, you know."

"So I've heard."

"You must find her." Birdie's eyes glistened with early tears.

Pike grunted. He sat at the end of the sofa, legs and arms crossed, one eyebrow up.

Not once had he engaged in the conversation or shown any of Birdie's enthusiasm for this investigation. Maybe he simply didn't take to me, or his masculinity prevented him from cracking a smile. How good could a private investigator be if she was a woman?

"I'm sorry." I lifted my head. "Did you say something?"

Drake's warning cough rolled through the laden atmosphere.

"Nothing. Go on." Pike pulled his shoulders in, but did so with a sneer on his lips.

A pressure burrowed into the place where my dominance should be, somewhere hidden inside my stomach. A push right now would show him I was twice the wolf he was. But nothing came. I clamped my jaw shut. Focused. Wished.

Not a single drop of pheromones evaporated off my skin.

God, I hated this, this total absence of power. It made me feel weak. Hell, it proved I *was* weak.

I turned my back to him, wolf-speak for *you're not even worth bothering with*, and smiled at Birdie. "Where did Raven like to go? How did she spend her days?"

Her lips trembled. "I don't know. We used to be close, but then…" She cast a fleeting glance at her husband. "You know how it is when girls get to that age."

I twisted to fix him with a glare and sharpened my pitch. "Did she go out often, stay out late?"

"I don't like what you're implying." Pike leaned forward and clawed his fingers into his thighs. "My daughter wasn't like that."

"What *was* she like then? You say she was into music. Why didn't she go to college to pursue her interest?"

"She's too young for that." He glowered. "She was better off staying at home, working for me."

A wolf's natural lifespan ranged between one-hundred and fifty years and two hundred years. "I agree she was young, but old enough to get her feet wet in life, don't you think?"

He surged up from his seat. "Do we need to go through this again? What is she going to find that you and Leo didn't?"

I whipped my head around to Drake, and for a second, control over my face slipped. Jonah had implied I wasn't the first wolf looking into Raven's disappearance, yet it hadn't occurred to me that Leo and Drake had been involved. They'd sure kept that quiet.

Drake kept his cool. He lowered his head, not in submission, but as a lead-in to the meanest glare this side of the equator. "Settle down, man."

But Pike's outburst had given me what I needed—the conviction that Raven did have reason to run away, even if it was dangerous to leave her alpha's protection behind. Luckily, I had found a handful of runaways and returned them safely to their parents over the past few years. If this was all there was to her disappearance, I'd be back in Chicago long before the Moon Festival.

"Do what you like." Pike waved off. "Raven's gone. Probably lying dead in a ditch, and this girl's not going to do any better than you did."

Drake exploded to his feet. His dominance shot across the room—an invisible bundle of thorns flung with perfect marksmanship. Pike and Birdie straightened as if yanked upright by a rope.

My arms itched, my shoulders stung, but he'd lobbed worse at me. Either I was getting used to his power, or he was going easy on his friend's parents.

"You *will* show respect." Despite everything, he kept his voice steady and polite.

Pike quickly dropped his gaze. "I apologize. I didn't mean to overstep my mark."

As fun as it would be to watch Drake flex those delicious biceps of his, Pike didn't deserve his anger. He was acting like a complete dick, but years of investigating disappearances had shown me this explosive anger again and again. Pike was a grieving father, discouraged by the lack of answers.

I got up. "Listen. I understand that raking over the past is tough, and talking when everything in you screams for action is frustrating, but we're nearly done here. Would it be possible for me to see Raven's room?"

"Of course." Birdie scuttled up from the sofa, her face ashen.

Drake's dominance waned.

If it were my choice, it would rage on. Drake had defended me. No one had ever done that. Most of the time I took care of business myself. It was expected, and I was good at it. Hell, I was proud of it. My father was the first to insist I fight my own battles, but just once it would have been nice to know someone cared enough to shield me. Just once, I wanted to not be at DEFCON 1 around other werewolves.

I signaled Drake to remain with the husband, and followed Birdie up the stairs.

She pointed at the first door on the left. "This is Ralph's room. We were going to turn it into a guest room, but I couldn't bring myself to pack up his belongings." She turned away and let out a small sigh.

These people had been put through the wringer. Birdie wasn't so different from my dad. He also hung on to tokens of the past as if they could take him back to a time when his loved one was still alive.

I was five or six when Mom died, too young to fully understand what had happened. How a man could love her without ever having spoken to her, and how he could kill her because she loved my father and me instead of him. What I did get without any need for an explanation was that when love and death collided, the fallout was on a nuclear level.

Love was like a drug that brightened the world for a while, but the minute it left, as it inevitably did, all that remained were pointless souvenirs and a dull, dark existence. But the true victims were the forgotten ones, the *other* sisters and brothers, or the sons and daughters who spent their lifetime trying to matter again.

"And this is Raven's room." Birdie stopped a few feet short of the door. "It's exactly the way she likes it, so please don't disturb anything."

"I won't." I waited until she'd gone back downstairs before I opened the door.

The young woman who lived in the room I entered was tidy, exact, and more like me than I'd thought. We were both victims of a lost love, and we were both anal about keeping everything in its place. To be fair, she didn't have enough possessions to cause a mess. Her closet was small. Three pairs of shoes stood in front of the almost empty shelves. A violin case leaned against a chair, which stood in front of a stand with sheet music.

Pinned to the corkboard above her desk was a schedule, which revolved around violin practice. Other than that, the walls were bare, probably because Raven was too old for anything cutesy. Music books lined the shelves. Not a TV or game console in sight.

If this room truly represented Raven, she abided by a set of rules. The only question was if these rules were set by her, or by overbearing parents. Understanding this aspect of her mind would tell me whether it was likely she'd run away and, if so, why.

My phone rang. "Hello?"

"Kensi? Hi, it's Natalie. From the library."

"Oh. Um. Hi."

"I was wondering if you wanted to meet for a late lunch tomorrow if you're still around? I figured you probably don't know anyone yet and I could give you the scoop on the town."

After a day with Drake, human company was exactly what the doctor ordered.

"That sounds great. All I need are the time and place." I grabbed a piece of paper from the memo block on Raven's desk and jotted down the details Natalie gave me. "Great. See you tomorrow afternoon."

I'd known Nat was a diamond the minute I met her. At worst, I'd have a break from work and wolves. At best, I'd make a friend and catch the one-oh-one on the human portion of town.

I rummaged through Raven's drawers, checked behind the organized papers and pens. Even someone like her—or like me—kept guilty secrets, the personal stuff with meaning. Photos. Movie stubs. Letters. Junk to outsiders, but valued possessions to us.

The space under her bed was empty, and the mattress didn't yield anything either. A diary would have made my life too easy.

If this were my room, where would I hide my treasures? The floorboards looked solid, and the furniture was sparse. Besides, I'd want to keep my stuff close by, not hidden in a place that required a tool belt.

I stepped back over to the desk and lifted the bottom of the corkboard off the wall to feel behind it.

Bingo. Two photos were taped to the back. I retrieved them and straightened the corkboard as if I'd never been here.

In the photos, Raven sat on grass between a guy's knees, her arm outstretched for a joint selfie. A tree with full foliage in the shape of an almost perfect sphere stood in the distance behind them. Long dark hair curled around her smiling face. Brown eyes glanced up from under full lashes. Her necklace shimmered in a deep blue, more sapphire than topaz.

The photo in Jonah's file hadn't done her justice. Shoot. When pretty women disappeared, the chances of a stranger being involved increased. A guy who'd sweet-talked her, an offer for fame that was too good to be true, or a sicko who stuffed her into his trunk—suddenly, these became potential alleys I had to explore.

The man wasn't anyone I recognized from Birdie's photo album or Raven's social media presence. He looked older, maybe early to mid-thirties. Asking her parents about his identity would be pointless, because they were obviously clueless about who their daughter was or who she hung with. Maybe Drake could help.

I slid the photos into my pocket and returned downstairs.

Drake, Birdie and Pike got to their feet.

"Ready?" Drake asked.

"Yes." I took Birdie's hands between mine. "Thank you for letting me get to know your daughter a little."

"Of course." Birdie beamed her flushed face at me. "If you need anything else from us, please ask."

Drake coughed loudly.

Pike stepped forward and bowed. "Thank you for your help, my lady."

My lady? Pike's new-found civility was Drake's doing, no doubt.

"We'll be in touch." I headed along the corridor, which was decorated with framed pictures of their children. School photos, judging by the cheesy grins and generic gray backdrops.

At the door, Birdie gave Drake another hug "Don't be a stranger."

Once again, he smoothly escaped her embrace. "I'll see you soon."

Drake and I filed down the drive. The heat had hit its predicted high, according to my app, which was a good thing because the dry air made breathing more difficult. Another degree or two, and I'd need an oxygen tank.

Drake grabbed my arm and dragged me behind the tree. "Why didn't you use your dominance when Pike challenged you?"

His scent blocked all others, his broad shoulders narrowed my world.

"You told me to go easy on them." I yanked myself free. "Besides, dominance is such a heavy-handed approach, don't you think?"

"I admire your grace under a full-on assault by an alpha or a protector." His gaze drifted up to the dark blue sky, then back to me, and he exhaled undiluted frustration. "But Pike's neither. A heavy hand would have put him in place *and* reassured him."

"He'll be reassured of my abilities when I find Raven."

He took hold of my arm again. "Listen, princess."

I surged up to him and stood nearly nose-to-nose. "For fuck's sake, stop calling me princess. It's Kensi. And while we're at it, don't tell me how to do my job, unless you want me to tell you how to do yours."

He let out a low growl that skittered down my spine. "Whatever you say."

"Good then. Now let's get going."

I stormed to the other side of the truck. This recent blowout was going to be one of many, unless both of us learned to chill. But that wouldn't happen until I made him understand I was every bit the potential alpha he was. If not by nature, then by title.

In fact, this was my gig, not his. I was the one who was meant to boss him around.

We climbed into the truck, hot and stuffy as it was, and avoided looking at each other.

"Find anything in Raven's room?" Drake's tone had returned to normal.

I fished the photos from my pocket. "She hid them behind the corkboard."

"Leo said he'd searched the room."

"He's never been a young woman with a no-nonsense father. Know the guy or the location?"

He angled the photo. "I know the place. It's by the lake, about twenty minutes from here by car. Lake Marvin."

"And the guy?"

"Hang on. Dammit. That's Cody. We went to school together. A mixed school."

"Girls and boys?"

"Werewolves and humans. Cody's human."

I took the photos back. "You say that like it's important."

"It is. For Birdie and Pike, it definitely would have been." He started the engine.

Cody looked cute and a little dirty in the way girls liked. Thick eyebrows, messy hair, worn-out jacket. Human or not, he was a crush waiting to happen. At least this explained the apparent age difference between Cody and Raven. Cody lacked the benefit of age-defying wolf genes, which is why he looked close to thirty-three, thirty-four.

I stretched out my legs and lowered the window. "I'm the second cavalry, huh? Your second chance of finding your buddy's sister."

Drake used his override to roll the window back up "You could say that. We struck out. I talked to Sable and everyone from those days, at least the wolves—some of the humans have long since left town—but nothing came of it. Leo searched their house and came up empty, too."

"School was a long time ago."

"I told you. Our community is tightly knit. Once you know someone, you know them. And there's not enough people here to meet new ones all the time."

"Tourists. You told me yourself about how much this area offers in terms of nature. And Raven was heavily into protecting the environment, so even with meddling parents, she could have crossed paths with strangers."

"How do you know about her interest in the environment?" He didn't sound happy I'd uncovered stuff about Raven without his help.

"I'm a P.I. It's what I do."

Despite my glee at getting one over on him, Drake didn't strike me as incompetent. If he wanted to, he could charm the pants off an old lady. And anyone he couldn't twist around his little finger would feel his dominance.

What were the chances of my succeeding where he hadn't?

My advantages were years of experience and a natural aptitude for snooping. The ability to navigate human habits would help me in my mission. Drake and Leo might have given the wolves a semi-decent look-see, but by their own admission, humans hadn't been on their radar. That meant thousands of potential witnesses even in a small triangle of towns like this. It also explained how their population had been upgraded from minor annoyance to prime suspect in Raven's drama.

Maybe Jonah had known what he was doing when he'd crammed me and Drake into the same boat.

I flicked my index finger at the photos. "I'd like to talk to this Cody."

Drake pressed a button and the radio display lit up. "That'll have to wait until the day after tomorrow. I promised my brother I'd look in on him."

"I assume that can't wait?"

"No."

I rolled the window down again and fanned my head with the photos to drive home the message that I needed ventilation. "I have little choice then, do I?"

Not that I didn't have plenty to do at home. My email inbox had to be bursting with messages that needed my attention, plus I still had to call hospitals and morgues.

Once again Drake closed the window and then reversed out the drive. "Give the air a moment."

I eyed the vents. Perspiration coated my back and without a flood of cooling air, I might end up glued to the seat forever.

At least we'd made progress. Taking a day to do my due diligence and meet up with Nat could only help. I shoved the pictures into my pocket, yet even this small movement felt like taking a bath in my own sweat.

Drake swerved around two kids playing ball on the street. Why didn't his face glisten?

A grumble behind the dashboard led the way for the first blast of icy air. At least it vaguely blew in my direction and dried my front.

"Tell me about the wolf outside the library." I held my hands and arms into the air stream and guided it up to my face. "Did you model for it?"

"They asked, but couldn't afford me. It's a recent addition. The unusual number of wolf sightings in the area hasn't gone unnoticed. But since a heavy werewolf presence fends off natural wolves, there have been zero attacks on humans. Their superstitious community concluded the wolves are their friends."

"That's handy. So no one goes out with guns to 'protect' themselves?" I added air quotes.

"Five years ago, an old rancher went out hunting under the pretense he was protecting his livestock. The law never got involved, but the rest of the town made his life so unbearable, he was forced to move. Our pack didn't have to lift a finger to get rid of him, and no one's tried to hunt since. Plus, humans stay largely out of the woods, which means we can run free anywhere."

One day, I'd run free, too. Maybe I'd come back to this place and challenge Drake to a race. By then, he'd probably be mated, have a handful of ankle-biters, and forgotten all about me.

Unless I found a way to make myself more memorable to him…

But I wasn't here to socialize or seduce unsuspecting men. Besides, Drake might be out of my reach. He'd shown zero interest in me, and while I didn't lack sexual confidence, I was a realist.

"Tell me about the locals," I said. "How much tension is there really between werewolves and humans?"

"It varies. It used to be just us with a lot of land to call our own.

Marlontown is still werewolves only. Denville and Robson's Creek are the rookies and started out as human communities. Then, with the loss of private land in Marlontown, some of us were forced to move into the new towns. Mostly, we get on with things and don't concern ourselves with our neighbors. Jonah's the one dealing with the worst of it."

"You mean the land issues."

"Yeah, that's a sore spot." He hooked the tips of his fingers into the bottom of the steering wheel and still avoided any of the bumps in the road.

"Why does Jonah need to sell land? The pack's making their own money, right?"

"First off, we need cash for emergencies and to pay off the drifter hunters."

I twisted my face into a grimace. "I hate those guys."

The few drifter hunters I'd met had assumed that, since I lived among humans, I was a drifter, too. Once I had to get my dad's protector involved to make sure a particularly stubborn hunter left me alone. Since then, I'd been carrying a license that evidenced I was allowed to do as I pleased while still enjoying my alpha's protection. This was all the more embarrassing since my alpha was also my father. Not many grown werewolves needed a permission slip signed by their dads.

"The hunters got a job to do, same as everyone else." Drake shrugged. "Drifters don't necessarily obey human laws, and the risk that they will expose our existence is real."

"No, I get they're needed, but so are taxes, and I'm not a fan of those either."

"I used to be a hunter for a few months. Before I started working for Jonah."

"Oh. Sorry." If I ever published a book, I'd call it *How to Never Make Friends but Piss Off People*. "I guess you're not as creepy as the hunters I've met."

"Not as creepy, huh?" He chuckled. "Do they make cups with that slogan?"

"I seriously didn't mean to offend you." Damn. "Anyway. Did your people move to Denville and Robson's Creek because the pack needed the money?"

"The 2013 flood didn't pass Marlontown by. We didn't have the money to rebuild our pack members' homes, so the town council in charge of the Triangle offered to resettle them to Denville, and in turn, took away the land the original buildings stood on."

"That hardly seems fair to Jonah. It was his land."

"And his responsibility to do what he must to ensure his people have a roof over their heads." Drake's voice left a melancholic, almost sad, note hanging in the air. "Anyway, our main problem is the government. Businessmen see untapped potential in our towns and want to build malls and condos, and encourage large companies to build here and create jobs. The political bigwigs put pressure on us to sell, claim they must seize land in the public's interest, or even dispute our ownership. The paperwork, the lawsuits, the negotiations, they all sap the life from our bones and the money from our accounts."

"That sucks."

"That totally sucks, dude." He gave his voice a teenage twang.

"Very funny." I shoved him, but not hard enough to make him lose control of his truck.

Drake's playful side was new, and I didn't disapprove.

"We're here." He pulled onto my street and rolled up to the curb. "I'll pick you up at lunch time. Say, around one?"

"Okay. Enjoy family time." I got out and waved goodbye before walking up to my house.

He didn't drive off until I'd closed the door. No, he'd learned his lesson.

Seven

That evening, I checked my fridge. It was stocked and the TV worked, so my "day off" might not be a total disaster. I was lounging in my old jeans with a strappy top and dug into a pot of mascarpone ice cream. The crime drama on TV was a rip-off of a book I'd read not long ago, but kept me moderately interested.

At quarter to seven, the doorbell rang, just as Detective Blaze got ready for the showdown.

I placed the ice cream aside and padded to the door.

"Hi." Leo beamed at me over a small bunch of flowers. "For you. A little welcome."

"Really? Wow." I accepted and took a whiff of the subtle floral scent. "Sorry. Where are my manners? Come on in."

He closed the door behind him.

I dug up a suitable vase in the kitchen. "I don't know what to say. They're lovely."

"Well, they're a token. I figured strange town, strange people. And then I heard Drake abandoned you."

"His brother's injured, I believe."

"No excuse to neglect you."

I filled the vase with water and arranged the flowers Who knew Leo was such a flirt? With Drake showing little interest in me, I didn't mind the ego boost.

And Leo was a mighty fine-looking guy. Tall, strong, blond, with a sense of the unpredictable. Turning up on my doorstep out of the blue? Yeah, I hadn't seen that coming. Plus, he had a certain quality, a quiet confidence that didn't need dominance to tell me he was a serious guy.

"Tell you the truth, I was a little upset." I centered the vase on the island. "The moment I found a clue, I had to abandon the investigation."

"Oh, really?" Leo placed both his forearms on the counter and leaned in. "What clue? Spill."

"I found a photo of Raven with a guy. A photo she kept secret from her parents."

"Raven had a boyfriend?" Leo whistled. "Well, that's great. Not for her parents, but an awesome find. Pretty good going for your first day. Almost like you're a real detective."

I grinned. "I know, right? But now I have to wait until the day after tomorrow because Drake has family obligations It's not his fault, but I'm not a patient woman."

"I'm sure you have plenty of other virtues." He straightened and turned a little to the right, giving his cocked head the right amount of *ooh-la-la*.

My grin expanded into a red-carpet beam. "It's what I keep telling people."

"But hey, I'm a protector. How about you and I do a bit of sleuthing tomorrow?"

"Would that be okay?" I asked.

"Why wouldn't it be?"

Ditching Drake had been an ambition of mine, sure, but not one I'd reasonably believed would happen. Now that the prospect was near, my expected enthusiasm wasn't doing somersaults. It wasn't even as if I was cheating on him.

I bit my lip for a second. "Won't Drake be pissed you're taking over?"

"Do you care?" He gave me a shrewd glance before glancing at the kitchen clock.

I had no reason to care. Drake might even be relieved he was finally rid of me. "Of course not. And it's only for a day, right?"

"Exactly. And look at it this way. Would you rather spend the day alone?"

I had plenty of people to call and Natalie to see, but why break his flirtatious little heart?

I shook my head. "I can't begin to tell you how much I don't."

"Great." He headed toward the door, while shooting me a panty-melting grin that made sure I was following. "What time do you want me to pick you up?"

"How about seven?"

"It's a date. See you then."

That night I didn't sleep well. Jonah and his people ran through my dreams, blocking the view of a woman, who stood forlorn in the woods. It was my mother, yet she looked pale and ghost-like.

I woke with a start and took measured breaths to slow my racing heart. Traveling didn't become me. If I didn't end up with stomach troubles, my dreams robbed me of my sleep. This was how my mind processed the events of my life.

The clock said it was eight. I rubbed the sleep out of my eye and got started on my morning routine.

After a decent breakfast, I tackled my inbox, while my voice recorder downloaded my previous day's conversations to the cloud and recharged. My assistant hadn't yet found any trace of Raven's enrolment in a college, but the country was large, and it could take a few days until I knew for sure.

I replied to job offers with a politeness that I hoped made me sound busy but accommodating. Just because I was unavailable now didn't mean I couldn't line up jobs for once I was done in Marlontown.

Following a light snack, I spent a few hours calling hospitals and morgues. One hospital in Denver had found a Jane Doe, a homeless woman on life support who resembled Raven by description. Once they saw the photo I'd emailed them, they ruled Raven out. I struck out everywhere else, too. All I could do was leave my number and hope they wouldn't call.

Jonah had asked me to do a job, and I would see it through. Still, finding Raven alive and well would make his support for my claim to the throne a shoo-in. For the royal packs to live in peace, the two giants both sides of the aisle needed to continue their friendship: my father's Boroughs Pack was the most numerous and stable pack of the monarchies, of the free packs, none was stronger than the Wild Pack.

Having learned my lesson the previous day, I set out early enough to make the long trek to the BBQ joint in Denville for my meet with Nat. The temperatures showed no mercy, and once again, I felt like a walking puddle of sweat once I finally got there, with ten minutes to spare. Despite the heat, business was in full swing. The parking lot was at least half-full, and finding a space on one of the outside tables was a pipe dream I immediately abandoned.

Natalie was already inside. I joined her in the booth near the entrance, glad to have somewhere to park my butt, even if it was inside a hot diner. The table was lined by a single bench, leaving the other side open for easy wheelchair access.

A smoky fragrance of sweet 'n meaty hit my taste buds hard, and my stomach growled loud enough to be heard over the Country tune playing in the background.

Natalie pointed at my stomach. "You're starving, aren't you?"

"You have no idea." I slid into the bench and checked out the menu.

Pulled pork, brisket, fritters, corn bread, as well as coleslaw, mac and cheese, and potato chips—they had it all. Nat waved, and the waitress made a beeline for us. Once they'd exchanged pleasantries, we placed our order. Natalie seemed more concerned with filling her stomach than with saving her bikini-ready figure and, like me, ordered half the menu.

"How are things going with Drake?" Natalie shot me a shrewd glance. "Has he been able to help you?"

How could a warm, intelligent woman be so smitten with Drake? Jonah had told me Drake got on with everybody, yet the protector's attitude toward me singled me out. That didn't make me feel special in the least.

I plastered on a smile. "I don't know. He seems to know what he's talking about, but it's a little abstract, you know? The history of something is only half as fascinating as the history of a particular living person."

Like my mother, for example.

"Yes, for that you need to read memoirs or biographies." She grinned. "What about you? Do you think history will remember you?"

I waved her off. "Good God, I hope not. How embarrassing to have your mistakes laid bare in black and white."

"True." She leaned back to allow the waitress to place our food on the table. "Like what mistakes?"

"Yeah, right. The only reason my lips aren't sealed is the grub. Christ, that smells good." I lifted the top bun to check that my smoked bacon and cheddar cheeseburger was sufficiently cheesy to warrant the name, which it did. "Anyway, tell me about the Triangle."

"We refer to Marlontown as a town, but strictly speaking it's a community built on a huge chunk of private land."

"Why didn't I know this?"

"Maybe because in reality, it doesn't matter. The State has declared Marlontown part of our Triangle, which is ruled by a single Town Council. In many ways, the Triangle is a compact place. The movie theater is in Robson's Creek, the school's in Denville. For all intents and purposes, we're one town. But on a human level, we're deeply segregated."

I shot her a quick but thorough glance. Did she know about the werewolf-human split? Yet her expression didn't indicate she was hanging on to a secret she was eager to spill. Instead, a light frown had worked itself onto her face.

I patted sauce off my mouth with a paper napkin. "In what way segregated?"

"There's a divide between the old and the new. Mostly, tradition is winning. I've lived here for the past fifteen years, and I still remember the upset when we got our first Internet café ten years ago."

"Seriously?"

"Sometimes I suspect the locals draw their selfies by hand." She tipped her head back for a full belly laugh. "Wish I were kidding. But it's more than that. Women are more likely to stay at home here than in New York, where I come from. Minorities? Some have come, not many have stayed."

I raised my eyebrows. "That bad, huh?"

"I'm exaggerating for political effect." She grinned past the drink she was holding to her mouth.

"Good, because I didn't know what to say, and that doesn't happen often."

"In fairness, people here by and large aren't racist, and no one looks at me with pity for sitting in a wheelchair. I've been welcomed and made a place for myself, but there's a feeling here. A sense that you only get sold half the picture, and it's nothing to do with color. That's what I meant by segregation."

"You're not making life here sound attractive." I slurped my soda and dipped a chip into the thick burger sauce.

A hundred extra sit-ups during my morning routine for the next ten years might burn off these calories, but right now, I relished every one of them.

"Not at all. You kind of fall in line with the rest. Women might not be fully emancipated here, but there's something nice about having big, hulking men acting all protective toward you."

If only she knew how quickly that got old. "Like Drake, you mean?"

She blushed. "A little. Harmless flirtation has never bothered anyone. Shame he's such a recluse."

"He seems content with his lot."

"Have you met his friends?" She focused on the fries on her plate, but her voice had sharpened.

"Some, yeah."

She lifted her gaze. "Have you met Jonah?"

"Um. Yes."

"What's your impression of him?"

Had I been wrong, and she crushed on the local alpha rather than Drake? In some ways, he was a better match for her, but he was still a werewolf.

I pushed the half-full plate away from me in an act of ultimate sacrifice. "He seems nice. Very diplomatic and persuasive."

"Right." Her gaze drifted for a moment.

"Why do you ask?" I went in for one last chip. One-hundred and one sit-ups then.

"I've noticed…" She washed down her food with soda. "It almost seems like he's leading the traditional brigade in this town. You know?"

A crumb got caught in my airway, and I coughed wildly. Natalie, meanwhile, observed my reaction with the eyes of a hawk.

Once oxygen flowed again, I wiped away a stray tear. "You were saying?"

"Whenever a new playground is to be set up or a hotel is due to be erected, he's the one opposing it. At first I thought he was simply a nature freak, like a member of POOF, or Protectors of Our Forests, that's active in these parts. You know, *that* I could respect. But now I think he's doing it by default. And half the Triangle follows his lead." She tapped her fingers on the table then placed her palm down emphatically. "It's weird."

What Nat didn't know was that every playground or hotel was taking away precious territory.

"You don't agree?" She tilted her head.

"What does Drake say?"

"Nothing. He can talk for hours about the origins of Marlontown or the architecture of some old building, but the minute you ask him about Jonah, he gets evasive. It's weird. That's why I'm asking your opinion."

"I only just got here." I shifted in my seat. "You know Jonah better than me."

"Actually, I've never met him face-to-face, but you have. What do you think? Is he an eco-warrior, or does he simply like complaining?"

I inflated my cheeks and then puffed out air. "He has a lot on his plate, but he's all right. I'm sure if you met him, you might change your mind about the kind of person he is."

"I'd love to, thank you. I didn't want to ask directly, but since you're offering…" She beamed.

Wait. What? Had she manipulated me into an introduction, or had I somehow issued an invitation that wasn't mine to make?

"Jonah is busy." I could tell my smile came across as uncertain. "And I won't be here that long."

"I'm almost always free. The library isn't crowded, and Elli, my neighbor, is available at a moment's notice to help. Any time would be good. Just say the word."

"What are you hoping to get out of a meeting?" And how could I let her down without hurting her feelings?

After all, Jonah might not be eager to have a powwow with a human librarian. Who was I to schedule his appointments anyway?

Natalie swiped the table with the edge of her hand. "I want to understand why half the people are so beholden to him. When I see him at town meetings or in the news, he almost comes across like a cult leader. He has charm, definitely, and the looks, but is there more to him?"

"If you've seen him around, how come you've never talked to him?"

"That's what I'm saying. He's always surrounded by people, chatting, asking favors, slapping his back. Trying to break through the crowd in this isn't easy." She slapped the armrest of her chair.

I sought advice from the wall opposite me, the rounded edge of the table, my hands. Finding none, I shook my head. "As I said, he doesn't have time for chats."

"I'm not looking…" She ruffled her hair before sitting up stick-straight. "Okay. Here's the thing. I was asked to weigh in on a recent proposal to build an activity center for disabled children. The nearby nature reserves and trails make our location ideal. It's a great cause, but Jonah has lodged an objection. There's some dispute about who owns the land."

"And you want to lobby him in person?" Yeah, Jonah was going to love me for this.

"Nothing as grand as that. As you can imagine, it's a cause I support, but before I get fully involved, I wanted to talk to him. Who knows, he might have a good reason for opposing the project. In other words, I don't want to start a fight. Maybe there's room to compromise."

I leaned back and crossed my ankles. "Is that why you invited me for lunch?"

If so, I could respect that. A clever move, especially for a human.

She lowered her gaze. "It was on my mind, yes, but it wasn't the only reason. It's tough to meet people my age. They rarely come to the library, and it's not like I'm a regular at the bar."

I slurped the last dredges of my soda through my straw. Maybe I could swing this for her, but should I? If I asked, Jonah might assume he'd be doing me a favor, and suddenly I'd be in his debt. That was the opposite of my reason for being here.

"Would you mind?" Nat's tone had lost its assertiveness. "I've been meaning to ask Drake, but every time I veer from history to something more personal, he blocks me."

He was a private person, all right.

I gave a one-sided shrug. "I'll see what I can do."

"Thank you."

Nat called over the server and paid our bill.

"Can I ask you for a favor in return?" I leaned back and waited for the woman to leave.

"Shoot."

"You mentioned POOF or something. If I were hard-core into the environment, that's the organization I'd join?"

"They run the show, as they say. They clean up the woods, write petitions, and give organized walks to tourists." She gave me a mysterious smile. "And still, they never go up against Jonah."

"Do you know where their headquarters are?"

"I know the place from which they operate, although I'd hardly call it a HQ. It's only a few blocks from here." She slid a napkin toward her, rustled up a pen from the small messenger bag slung around her body, and drew a map. "Here. They have a large sign in the window, so you can't miss it."

"Nice."

"Thinking of joining them?"

"I won't be here long enough. I'm just looking for information."

"On the travelers?"

"We'll see."

At this point, the humans probably hadn't given much thought to Raven's disappearance. Until I'd spoken to her friend Cody, I'd like to keep it that way. Investigations accompanied by a fanfare rarely went smoothly.

"This has been fun." I got up and shook her hand.

"It has." She leaned her head to the side. "You'll let me know about Jonah?"

I took a deep breath. "Sure."

I opened the door for her, and we went our separate ways.

Natalie had left me with a dilemma. If she hadn't given me a strong reason for wanting this meet with the alpha, I'd have brushed her off, but the cause was close to her heart.

Of course, there was the matter of Jonah maneuvering me into the whole Drake-babysitting situation. It would be only fair to show I was every bit as cutthroat and conniving as the alpha himself. Maybe I shouldn't look at this as a favor to Nat but as payback.

The prospect of pulling this off held an even greater attraction I hadn't yet considered. Drake would be totally pissed to discover I'd bypassed him. That in itself gave me a warm, fuzzy feeling and settled the matter.

𝒞IGHT

I SWITCHED OFF THE TV, SLUNG my jacket over my shoulders for at least the illusion of professionalism, and pocketed the keys on my way out. "Ready."

Leo rounded his sedan and opened the door for me. "So, care to fill me in on where we're going?"

We fastened our seat belts at the same time, and our hands touched. I pulled back my arm, but didn't miss his gentle smile.

Bad Kensi.

To overplay the awkwardness, I showed Leo the pictures of Raven and her boyfriend. "Drake says his name is Cody. He said he went to school with him, which I assume meant you did, too?"

Leo reached down and turned on the engine. "Cody's bad news. He drinks too much, he sleeps around. You know what humans are like."

Alcoholism and drug addiction were rare in werewolves, so for us, human behavior could be tough to understand. TV and the movies didn't exactly cast humans in a better light, either.

"I live among them, so I know how to handle them." I shrugged. "What else do you know about him?"

Leo checked over his shoulder and pulled into the road. "Well, not that much."

"Why is Cody being human such a big deal?"

"If Birdie and Pike had known about Cody, they would have been upset. Rightly so. She's from a good family, and after Ralph died, is it fair to disrespect her parents?"

"She's young. We don't always know what's good for us, and if we do, we tend to do the opposite."

"Oh, the voice of experience?"

"I'll never tell." I mimicked locking my mouth and throwing away the key.

Even though it wouldn't get dark for a few more hours, clouds dimmed the light. I removed my hair band and let my hair fall over my shoulders. Cody might get squirrelly when confronted with uninvited guests, and a softer appearance wouldn't hurt.

"What did Drake tell you about Cody?" Leo asked.

"Nothing. He and I, let's say there have been communication problems."

"He pissed you off already? It usually takes people a while to hate him."

That's not the impression Jonah had given me. In all fairness, I didn't hate Drake. He was funny, easy on the eye, and certainly wasn't stupid. In fact, if he stopped bossing me around, we might get on well.

"Let's say he keeps challenging me and throws his dominance around like confetti at a wedding." I shrugged. "No big deal."

Raindrops stippled the windshield, and Leo turned on the wipers. "Don't take it personally. Drake's got a chip on his shoulder about being a babysitter, while I get to sit in on the important meetings. He doesn't get that I have more experience. Jonah took me on as a protector when my father retired."

"Your father was Marlon's protector?"

The smile left his face. "Well, those were tough times. We

were practically at war, and Marlon barely kept up with his pack duties, you know, making sure the territory was safe, handing out emergency loans."

"So he stepped up?"

"Someone had to."

Leading a pack wasn't only about power, but also about the admin and order within the ranks. Dad spent many late nights grappling with red tape and minor disputes. He could delegate much of it, but he insisted doing the small stuff helped him keep up with the main issues.

"And Jonah wanted you to walk in your dad's footsteps?" I asked.

"Yes. He appointed Drake and me at the same time, about a year after we finished high-school. Drake's loyal to Jonah, no doubt, but he lacked the experience. My father trained me in all aspects of being a protector."

A tough gig. Around that time, our age-slowing genes that allowed us to live longer than humans were setting in. This was why werewolves were considered kids until well into their twenties. But Leo and Drake would have still been teenagers when they got appointed Jonah's protectors.

"Because of my special training, I became invaluable to Jonah." Leo's mouth tightened briefly. "In the end, he was glad to have two of us, though. I was okay sharing the gig, but Drake…"

"Not happy?"

"What do you think?" He gave me a sideways glance. "So don't take his manners to heart. Proving himself has become an obsession with him. Hey." He pointed with his chin down a one-lane street lined by trees on one side, with a wide grass strip on the other. "Cody lives down this road. If he's not in, he'll be in his usual watering hole."

Each house in this street had a quirk, be it a striking color or an unusual build. One exhibited horizontal stripes of green, white and blue. Shame Chicago didn't encourage such displays of individuality, but that's why they invented graffiti.

We got to the end of the road, and Leo slowed the car. The dull light struck his face and gave him a soft complexion. This guy wasn't here to play top dog, but as a partner. Men like him were rare.

He angled his head to look past me through the window. "The lights are on. You have a plan of attack?"

"I'm going to talk to him." I chuckled. "There will be little bloodshed, I assure you."

Leo parked and shut off the motor. "I'll hold you to it."

Cody's house was a washed-out yellow color, with a weed-covered short drive and an old beater parked out front.

The guy who answered the door looked older than he had in the photo. The crush factor had faded. His face had filled out, and his worn dark jeans and wrinkled shirt took his attire from the cool kind of dirty to just dirty.

His tall, slim figure clung to the door, his eyes glazed but wide. "Leo? What the fuck are you doing here?"

"Hey, Cody."

"My name is Kensi." I smiled and waved playfully. "We would like to talk to you about Raven."

"Raven?" He studied me, then nodded. "You'd better come in then."

He walked off, trusting us to close the door, and sank into a chair. The TV was on, blaring out a quiz show.

Leo gestured for me to sit on the sofa near Cody, while he took a seat at the far end. "You're not surprised we're here?"

Cody didn't move, yet looked as if he was about to fall out of his chair. "I'm surprised to see *you*, not the police. You've hardly changed at all, man." He wiped his palm across his face before turning his gaze back at me. "You're the detective chick, right? The one from the TV?"

A handful of empty beer bottles cluttered the small table next to his chair. The stale air inside smelled of wet dog, yet there was no tangible evidence another living creature depended on him. Small mercies, because the man in front of me hardly appeared capable of looking after himself.

I leaned forward in my low seat and clasped my hands against my knees. "You have a good memory. Most remember the Society Strangler's case, but not the people working it."

"If you didn't look like you, I probably wouldn't have."

I acknowledged the compliment with a smile, which faded fast. Breaking the ice with witnesses was a delicate business, and Cody could provide valuable clues—provided I handled this right.

"I would like to ask you a few questions about your relationship with Raven. You were in love?"

Cody lifted a bottle from a small table and picked at the label. "Have they found her?"

"No. But we're taking another run at it, and you can help."

He scoffed and briefly glanced at the ceiling. "If I knew where she was, don't you think I would be with her instead of in this shithole?"

I dipped my head. "Is it not possible she's run away without you?"

"I thought she did at first. Her parents were driving her crazy."

"And now?" I raised my voice over the applause coming from the TV.

"She would have called. Let me know where to find her. But she didn't."

"What do you think that means?"

"Do I have to spell it out? Christ, it means she's dead, lady. She's..." His lips trembled. He took a deep breath and looked into my eyes. "She's dead."

"You sound sure of that, Cody." Leo's voice shot across like a whip. "What are you hiding?"

"What?" Finally, Cody showed some sign of life. "What are you saying?"

Leo moved his hands in an appeasing gesture. "Just asking."

Cody glanced at me. "Do the cops know about me?"

"No, and no one's accusing you. You love her, right? You wouldn't have hurt her. I know that. We were simply wondering why you're so sure she's dead." I shot him a pleading look. "Anything you know, even little details, could help us."

He slumped back, seemingly depleted of energy. "We had this spot by Lake Marvin, where we met every day. Real private, you know. One day, she stayed behind. Last I ever saw of her."

"Can you tell me the exact location? Is there a marina nearby or a boat-launch ramp?"

His gaze drifted far away. "First I thought she didn't want to go home to her old man, always on her to practice that damn violin. For what, right? He'd never let her go to college anyway. Next day, she didn't come back. Just disappeared." His voice tapered off to a whisper. "If she isn't dead, where is she? You know, we talked about running away, starting a family."

"How were you going to support her, huh?" Leo scoffed. "I think she came to her senses. She probably saw you for the waste you are."

"Shut your mouth!" Cody's lips twisted. "You can't come to my house and talk to me like that."

The dark gray overall on the radiator proved he could hold a job, possibly even pay the mortgage on this house. Leo was blind to that, though. He didn't get that, to a young woman whose life had been dictated to by her parents, Cody had offered freedom and affection.

"Leo, go easy. He's grieving. Can't you see?" I turned back to Cody, who'd covered his eyes with his hand. "I'm so sorry about that. Leo's a friend of the family, so this is personal for him. But it's clear you cared about her. Now, you mentioned a lake."

"No, I'm not buying it." Leo tapped his thigh. "I mean, if you're innocent, why didn't you come forward after Raven disappeared?"

Drake wouldn't have got Cody so riled. He knew how to handle humans. Why couldn't I've waited until tomorrow?

Cody surged to his feet. "Fuck off. Both of you."

"Listen, Cody. We don't believe you did anything wrong." I gave him a reassuring smile. "But if you prefer, we'll leave. No problem. Come on, Leo."

My tone had turned acrid. Damn Leo had screwed up everything.

Cody stood with his arms crossed, watching Leo and me head toward the exit.

With the door handle in my hand, I turned around one last time. "I want to bring closure to her family and friends, and I know deep down, you want that too." I extended one of my business cards to him and, when he refused to take it, placed it on a waist-high cabinet. "If you do remember anything, please call."

Leo gripped my arm. "Kensi, maybe we should—"

I spun out of his hold and glared. "Don't push me."

Leo's dominance rippled over me, an uncomfortable itch across my skin, but my stance didn't soften. He'd have to roll out more than that to truly challenge me.

The sensation ebbed away a second later.

Why wasn't Drake so easy to put into his place?

Leo stepped back and glanced down in submission. "Sorry."

"Come on." I left the house, sure he'd follow.

The rain had moved up from mild drizzle to full-on shower, which pelted my head and turned me into a mess. I raced across to the car.

Leo unlocked the doors, and we hopped in.

"The thought of Raven with that guy?" He slammed his palm onto the steering wheel. "She was Ralph's sister. I've known her all her life. But the way he talked about her parents got to me. Notice how he didn't give us any information? If he and Raven were that tight, he must have known something. Right?"

"If he knows anything, we're not going to find out today." I wrung out my hair.

"That's my fault. I'm such an idiot. Ruined it all, and you were doing so well. It's just, I was so pissed at him, you know?" He breathed hard and shook his head. "No excuses. I messed up."

Yeah, he did.

But the guy did look crushed. His shoulders slumped, his gaze downcast. Poor little puppy. If he were in my line of work, he'd know that beating yourself up didn't accomplish anything. Of course, if he were in my line of work, he wouldn't have behaved like a jerk in the first place.

"It's done now." I forced out a smile. "Don't worry. By tomorrow, he'll have calmed down."

Leo had submitted to me. Bowed his head and given in. Weak-ass stamina for a protector. Drake would have stood his ground, whipped out his power, and proven his status. He wouldn't have beaten me, but Leo hadn't even tried.

"Thanks for not making me feel worse about it." Leo gave a soft laugh.

"You seem to do well enough without my help." My tone had taken on an unnecessarily sharp edge.

"And did you notice? I didn't push my dominance on you."

"I did notice." I glanced out the window, determined not let my expression reveal how I felt about that.

"You said you didn't like it, and I listen. Unlike Drake."

If I'd asked Drake politely not to unleash his pheromones every five minutes, he'd unleash them every two.

"Let's go home." I smoothed my wet hair. The car's display read twenty after eight. "I'm actually totally beat."

"Sure." Leo turned on the engine and pulled onto the road.

"Let me make it up to you. Breakfast tomorrow morning is on me. What do you say?"

I eyed him from the side. "Where I come from, that's a forward thing to say."

"What?" His face went pale. "Hey. I didn't mean that. I'm sorry. I would never assume that of you."

"Never assume what?"

"That you'd sleep with someone you've only known for a day. You're way too classy for that."

"True." I cocked my head. "How classy?"

"What do you mean?"

I stretched out my legs and shifted deeper into my seat. This was getting fun again. "How many days do you think I usually wait?"

"You're teasing me. All right." He hmm-ed. "At least five dates."

Leo was an honest country guy who made an attempt to be nice. To top it off, he was awfully handsome, with his straight mouth and slightly jutting chin. And judging him because he hadn't pushed his dominance after I'd told him how I hated it? Jeez, I could be such a bitch.

"Still, I'd like to see you again." He held the steering wheel firmly while he navigated the wet road. "If you'll let me."

At the beginning of the evening, his invitation would have left my heart beating faster. Now, as I listened for a thud or a bang, I wasn't even sure if I was still alive. That flutter was gone. The urge to flick my hair or make my voice more girly, nowhere to be found.

I exhaled sharply. "You know that I'm here to work, right? Even with five dates, nothing's going to happen."

His lips tightened, the air shifted, but he reined himself in before his dominance exploded. "I only meant I'd like to make up for my behavior."

We pulled up to my house. Maybe I'd got Leo wrong from the start. His flirting could have been well-disguised attempts at befriending me. Not exactly a boost to my ego, but not a surprise either. There was a reason I hadn't been kissed in months. Dad wanted me to smooth myself out more, be less abrasive. In other words, be mate bait twenty-four seven. Pity for him, I wasn't built that way.

"Okay." I released the seatbelt and let it retract into its housing. "Breakfast it is. Pick me up around nine?"

"Sounds great." He swiveled in his seat to face me. "And Kensi. This isn't my place, but don't close yourself off to new experiences. Living among humans is one thing, but here, you can be who you really are. At least with me."

"That's sweet." I gripped the door handle. "I don't mean to come across as aloof. Being a woman in a male-dominated world is a scary thing, though."

"I'm just saying, if you want to hang out, have fun for a while without judgement, that's okay." His chest lifted, and he blew out a stream of air. "Anyway. Nine o'clock?"

"I look forward to it." I stepped out of the car, then leaned back in. "And I appreciate your taking the evening off to help me."

He touched his forehead in a salute. "It's my job, ma'am."

I closed the door, and he sped off.

A complicated man. Certainly a temperamental man. He'd said all the right things, even submitted to me once, but at Cody's place, he'd almost exploded with uncontrolled frustration. What was beyond doubt was that, in his own way, Leo presented a challenge. Another mystery to be solved.

Goodie.

Nine

AT EIGHT FIFTY-FIVE A.M., I sat dressed in a pair of blue capri pants and a strappy top on the swing on my porch, with my jacket draped over my lap. The rain had cleared and been replaced by fresh air and a strong breeze, which tickled my bare shoulders. My bra's thin straps showed, but going without wasn't an option. My tits might not appear massive on my tall frame, but my cup size told a different story.

To help sell my look of debonair visitor, I'd put my hair back up in a bun and covered my eyes with shades.

Leo pulled up in his sleek black sedan a few minutes later. After last night, I still wasn't any clearer on how he regarded me. As an investigator, a friend, or a woman he might have a shot with?

I made a beeline for the passenger side and got in.

"You look nice." Leo steered the sedan into the road and accelerated. "Did you sleep well?"

"I did. Where are you taking me?"

"A diner in Denville." He shot me a glance and waggled his eyebrows, man-of-mystery style. "It's owned by one of us and makes the best breakfast in the state."

"Sounds promising." I stretched out my legs and crossed my feet at the ankles. "I meant to ask. How do *you* get on with the humans? As Jonah's protector you work with them, don't you?"

"Well, tricky question, that. Marlon's old tactics of creating an uncomfortable environment for the humans died with him. Since then, they've been taking more and more of our land, but it doesn't stop there. One school between three towns means humans and werewolves mingle, yet lessons are of course geared at human history. My father told me about our origins, but not everyone is as lucky. No surprise that many of us dream of living like humans."

He gave me a sideways glance.

Jonah clearly was a bad influence on Leo, but being the alpha, he could get away with openly judging me. No such luck for his protector.

"I have to live somewhere." I tightened my tone. "You may not know this, but it's a rite of passage for royal alphas-to-be to live outside the pack. My dad encouraged me to move out. And just so you know, I like living among them."

"Hey. I didn't mean anything by it." Leo lifted an appeasing finger off the steering wheel. "But you could have lived with another pack instead of humans. That's the way it used to be done, isn't it?"

"Maybe. Yes." I exhaled slowly. "Back then, the alpha-to-be would spend years with a different royal pack on the promise that he would mate with one of the dominant females there. But since the free packs declared their independence, not many royal packs remain. Besides, I'm going to choose my own mate."

The lie flowed from my lips like a lullaby. The true reason I'd left Germany was that I had no choice. When I was young, Dad told our pack I was forbidden from using my dominance so I might learn the art of diplomacy instead. But once I got older, the whispers grew, and hiding what I was—and what I wasn't—became increasingly complicated.

Moving in human circles bought me time until my alpha powers broke.

Whenever that might be.

"You could have lived with a free pack." Leo underlined his argument by moving his shoulders, while his hands remained glued to the ten and two spots.

"Outside the crown, alphas rise to their position by aggression and fights. Don't get me wrong. I've trained all my life to take out guys bigger than me, but despite that, I could be at a disadvantage in a free pack, or at least subject to repeated challenges. That doesn't sound like fun to me."

"That makes sense."

"Besides, a good alpha needs more than the werewolf strength nature provided. She needs diplomacy and tact, empathy when needed and moral strength when called for. What better place to learn these virtues than in a society that doesn't resort to physical challenges to figure out their problems?"

Leo turned into a parking lot by a long building with a glass front. A huge sign over the entrance read *Breakfast Bar*. Several other cars had beaten us to it, and the diner's popularity gave me hope for a mouth-watering breakfast.

Inside, the scent of fried bacon and strong coffee, accompanied by a soft poppy tune from the speakers, combined into what could have made for a relaxed atmosphere, if not for the busy splatter and chatter coming from the kitchen.

We took a seat near the entrance. The benches were narrow, the dark floor scuffed, but the coffee was steaming hot and the plates seemed generous.

The menu came printed in small letters on a single laminated sheet, and the breakfast section comprised too many options. Leo ordered pancakes. In many respects, I'd acclimatized to life in America, but this obsession with sweet stuff on a sober stomach was one I didn't share. Instead, I ordered a breakfast plate with bacon, sausage and eggs, and a coffee to wash it all down.

"Tell me about Raven." I leaned back and arranged one arm on the back of the empty seat next to me.

"Do you want to spoil breakfast with talk about work?" Leo's charm was back on form. Flashing a white smile, he tilted forward. "We could talk about you. There's much I don't know about you."

"What you see is what you get," I said. "I'm basically all surface. But you agreed to give me the one-oh-one on life in Marlontown."

The server brought our food, a delicious heap that seemed twice the amount I'd ordered. Marlontown had become a location determined to fatten me up.

"Did you see much of Raven?" I sipped coffee before attacking my eggs.

"Not really." Leo chewed on his pancakes. "I used to hang with Ralph and the guys. Raven and her friend Sable would sometimes accompany us. Our pack is small nowadays, so we kind of all know each other."

"Does Raven have hobbies?"

"Well, she'd get really lost in music, but not in a relaxed way. More as if she was concentrating." He put down his fork and, elbows propped on table, folded his hands before his face. "You get that same expression. I noticed the similarity first time I saw you. Same long hair. Same smile. In fact, you and her could have been sisters."

I grinned. "That would be unfortunate for her. I'm an only child and don't like sharing."

"I bet she could have learned a lot from you." He held my gaze, maybe a second too long to be dismissed as casual.

What did he want from me? A fling? A relationship? Nothing at all? When I liked a guy and wanted to be with him, I usually told him. At least that was what I did with humans. Werewolves were more complicated. Maybe they were too complicated.

I moved my butt back in the seat and crossed my legs. "Is there anything else I should know about her? Anything that helps me paint an image of who she is?"

Leo picked up his fork and used it to stab at his plate. Once or twice he started to talk, but in the end, he gave a half-assed shrug.

"I'm not part of your pack and very discreet." I briefly touched his arm to encourage him. "You can tell me."

He wobbled his head from left to right. "All right. I mean, I don't know about hobbies, but she and Sable weren't as wholesome as you think."

"Interesting. Did you and Raven ever…"

"No." He directed his gaze to the side. "We did not."

"But?"

"But Sable and I, well, we kissed once." He took a deep breath. "It was that one time, that's it. She kind of waylaid me in her father's barn. Did it for a bet, she said. You know, making out with the older boys. I only mention it to make sure you get a clear picture of the kind of girls they were."

Picture received clear as glass. If Sable and Raven toyed with boys, maybe Cody wasn't Raven's only secret relationship. An ex could have harmed her, or some other guy could have lured her to a new life.

"That helps." I rewarded Leo with an indulgent smile. "Was it mainly Sable, or do you know if Raven sneaked around barns with anyone?"

"This looks cozy." Drake's voice cut our twosome into pieces.

A darkness swept his expression, the sense of untamed danger barely suppressed. My skin tautened while the burn of his dominance raged through my flesh. Had my unsanctioned excursion with Leo pushed him to breaking point?

The voices inside the breakfast bar fell quiet. About a third of the clientele sat hunched on their chairs, with conversations suspended mid-word. As werewolves, they'd sense that trouble was brewing. The humans, meanwhile, craned their necks to pinpoint the source of the change in atmosphere—and they were shifting their focus to Drake.

Fighting the tightness in my chest, I forced a smile onto my lips.

Defuse the situation. Deflect attention. *Nothing to see here, people.*

I touched Drake's arm. Maybe I shouldn't have. Anything could set him off.

The pressure in Drake's lips ebbed away, his fierce squint smoothed into a look of mild consternation. At the same time, his pheromones collapsed back into their source, somewhere inside his powerful chest. Once again, his control was absolute. The mark of a true alpha, not only by nature, but by position.

How was this man still a protector?

Whispers turned into normal conversation as our fellow diners resumed their lives. If I had to guess, I'd say this wasn't the first public display of dominance in the Triangle.

The blockage in my chest cleared, and I took a deep breath. My father's pack lived side-by-side with humans, on neighboring estates, but we didn't mingle. Not like this. Jonah and his protectors clearly had cause to worry after all. One misstep, one careless word, would reveal their existence to humans.

"It's breakfast," Leo said. "That's all."

He should have been more confident. If he and Drake were truly of equal status, his own dominance would have erupted. Instead, he'd remained passive.

I was a dud. What was his excuse?

"*I* am the princess's protector." Drake stabbed the air in front of Leo with his index finger. "*You* are supposed to organize a meeting with the town planners."

"I will. Later. This seemed more important."

"Weren't you the one who insisted we stop looking into the disappearance of a moody female and focus on real business?"

Leo turned his head toward me, his eyelids low. "Well, things have changed, as you know. Kensi has made progress. I, for one, think that's important."

"I don't even want to know what you two have been up to," Drake aimed his dark glance at me. "But I hope he made it memorable."

"Hey!" I thudded my fist on the table's surface. "I don't know about the women you know, but I'm not that easy."

What a cheap attack. And if Leo were truly into me shouldn't *he* have defended my honor?

I took my time taking tiny sips of coffee.

Drake crossed his arms and stared. His mouth moved as if he was sucking candy—probably one of the peppermints he kept in steady supply.

I placed my nearly empty cup down emphatically. "How did you find me anyway?"

"Back in the library, I put an app on your phone. Good thing I did." Drake's look was ice, but burned like fire.

Was big, scary Drake actually jealous?

I wished.

It was more likely he kicked up a fuss because I didn't bow at his feet. Peel the onion, and what you got was a bully. An absolutely lickable, dead sexy bully.

I slowed my breathing, lowered my voice. "You're spying on me?"

"Doing my job. Now that you've finished breakfast, let's go."

Leo got to his feet. "We're not done."

Nice. Dominance when it was directed at me sucked, but watching two hotties slug it out made for fantastic viewing. Shame I hadn't ordered popcorn.

"Jonah wants you home." Drake lifted his chin to play his two-inch advantage over Leo. "Chop chop."

Leo inhaled sharply. Finally, he turned to me. "Sorry. It looks like Jonah needs me."

I waved him off. "Some people are indispensable when it comes to running a pack. You should go."

"I'll see you soon?" Leo leaned over the table and placed his lips on my cheek.

I kept my surprise to myself. Whatever the reason for Drake's mood, I liked seeing him on edge.

Leo walked off with a stiff gait.

Drake slid onto the bench opposite me. "You sure know how to pick the bad ones."

"Most people would think of *you* as a bad boy." I pointed at his tattoos.

"I said 'bad one,' princess, not 'bad boy.'" He tapped the table with his fingertips. "There's a difference. Anyway, back to business. We should go to Lake Marvin. Where the photos were taken, and the last confirmed sighting of Raven."

I squinted. Once again he'd assumed the lead in this investigation, and once again, his was a good idea.

Damn him.

"Maybe some other time. Today, I have other plans."

"Without me? That's not going to happen."

"I'm not your prisoner. But if you want to come, come."

"Really?" His mouth opened again and closed.

I could have pressed my advantage, shut him out, but since I'd escaped his alpha-mandated babysitting duties once again, he deserved a break.

"Raven was interested in protecting the environment, and Natalie told me POOF is the place to go."

"Who?"

"POOF. Protectors of our Forests."

"Right. And Natalie told you this when?"

I smiled mysteriously, because guilt only took my courtesy that far. "Cody is one human element you hadn't considered in your prior investigation, and POOF might be another one, so I'd like to get it over with."

He shrugged. "Fine. Do you have an address?"

"Even better. I have a napkin." I retrieved the directions Natalie had drawn.

He stared at the map, nodded, and returned it to me. "Okay. Let's go then."

I once again picked up the cup and let the last drops of coffee flow into my mouth. He'd nearly made it two minutes without ordering me around—and then spoiled his record with three little words.

I lowered my hand. "Good coffee. Maybe I should have another."

"Kensi." My name wasn't easily growled, yet Drake managed it beautifully.

Maybe I was getting altogether too much pleasure from riling him.

"Hang on." I called for the check and paid for my food and Leo's. "Now we can go."

Drake frowned but followed me out of the restaurant without any more grumbles.

POOF headquarters weren't what I'd expected. Despite being discreetly located inside what used to be a store, plenty of desks set the scene for a manic rush. Eager fingers attacked keyboards, while whispered conversations and the smell of printed paper saturated the air.

No one took any notice of us at first. How this was possible given that Drake was by my side would remain a mystery.

"Drake? What are you doing here?"

"Buck?" Drake turned his head.

Buck winked at me. "Are you thinking of joining us?"

"Hardly." Drake jerked his head. "We're here to find out if Raven was a member."

"She was, yes." Buck eyed his fellow POOFers, who were largely people in their twenties and thirties. "How do you know?"

Drake widened his stance and pulled back his shoulders. "Why the hell didn't you tell us? I asked you to tell me everything you know about her."

His voice rolled through his throat, but he kept his anger under control.

A shame, because his dominance would have shown me at one glance who at POOF was a werewolf and who was human.

Buck stared at the toes of his shoes. "She asked me not to tell anyone. Her parents would go ballistic if they knew."

From everything I'd seen and heard, that seemed a fair assessment.

"Mind coming over here?" I nodded toward the entrance, out of earshot.

Both Buck and Drake followed.

"Is this more a human organization or more werewolf?" I asked.

"Half and half." Buck leaned toward me. "The humans here are really into the outdoors and into fundraising, but their efforts definitely benefit werewolves. A couple of guys have good connections, and I use my influence on them, you know, to see things our way." He rubbed his nose, while his gaze focused without blinking on my face. "It's why I joined, you know."

I'd been around enough liars to spot the signs of lying—covering the face, avoiding contractions, manic stare—and Buck displayed all of them. Pushing him in front of Drake wouldn't do me any good, though. He'd clam up.

"Did Raven make any friends in particular?" I kept my voice casual. "Anyone we should speak to?"

"She just got on with it, really, but you could speak to Andy. He's the unofficial leader here." Buck pointed at a guy with red hair. "They worked on a couple of projects together."

"One last thing. Can you get me a copy of your membership list?"

"I think that'll be okay. I'll send it to Jonah, okay?"

I nodded my thanks at him and made a beeline for Andy, who was poring over a leaflet with another woman.

"Are you Andy?" I clasped his hand between mine. "My name is Kensi. I was wondering if I could talk to you about Raven."

"Who?" He squinted.

"Raven." I removed my hands just as his pulse spiked.

Interesting.

"What about her?" He stepped away from his friend and herded us into an empty corner of the office.

I exchanged a furtive glance with Drake, then focused my full attention on Andy. "When was the last time you saw her?"

"Not for months. Why?"

"Neither have her parents, and they're getting worried about her."

He crossed his arms and pivoted his head to the side. "I didn't know. Sorry to hear that."

"Do you know anything that might help us? People she hung out with, hobbies, that sort of thing." I counted off on my fingers.

He slowly dragged his gaze to me. "Who are you again?"

"I'm Kensi. Raven's mother asked me to look into her whereabouts."

"Right. I don't know much about her. We didn't hang out or anything, other than in the woods or here in the office."

Drake gave a quiet growl, too quiet for Andy's human ears, but a sign he was losing patience. Guess it didn't take a super-sleuth to realize Andy, too, was holding back. Then again, Raven was a pretty woman and Andy an average-looking guy.

"You like her?" I put on a charming, conspiratorial smile.

Andy scratched his chin and angled his body toward the main door. "She's nice, yes."

"Yes, but you *like* her?"

"I don't see how that's any of your business. Besides, she has a boyfriend. Why don't you go and bother him?"

Been there, done that.

Still, at least I'd confirmed my suspicion. He was a spurned admirer, and probably not a homicidal maniac.

"I'm not making any accusations." I fished a business card from my pocket. "If you can think of anything, anything at all, please give me a call, okay?"

"Okay." He took the card. "Do you… Do you think she's okay?"

"I hope so." I patted his shoulder. "And please ask your friends if they know anything. We're getting worried about her."

He nodded and relaxed his posture. His secret was out, and there were no more skeletons for me to find in this particular closet.

I was back at square zero.

TEN

RAKE'S TRUCK PUMPED COLD AIR into my face and onto my arms the second he turned the ignition key. "You've fixed the air con *and* the blower.' I beamed at him.

We were on our way to Jonah to report in, even though my time would have been better spent catching up on emails.

"Yeah." Drake waited for a car to pass, then reversed out of the parking lot to join the road.

I crinkled my nose. This would not be another drive in silence.

"Do I look like Raven?" I leaned forward. "Leo thinks so."

"Leo is delusional."

"Hell, you're making this partnership difficult than it needs to be," I mumbled loud enough for him to hear. Still, I wasn't beaten yet. "How is your brother?"

"He's a mess. One broken leg, and he's falling to pieces. Can't cook, can't do anything."

"Good thing he has you."

"I can't be there for him all day." He slammed the indicator into the on position and turned onto a different road. "Sometimes

I wonder which of us is the older brother. Then there's the trouble with the house."

I reclined into my seat and motioned with my hand. "Go on."

"He inherited our parents' house in Denville, but the plumbing is old, and so is the wiring."

"That sucks."

"I'd tell him to move in with me, but we'd end up killing each other."

"What does he do?"

"For work? He's a lawyer and helps Jonah through the legal landmines. With him incapacitated, Leo's supposed to step up, but clearly he'd rather spend time with you." His sideways glance was unreadable.

It took more than a look to make me feel guilty.

"Land negotiations?" I scoffed. "You can't blame him for preferring my company."

"It needs to be done. Let's not forget, Leo told everyone who'd listen that he's the guy for the job. You know, the guy who keeps the machine oiled. That's how he sells himself. But he keeps finding excuses."

"I don't know." I adjusted the vents, which moved smoothly into the correct position. "Leo strikes me as a guy who does what he has to do."

"Leo's an empty shirt. The only reason Jonah hired him as a protector was to make the transition easier on Marlon's followers."

Where did all that venom come from? There might be a part of their history they hadn't shared with me yet.

"You talked to Natalie, you had breakfast with Leo." Drake gave his steering wheel three sharp taps with his fingers. "Anything else I've missed?"

"Not really." My grin grew wider and wider. "Unless questioning Cody counts."

The truck jerked.

Drake's head spun toward me. "You did what?"

"Keep your panties on. You were otherwise engaged, remember? Leo took me. Anyway, Cody admitted to dating Raven. They were supposed to meet up, but she never showed. He thinks she's dead."

I fished the USB recorder from my pocket and rewound to the beginning of the conversation, so he could judge for himself.

"Clever device you have there," Drake said afterward.

"It cost me a fortune, but it was worth every cent."

Drake scratched his chin. "Cody thinks Raven's dead, and yet he never alerted the police."

"That's what Leo pointed out. Unhelpfully so, I might add, because as you heard, once Cody thought we suspected him, he shut down."

"Total idiot, that dude. Told ya."

This time, I settled for a reproachful look. "Anyway, I want to try again, but Cody needs space to calm down."

"Okay. We'll wait." Drake turned into the long, bouncy road leading to Jonah's home.

The butterflies that had plagued my stomach when I arrived had flown away. Even the fields didn't strike me as eerie today. Sure, Raven was still missing, and I had zero leads. My information-gathering about my mother's past had also stalled. But at least I'd figured out the pack's major players.

Maybe not all of them. Drake continued to be a mystery. He made me chuckle one minute, and wish for my dominance the next. Right now, his relaxed posture contrasted with his focused look onto the road ahead, yet I'd been around him long enough to know that driving didn't take up all his concentration. Which begged the question, what was he really thinking?

"One more thing." I shifted forward slightly to better catch his expression. "Leo mentioned that Raven and Sable once had a bet about seducing older boys. Sable tried it on with Leo. I wonder who Raven picked."

"You don't know what you're talking about." He shot me a shut-up glance.

I poked him with my index finger. "Ah, it was you. *You* fooled around with her."

He braked. For a second the engine idled while Drake stared into the distance. "Raven wasn't the girl Leo makes her out to be. He may have hoped she was, but she was all right, not easy like some."

"You think she's dead, too?"

"What? Of course not." He shifted in his seat to let me feel the full force of his accusing glower. "Why do you say that?"

"You said she *wasn't* the girl Leo made her out to be."

Drake sucked in air and then got the truck moving again. "She wasn't that type of girl back then."

"I'm not saying she was evil. But she sounds like a woman forced to live a life separate from her family. A woman with a secret boyfriend who made plans to elope. How do we know there weren't other guys in the picture? An angry ex, maybe."

"Raven's different. She wanted love, romance, a big wedding, the whole enchilada. Ralph was the same, you know. Idealists. Dreamers. Always thinking something great was waiting around the corner, and always looking at the past through rose-tinted glasses."

I puffed out my cheeks. Dreams were for those without perspective. Dad ignored reality enough for the both of us. *Don't sit there, it was your mother's favorite spot. You can't have the music box, it was your mother's.* As if she didn't lie dead six feet under, but had merely popped out to the supermarket.

Drake pulled into the sizeable drive and turned off his engine. He checked his phone and made a sound of dissatisfaction. "I gotta call my brother. Can you find your way in?"

"Sure." The perfect time to tell Jonah about Natalie's request.

I got out and rang the doorbell.

"Kensi." Leo opened the door and immediately leaned in for a peck on my cheek, while resting his hand on my arm. "Nice to see you again so soon."

"I'm here to update Jonah." I kept my voice light, but twisted slightly to shake off his touch.

"Where's Drake?" He lowered his voice. "Did you finally kill him? Because no jury would convict you."

I laughed and aimed my thumb over my shoulder. "He's on the phone. Besides, my investigation, my report."

"All right. Come on in."

We headed to the same room in which Jonah had given me his good ol' werewolf welcome.

The alpha sat in his chair, barely glancing up when we entered. The large windows bathed half the office in light, while the front half, where the table was located, relied on the high ceiling lamps for illumination.

Finally, Jonah put down his pen and pushed his papers aside. "Kensi. What have you found?"

His tone demanded not just news but answers. If only investigations were that simple.

I followed his outstretched hand and sat in the chair opposite him. "All I can say at this point is that Raven did intersect with humans. She has a human boyfriend and is a member of an environmental group that's fifty-fifty human."

"Okay." He repeatedly struck the table with his pen. "What does that mean?"

"Nothing without context, and I don't have anywhere near enough of that. The good news is that these are solid leads, or starting points."

Jonah crossed his arms and tilted his chin up. "How so?"

"I can check out the other members of the group, look for unusual behavior or a break in patterns." I lifted my shoulders and straightened. "Cody, her boyfriend, is due another visit, too. And we'll have a look around the spots where Raven used to hang."

"In other words, you have nothing solid."

My fists clamped tight, but I kept my expression smooth. In a couple of days, I'd achieved more than his protectors had in months. "I already checked with the morgues and hospitals in the area and put a bulletin out to the remaining ones in the state. My assistant is working a few angles from Chicago, and I will check in with her this afternoon. Eliminating possibilities is as important as confirming them. We're making progress."

"I wasn't criticizing you." Jonah waved off before letting his hand re-join his folded arms. "Forgive me. I'm not a patient man."

"It's okay," I mumbled.

"But I'm a grateful one. Really." He impishly fluttered his eyelids.

I couldn't help but smile. Was this the real Jonah? The guy he was when he wasn't playing mind games?

"No biggie." I gave a one-sided shrug. *Jonah unplugged* was a man I liked.

An elderly woman carrying a pot of tea entered the room through one of the side doors.

"You see?" Jonah said. "All will be well. I spent a year in England and firmly believe in their national motto that tea heals all troubles."

The woman's warm smile was directed at the room, but her shrewd gaze targeted only me. Her large irises were a deep brown, bursting with the things they'd witnessed in her long life. No makeup altered her smooth light-brown skin. She was a stunner now. In her youth, she must have been downright devastating.

"Thanks, Liza." Jonah pushed a second cup forward to be filled. "How about cookies?"

"Of course." She retreated through the same door.

Transfixed, I watched her graceful gait.

"Is she human?" I asked once she was out of earshot.

"Who, Liza? No. Why?"

I reluctantly returned my attention to the alpha. "Her name isn't an animal name."

"She wasn't born into our pack." He narrowed his eyes. "No one knows where she was born. She doesn't talk much, but she's an excellent cook."

The sight of another outsider could have sparked her interest in me, or maybe she was excited to meet a princess.

"Before I forget." He pushed a small stack of papers in front of me. "Buck emailed a copy of the police report, a form you need to sign—" He pointed at a page and gave me his pen.

I skimmed the insurance document and added my signature.

He retrieved both pen and sheet from me. "—and a list of names for POOF. He said you asked for it."

"That was quick." I folded the two sheets and slipped them into my pocket. "I have another request, if I may. It's not actually for me, though. Consider me the messenger."

"I'm intrigued." He bent forward, letting his forearms slide along the table.

"I had lunch with Natalie Daniels, the local librarian. She told me about this town, about the deep rift between old and new—or werewolves and humans, as you would say—and she fingered you as the sower of discontent."

"Excuse me?"

"Again, I'm not being disrespectful, only relaying a message. So no shooting, okay? Nat claims you and your followers oppose any of the town's efforts to hop into the twenty-first century."

"My followers?" He gave a subtle shake of his head, then rubbed his eye with the heel of his hand.

I cocked a finger gun and clicked my tongue. "Pretty astute for a human, isn't she? I believe she mentioned the term 'cult leader.' "

"Is she going to be a problem?" Leo pressed his hands tight against his thighs. "Do I need to pay her a visit?"

"Whoa, stand down, soldier." I raised an arm. "She's not dangerous. Jeez."

He lowered his gaze.

Jonah coughed, yet a grin radiated across his face.

"Sorry." I crossed my arms between me and my cup. "Your protector. I get it."

"No, that was good." Jonah made an inviting gesture. "You certainly have the dressing-down part down for when your time comes."

I chuckled. "Practice. Dad says I was bossing him and Mom around the second I popped out of the womb."

"Like mother, like daughter." He shook his head. "Man, Aldwych wouldn't stand a chance against you two."

The laughter left my lips and my heart. Of course, Jonah would have known my mother. He'd have been young back then, even younger than my dad, yet old enough to have a grown-up conversation with her. Here I was, her own daughter, and I couldn't even remember her voice.

"I'm sorry." He pushed a white bowl of sugar toward me. "I shouldn't have mentioned her."

Although a sweet tooth wasn't one of my vices, I heaped two spoons of sugar into my tea. The mood change that occurred when someone spoke of my mother wasn't one of the better traits my father had passed on. Shouldn't I be over her death by now?

"It's okay." I lifted the cup to my mouth and promptly burned my lips. "What do you know about my mother?"

"She was pretty, funny, and confident as all hell. As I said, you remind me of her." He twisted his expression into a wince. "When her pack moved into this area, they caused upheaval, though, and she was of course at the center of it."

"Must have been overwhelming for them." I stared out the window at the large back yard. My knowledge of travelers was limited, but constantly being on the move had to be tough. I focused back on Jonah. "The minute you get settled in a new place, a bucketful of tension erupts not with humans, but with your own kind."

"That's not what I meant." Jonah fumbled with his pen and didn't meet my gaze. "Your mother was the reason—"

Liza returned with a small plate of baked goods.

"Thank you." Despite Jonah's ominous words, I smiled at her.

She touched my arm for a few seconds, and then quickly left the room again.

I sucked in air and steeled myself. An atmosphere like this, heavy with unspoken words, rarely led to a barrel of laughs.

"Okay." I prodded my finger against the table, beckoning Jonah to spit it out. "You were going to tell me about my mother."

"Forget it." He waved me off repeatedly. "It's not important."

"Seriously?" I shook my head. "It sounded like what you had to tell me was pretty damn important. I know so little about her."

"If your father hasn't told you about this, he must have a reason. Whatever that reason is, it's between you and him." His thin lips would divulge no more.

"Dad doesn't talk about her. Period." I slipped down an inch on the smooth chair and averted my gaze.

Jonah had said my mother had been the reason. The reason for what? That man was infuriating, but he was right. It was time Dad and I had a proper conversation. No more vague excuses.

"Anyway. You mentioned your friend from the library." Jonah's frown disappeared, and he was back in amiable alpha mode.

If only I could compartmentalize that easily. "Yes. You're currently opposing a project that is of special significance to Natalie. An activity center for disabled children. If she's the person I think she is, she's going to fight you tooth and claws on this if she has to. But for now, she's going to try diplomacy."

"Meaning?"

"She wants to meet with you."

Leo made a move forward, but his alpha's raised finger warned him off. One move was enough. Jonah knew how to keep his people in line.

Leo shrugged and ambled out of the room.

Jonah looked at me like I'd lost my mind. "Is this still because I went over your head to engage your services, or do you just hate me?"

"No, this is about you giving up a few minutes of your time to be a good guy." I'd failed to check my tone, but it was too late.

Jonah's eyes narrowed into cold slits.

"Why should I meet some woman who has a stick up her ass about one of my land deals?" His dominance swept over me with the force of a hurricane. "What the fuck do you think I do here all day? Fluff cushions and cuddle kittens?"

Keeping my chin raised and my gaze steady, I let the prickling heat tear across my skin.

"I don't want you to meet with *some woman*." I countered Jonah's power with my alpha voice. "She's a canny lady who's spotted that you hold a special position in the Triangle, and with it, the key to influence half the locals. A woman who, as a librarian, is a wizard at doing research and finding dirty little secrets if she put her mind to it, and someone who's decided to use anything she can against you to make this project a reality."

His dominance slowly ebbed away.

I relaxed my legs, where I typically concentrated my resistance so none of the strain would show on my face. "Meet her, be nice, serve cookies. Twenty minutes to save you serious trouble down the line."

"Surely you're not considering this?" Leo returned to the room. "We've invested too much in the paperwork already. You can't allow this woman to derail our progress. I mean, if we concede any more land to these humans, the pack will revolt."

I gestured *there you go* with my hand. "All the more reason to compromise. Deflect the ball before it gets anywhere near the ten-yard line, and you might be spared grief."

Leo's eyes widened. "Oh, you know about football?"

I scratched my chin with my middle finger. "The things I know would astound you."

"Kids, please." Jonah raised a hand. "I'm not entirely convinced it's necessary, but you make a good point, Kensi. Set it up."

"Any particular time?"

"She's not already here, is she?" Jonah tilted his head as if to check for her presence through the solid wall of his office.

"Of course not." I dialed her number before he could change his mind. "Tomorrow okay?"

"Three o'clock." He rubbed a circle over the spot between his eyebrows. "And you'd better be here, too."

Natalie was delighted at the good news.

After I'd hung up, I pushed my cell back into my pocket and got up. "I'd better leave you to it. Where's Drake?"

"Gone to run an errand for his brother. He'll be back in an hour." Leo smiled. "If it's okay with Jonah, I can give you a lift home."

In a bizarre reversal of emotions, my instinct was to wait. I was way past any interest I might have harbored for Leo. He was too polite, too soft, and…Heaven help me…he wasn't Drake.

"Good idea." Jonah studied me, probably to ensure I wasn't going to leave the room again without his permission. "You may go."

I gave a courtesy bow and left. Maybe this turn of events was for the best. I was dying to visit the travelers' camp. Drake would make a song and a dance out of it, quiz me about my motivation, and drill, drill, drill until he struck the truth. Luckily, one of Leo's defining traits was his eagerness to please—a weakness I was fully prepared to exploit.

Eleven

Leo passed me in the hall and opened the door. At once, the heat knocked me back a few inches.

"You okay?" he asked.

"Sure." I rallied and stepped into the inferno. "Feeling guilty for opposing me when I asked about Natalie?"

"Should I? It's my job to schedule Jonah's time."

"And that's why I'm giving you the chance to make it up to me." I hurried to his sedan, driven by the prospect of its excellent AC.

Once again, Leo overtook me within seconds. "What did you have in mind?"

If the way he drawled his last words was anything to go by, his thoughts had fast-forwarded to romantic activities.

My expression no doubt showed little enthusiasm. His suggestive question should have brought out my flirtatious nature, but there was a disconnect between us, something that had broken the initial attraction. If anything, he was standing too close, the smell of his aftershave so pungent it blocked my nose. Another area in which he could learn from Drake, who'd found the perfect balance—a constant tease between sexy store-bought fragrance, refreshing peppermint and panty-melting wolf.

Still, I had a plan, so I looked up at Leo from under my eyelashes. "I need a change of scenery."

"Oh, okay. Sounds good." He waited for me to climb in and then got behind the steering wheel. "Where would you like to go?"

Bingo. Wrapped around my little finger. "Natalie told me of this lovely spot where travelers used to live."

"In the woods?" He sucked in an audible breath. "Did you… want to run?"

"No." I gave a childish giggle. Running in wolf form with a man wasn't just an intimacy I wasn't prepared for, it was of course also impossible. "I would like to talk about something other than Raven or land disputes for a while. That's all."

His glance swept over my neck and mouth before landing on my eyes. "Then let's not waste time."

Leading him on carried the stink of an underhanded, even cruel maneuver, but my situation didn't leave me many options. I had no car, and I couldn't risk this trip with Drake in tow. If Drake continued reading me like a book, he'd discover what I was—a dud—and that my shows of bravado were make-believe. I had nothing to counter his dominance with, except for a greater-than-average willpower that faded fast in his presence.

Leo had done nothing wrong. He'd respected my space every inch of the way, so at least I should be kind and show him the respect he'd earned.

The sun stood high, and I put on my sunglasses. The search for my mother's past had reached a dead end, but Jonah had let something slip that could open up a new lead. Something that seemed important. If I caught my father on a good day, he might simply tell me what he wanted me to know, rather than let this ridiculous hunt continue.

And if wishes were horses, beggars would ride.

Why did men insist on being a pain in the ass? The simple ones, like Leo, were rare.

His casual top suited him better than the suit he'd worn on day one. Even his posture was more relaxed, although he still held the steering wheel like a seventeen-year-old.

He smiled, probably because he'd noticed my prolonged look. "What do you know about the travelers?"

"I assume they traveled a lot, and yet they had a camp. Weird, huh?"

"Don't let the romantic notion of travelers fool you. They were a bunch of misfits, deviants, criminals even. People who, for some reason, refused to live in a traditional pack, accept pack law, or abide by the rules."

"They were still werewolves, so there had to be some rules they followed."

"Well, that depends on your definition of werewolf. I mean, some of them, sure. But through breeding with outsiders, many of them barely held even a drop of pure blood, I imagine. For all intents and purposes, they could have been as human as Cody."

My shoulders stiffened in a painful attack. Was he right? If my mother's people hadn't been pure werewolves, what about her? I gripped the side of my seat, buried my fingers inside until they burned. Suddenly, everything became clear. Her ancestors had diluted their genes to the point that I was a dud.

Was this what my father wanted me to discover? He hadn't sent me on some crazy, uplifting personal journey. No, he was too chicken to tell me the truth.

I was at least part human—and there was no *cure* for that.

"Hey. What's wrong?" Leo frowned and placed his hand on my arm.

My lips trembled, my throat tightened to the size of an eyelet. "Nothing."

"You're pale."

I lifted my hand. "I guess the heat is getting to me. That's all."

"Hang on." He pushed a button, and the air blowing through the vents cooled. "Better?"

"Yes. Thanks." My sunglasses shielded my burning eyes from his attentive gaze.

Drake wouldn't have believed my half-assed lie, of course. He'd have parked up and shaken me by the shoulders until my secrets fell out.

I took a few deep breaths. All was not lost. I was my father's daughter, so wolf blood did run through my veins. Alpha blood to boot. My mother had been able to shift into wolf shape, too. Besides, would Dad have married her if her own background had been sketchy? If the blood in her veins was partly human?

Wrong question. The guy had been too in love to make a rational decision.

In any case, Leo might be wrong. Who really knew another person's genetic makeup? It wasn't like you could tell by looking at someone.

As we approached the woods, tall trees increasingly blocked the sun's relentless glare. Leo parked his sedan on a narrow piece of grass. I opened the door and inhaled the familiar scent. This trip might not answer my questions, but it might clear my mind.

Leo ambled over to stand in front of me. "We're here."

"I can see that." I pointed my thumb at the tree line. "Ready to head in?"

"In a second. First, there's something I meant to say to you."

With his right hand on the door and his left on the roof, he leaned in to kiss me.

I pushed back into the car.

Dammit. If I hadn't been vague about my feelings, I could have spared both of us a bucketful of embarrassment.

"That's not a good idea." I patted my stomach. "Still feeling queasy."

He let go and frowned. "I wasn't thinking. Sorry."

"Yeah. Um. I'm also a little surprised," I said in a low voice. "Actually, a lot surprised."

"I liked you from the moment I saw you." He kept me immobile between his body and the car. "I wanted to make sure you feel the same way."

"That's sweet of you." I placed my hands high on his chest and gently put distance between us. "For now, all I feel is—."

The sound of an approaching engine saved me.

Drake's pickup blasted up the dusty path, spraying a pinkish dust out to the sides. He came to a stop, killed the engine, and climbed out of his truck. His face was all thunder and no flash.

"We had a deal." Drake drew me aside. "You said you weren't going to wander off again."

"Give her a break." Leo stepped up. "Jonah gave his okay, because once again, you had better things to do. She's safe when she's with me."

As much as I didn't like the "she's with me," factually, I wasn't in a position to deny it.

Drake unfolded his full height and stature, and stared down his fellow protector. A few seconds later, Leo moved aside with an awkward shrug.

"You couldn't have waited one lousy hour?" Drake swiveled his head toward me.

Did the flare of his nostrils warn of danger—or was he inhaling my scent? His natural fragrance edged through, too, spinning my head into whirlpools. A touch, a wrong word, even a look could dissolve his control.

I knew it.

He knew it.

My head cocked, I watched him as his gaze moved slowly away from my eyes and settled on my mouth.

"I needed to get away." I licked my dry lips. "Clear my head."

"And you came here of all places. A total coincidence?"

I slow-shrugged and looked to the side. "Maybe not a *total* coincidence."

"Leo, head back." He spun his head to the other man, whose presence had slipped my mind. "Your meeting starts in half an hour."

"All right." Leo sneered. "I'll pick you up tonight, Kensi. Okay?"

I frowned. "What for?"

"A restaurant. Do you prefer Greek or Italian?"

Had I agreed to that? Hell, the heat and Drake's dramatic appearance had truly done a number on me.

"Today, I'll need an early night." I pulled back, now using Drake's build as a shield.

Leo's demeanor registered no disappointment. "Maybe—"

Drake barely moved, but a tiny shift was enough to command attention. "Time to do your job, so I can do mine."

"Fine." Leo stalked back to his car and got in. The sedan's engine rattled as he reversed, a hair's breadth from bumping into Drake's pickup, and sped off.

"You can flirt when the job's done, princess. We're not paying you to make out with Leo." Despite Drake's harsh words, his voice yo-yoed.

A rare glimpse of emotion?

I took off my sunglasses. "I wasn't making out with Leo."

"So I didn't see you two kiss?"

"No. What you saw was Leo making a move, that's all."

"Right." His gaze drifted past me to the trees. "Good. What I was trying to…you know. Why are you here anyway?"

"I wanted to see the place for myself."

Drake stilled for a moment.

In the corner of my eyes, small branches bobbed up and down in the breeze. Even though I'd never known the pleasures of running free, the forest was in my blood, part of my DNA. Under the dimmed light, my perception shifted its focus away from the eyes to my ears, my nose and my skin. A whole new world existed under that impenetrable foliage.

"Come on then." Drake jerked his head. "Let me show you the old camp."

We followed a path wide enough for grass to grow, but as the trees grew denser, vegetation on the ground became sparse. My pulse quickened every time I picked up a new scent or the sound of a scurrying animal, and within minutes, I'd lost myself in my new surroundings.

Drake moved with purpose. He knew when to turn right, when to turn left, when to duck a branch or simply push it out of the way.

"It was in woods like these that the first modern werewolves first crowned a king." Drake gestured for me to catch up. "In their united form, the pack grew and expanded. The king's two sons later each took charge of one half, with both halves now numbering in the hundreds. As resources became sparse, the younger one moved his werewolves away."

I divided my focus between my environment and Drake's butt. "Away from the area?"

"To what would one day become Germany, where the werewolf monarchy endures to this day. Back then, both here and in Germany, we lived apart from pure-blood humans and sustained ourselves through farming and foraging. But the world soon became crowded—too crowded to avoid mingling with humans."

A scary time for my kind, I imagined. Even now, centuries later, werewolves found co-existing tough. Back then, it must have been downright terrifying to be faced by new worldviews, cultures and rituals.

"What did they do?" I hopped over a thick branch on the ground. "Hang on. Was that when they signed the Treaty of Frankfurt?"

"Yes. In Frankfurt, Germany the two packs decided to give up their isolation and allow our human form to live alongside pure-blood humans. Only our wolf forms would remain hidden. Not everyone loved that idea, and the two kings struggled, and failed, to keep peace."

"The two packs splintered into groups and some declared their independence from the crown." This was one part of history even I had known.

"Indeed." He turned around and grinned. "Who's a clever girl?"

I raised my eyebrows and glared in mock outrage. "I don't know, but I'm a grown woman with an overwhelming urge to kick you where the sun doesn't shine."

"You want me to shut up?" His grin widened.

"I'm torn, but it seems you're a half-decent history teacher, so please go on."

He whistled. "A rare compliment."

I pushed him along the path. "Shut up and keep talking."

He laughed. "Okay. Anyway, after the Treaty of Frankfurt, about six smaller free packs split from the two royal packs, and over the next few years, the remaining royal packs themselves split into different monarchies in various countries, initially with the Germans as their supreme king."

"My dad has enough problems keeping his people in line." I chuckled. "Being in charge of several packs would drive him into an early grave."

"No surprise then that, when the individual monarchies soon declared their independence from the supreme king, he quickly assented. No war, nothing. The problem was, every group had their own idea of how to deal with humans. Some avoided them, others embraced the human world and even became indistinguishable from them."

"Did they mate with them?" I stopped walking as a sudden chill seized me. "Become human?"

Drake lifted a branch and let me pass first before dropping it and retaking the lead. "Sure. Their wolf genes faded, and the wolf in them went to sleep."

The warmth left my body. I stopped mid-step and stared at Drake without seeing him, without seeing or hearing or smelling anything. My senses had shut down, locking me inside my brain, which was shouting I'd never be an alpha.

TWELVE

LEO HAD BEEN RIGHT. My mother's ancestors diluted their DNA. Diluted it until I was unable to wake up my inner wolf.

All my life, my father had convinced me I was going to be an alpha, that one day my dominance would break free. I rested my hand on a trunk, braced my feet against its immovable mass until the bark dug into my palm. Dad should have told me the truth, damn it. I deserved to know the truth. Hell, my whole future rested on the notion that I was a real werewolf.

"Kensi?" Drake's face popped into my personal space. "Are you okay?"

I recoiled. Of course, Drake had no clue as to the turmoil his tale had unleashed on my stomach, which was spinning itself into knots.

"I'm good." I waved him away, unable to believe my own words. "I'm good."

"If you're not up to it, I can take you home." He touched my arm, high up near my shoulder, and rubbed small circles into it. "There's not much left here anyway. Just trees."

His kindness didn't make finding my composure easy. The

muscles in my face had tightened into a grimace, but I forced them back into their original position, the one that would convince Drake I was ready to continue.

My mother might be the reason my hopes had crashed and burned, but she was still my mother, and this might be the one chance I'd have to see a place where she had lived and laughed.

Once my breath flowed smoothly and my heartbeat had settled, I straightened and stepped away from his touch. "Just the heat playing whack-a-mole with my nervous system. I'm good."

Drake studied my face, then nodded and continued along the path. "If you say so."

Thank heavens.

"You were telling me that the various monarchies separated." I followed close behind him, opening and closing my hands to draw blood back into them.

"The individual packs based themselves in Sweden, England, Scotland, Spain and so on, and once Western Europe could support no new packs, they moved further east into the Baltics. For about a century, a status quo was reached. Then the human world wrecked their peaceful existence. The USSR splintered, wars broke out... About forty years ago, one group of wolves returned to America under the guise of a tribe of Roma."

That pack would have been my mother's. "They'd come home to where the journey had started, but the welcome wagon was missing."

"You could say that. The United States of America, as their old land was now known, was a different country from the one they'd left so many years before. Despite help from their European cousins, the American monarchy had been destroyed in a civil war. Only free packs remained, and they had a long memory and clung to their hatred of the old ways."

The abundance of trees thinned to give way to an area that wasn't quite a clearing.

"This is it." He moved his arms to encompass the area. "This is where that tribe lived for a while."

I did a slow three-sixty.

Dead stumps, covered with moss and dry leaves, formed a semicircle to my right. Be it coincidence or a deliberate move to create seating, it would have served the tribe well.

Drake described a vague shape with his hand. "This area was used as a communal living area. It's sheltered, a great place to get together, and to meet strangers as a united front."

"But they didn't sleep here?"

"Each family entity made camp further back in the woods. Far apart, each claimed their own territory, but close enough to get safety through numbers when needed. Some built shacks or cabins, others roughed it in tents or lived in caravans."

People had lived here, cooked here, laughed and cried here. Had my mom been one of them? She could have stood where I stood, felt the breeze as I felt it.

I shook my head, swaying lightly. Fervent wishes made for a flimsy reality.

Drake took my hand and curled his fingers around it.

Even though my hand was small by comparison, it slotted neatly into his. A chuckle bubbled up in my chest. Who would have guessed that anything about us would fit? Yet my laugh didn't erupt, because the serious gaze from his silver eyes stole the breath right out of my lungs.

"Over there's a path wide enough for caravans." He dragged me deeper into the area. "I'll show you."

Maybe I'd been reading too much into this. Drake had taken my hand to guide and protect me, as Jonah had commanded. Nothing else. Besides, a man as guarded as Drake had secrets and baggage, and my carousel was already overflowing with my own crap. I was on a job. Find a missing woman. Then move on.

"Is this camp what you'd hoped to find?" Drake squeezed my hand.

I looked up, electrified. "I guess."

He strode with a confident pace, head high, not a frown on his face.

Why the squeeze? An unintentional spasm in his fingers? A reprimand for walking too slowly? Or had it been a personal message: *I've got you. I won't let go.*

I retrieved my hand, careful not to look at him. What was wrong with me? Had some strange magic cast me back into the body of an idealistic teenager who still believed in romance and love?

"You know this area well, don't you?" I crossed my arms, still avoiding his gaze.

"I come here a lot." His voice was deeper than usual. "Not only to run free, but to explore. To most, this is forgotten history. To me, it's a past we're still living."

"Is that why you're so into history?"

"Yeah. They say the past casts long shadows." He drew me close against his side. "That has never been truer. Your ancestors, your family, lived here. And they built these roads." He pointed to an area ahead of me.

"Not much of a road. Not on the ground at least, but you're right, they cleared enough trees to allow a caravan through."

"One of these roads leads to the greatest mystery of them all. You can see it already." Drake gripped my waist and shepherded me to a tall, moss-covered rock.

For a second, I pressed my cheek against his chest and inhaled. The homey fragrance of nature mingling with his minty-fresh scent spun my head.

The obelisk dwarfed Drake by a few inches. While the rear was covered by moss, the front was highly polished, save for scores of letters chiseled into its surface. I ran my fingers across the contours and moved my lips to sound out the words.

"Herra means mister." I pointed at the ones I recognized. "And down here, raamatutoku is a collection of wisdom or books."

"How do you know that?"

His scent lingered, and I slowly lifted my gaze to his face. "My parents taught me a few things."

"It sounds Estonian." The space between his mouth and mine was no wider than a tree trunk.

"It is, but apart from those words, I don't recognize any others." I stepped around the obelisk to create distance between me and temptation.

A notch at the base of the large rock caught my attention. I kneeled and scraped off the moss to reveal a sentence.

"*Hundist ei saa karjakoera*." My pronunciation would have burned holes in any Estonian's ear canal.

"What does it mean?" Drake approached and leaned over me, his breath warming my head.

"Not sure. *Ei* means *no*. *Hundist* looks like the German word *Hund*, or *dog* in English, but I seem to remember it means wolf." I placed my hands on the ground to steady myself. "Sorry. Estonian wasn't on our curriculum."

"I'm surprised you know any words." Drake straightened, taking his warmth with him. "Was it your father or your mother who taught you?"

I got to my feet, and he immediately spun me toward him.

Dad had told me that my search for my mother's past was a personal one, to be undertaken by me and me alone, but he'd failed to warn me about eyes of shimmering silver and a dominance so strong, even in its off-state, it controlled my alpha urges.

"My mother." The light pressure of his hands on my arms, even the weight in his gaze, made my legs weak. "She was…"

"She was what?" Drake blew his words onto my cheek as a soft caress.

"She was one of them. Her name was Maaren, or Maarah." I

swiped my hand back toward the Estonian sentence. "The words I remember were her words. And this, what you see in this camp, it's her story. My history. That's why I want to know about the travelers."

Drake let go of me and retreated. "You're Maarah's daughter?"

A gust of wind came out of nowhere and brought a chill to my bones. "I thought you all knew how my parents met. Jonah certainly does."

"He never told us." He crossed his arms. "If everyone knows, why are you sneaking around behind my back?"

"I'm not sneaking. It's not even that important. My mother has always been a memory, and I simply wanted to make her real. Find out what she was like, how she lived." I gave him a pointed look. "My priority has always been to find Raven. This here…" I gestured around me. "This is personal."

Drake remained silent for a few seconds too long.

Had I said the wrong thing? He was Jonah's protector. Even the suggestion that my eye wasn't on the case for which I'd been hired could ruin everything. I needed the alpha in my corner, ideally with a dollop of gratitude on his part.

Finally, Drake gave a curt nod. "I get it, but I don't know why this has to be done hush-hush. Are you ashamed about your mother being a traveler?"

"No. I don't know." I pressed my fingers against my forehead. "I'm not even sure what this means. They don't have a good reputation. Leo says they were mostly humans, not wolves. If anyone found out the German princess came from weak genes… No wonder Marlon wanted them gone."

A crack slashed through the calm of the forest.

I twirled. "What was that?"

He chuckled. "The woods make sounds, even if no one is around to hear them."

As a native of the Black Forest, I knew the noises that filled the woods back home, but America had different trees, bushes, and animals. Dangerous animals.

"You look spooked." He lifted my chin. "Apart from werewolves, no natural predators run in the woods around the Triangle. Besides, I've got your back, princess. Thought you knew that by now."

I swayed, not in body, but in mind. "Don't call me princess."

"But you're *precious*." Drake's eyes shone a dark gray, the color of tarnished iron.

Dammit. He was all tease, no action. I inched toward him, keeping my breaths even.

He didn't run. In fact, his mouth pulled into a hint of a smile.

The first touch of our lips was velvet, a caress that turned my legs into juddering limbs. A primal yearning raced through my length, leaving goosebumps on the inside of my spine. Why had I waited so damn long? If I'd been half as stubborn, we could have skipped the arguments and moved on to the dizzying, electrifying part days ago.

The tip of his tongue crossed the threshold, and my blood sped so fast it hummed. I'd been kissed many times, but never before had my stomach quivered this way.

Too soon he withdrew, but the gray of his eyes remained, watching. Waiting.

Was this real? Had I made out with Drake in the middle of a case? I leaned back, away from him, still trapped by the lingering memory. He hadn't touched me, or gripped me and pulled me tight. Maybe I'd misread his look earlier. Maybe he wasn't into me.

Where did that leave me and the job I'd come to do? First I told him that my focus was divided between Raven and the travelers. Then, to prove my lack of professionalism, I kissed him.

Had I eaten stupid pills by accident?

"Okay. *That* happened." I gave him an uncertain smile.

So much for being a confident alpha-to-be. My first words after my world had tilted upside down could have done with a polish.

"About time, too." His voice held all the smoothness of smoky whiskey on ice. "Do you wish it hadn't?"

Had he been waiting for a kiss? Then why the hell hadn't he initiated it? Why hadn't he participated with more enthusiasm? And why, for crying out loud, had he finished it so soon?

"It wasn't professional, that's for sure." My tone remained steady—level and non-challenging.

He curled his fingers around my wrist. "That wasn't what I asked. Do you regret it?"

As if I was going to fall for that old chestnut again. He was still testing me. A yes would sound like an apology—weak. A no would be an admission that I'd got it wrong, overstepped my bounds.

I painted on a cocky smile and colored it in with arrogance. "Regret is for idiots. I stand by my actions."

"Good, because I think…" His mouth bore down onto mine like flint against steel.

Sparks zapped into my brain and down my insides, leaving my limbs weak and burning. He ran his hands down my back, held me as if his life depended on it, while I clung to his neck, drawing him deeper into me. Every bit of him teased my senses.

I'd been wrong, so gloriously wrong. Our attraction wasn't a figment of my overactive imagination.

We parted, and our grins spoke volumes without our mouths uttering a word. Even with his flushed face now inches from mine, my body still crooned.

"Yeah. I'm definitely good with this." He nudged my hair with his nose and breathed me into his lungs.

"So we agree. Not professional, but—"

"Worth repeating, over…" He pressed his lips against my temple. "…and over…" Then against my cheek. "…and over." He reached my mouth, which held on to him for a few more seconds.

I was a multitasker, and keeping it casual with Drake while remaining focused on the case would be easy enough. Only one problem with that plan: making out with guys got them all psyched up. Even one kiss could strengthen a man's antiquated ideas of what roles men and women played in their fantasies. The last thing I needed was for Drake to take the reins even more.

"What's wrong?" He wrapped his arms tightly around my waist and slayed my thoughts with his scent.

"I… It's…"

"Has the impossible happened, and you're speechless?" He chuckled.

"Shut up." Yet I didn't push him away. "Raven's murder should be my priority. You get that, right?"

"Of course. Stop worrying." He placed his lips against my nose with utmost tenderness. "What about your mother's history? Want me to look into it more? That Estonian sentence has me intrigued."

He was good at history and stuff, and an hour ago, I'd have begged for his help. But what if my mother had been too human? What if he discovered I was a poor excuse for a wolf, and that I'd never run free? If he knew the truth, he'd leave me in his dust and tell his alpha. Not only would it mean my utter humiliation, but unleashing my secret could also put my father's leadership on shaky ground.

"No." I swallowed down the roughness in my throat. "I know everything I need to know. I've found my mother's home, and I understand how she lived. What more is there? I'm content with that."

Children's laughter. Men singing. Women chatting. All of that lay in the past. What remained decades later were a few tree stumps and an empty place in the woods.

"We should go." I turned and stepped away from the obelisk and from memories that weren't my own. "Not much to discover here anyway."

Drake followed a few steps, and then his phone rang, startling a rabbit or mouse in the undergrowth. "Hello."

I stood patiently by his side, not least because he stroked my neck with his thumb while he listened.

"Is that Jonah?" I asked.

"Hang on." He pressed the phone against his chest. "Shh."

Did he just shush me?

He turned his attention back to his conversation. "Got it. I'm on my way."

"Something to do with the case?" I didn't even wait for him to stow his phone back inside his pocket and dragged him with me.

"No, my brother. He's so needy."

"That's okay. I have a ton of research to do anyway." In fact, the sheer length of my to-do list caused my shoulders to tense. "If you want, we can finally visit the lake tomorrow afternoon."

He kissed me. "We could bring a picnic, but I assume you'd say that's unprofessional, too?"

I brought my index finger close to my thumb. "A little."

He sighed. "Fine. What time?"

"I'm supposed to meet with Nat and Jonah at his place in the afternoon."

His steps halted. "I heard about that."

"Are you upset?"

"I would be, but you pissed Leo off, which is a good thing." He started walking again. "Come on then. No rest for the wicked."

We returned to his pickup hand in hand. Touching him had become second nature fast, but the absence of his lips also pushed the blood back into my brain at last.

If my fears about my mother's DNA were true, was the throne still an option for me? If my wolf was out of my reach, and I was unable to put my pack into their place, I'd be a poor leader. And even though physical challenges were rare in royal packs, my desperate claim could still lead to violence. Every contender with links to a monarchy could enforce ancient rituals—organized fights that left no survivors. Of course, I'd defend my inheritance tooth and claw, but my death would be all but certain. If not from the first challenger, than from any of those who followed.

But if being an alpha was no longer in the cards for me, what would I do?

Thirteen

Despite delegating the background searches relating to the members of POOF to my assistant, I took on Buck and Cody myself. Buck had conveniently left his name off the list he'd emailed Jonah, but a quick check on POOF's website filled in the gap.

After I'd shot a message off to my contacts at the Chicago police force, I made myself a cup of coffee and then called my dad.

"Hello, *Schatz*." His voice held a pinch of annoyance. "How are you getting on?"

Since I hadn't asked him anything yet, I assumed one of his advisers had pissed him off. If I wanted to get answers from him, I'd have to tread carefully. "Is this a bad time?"

"Not at all. I need a break." He hmm-ed, smacked his lips, then gave a satisfying sigh. Seems I wasn't the only one getting a caffeine fix. "How's your search going?"

"For Jonah's missing werewolf? Not great. For Mom's relatives or any information about her? Worse. It seems no one from the old pack is left. They've all moved away."

"All of them?" For once, he sounded surprised.

Dad always had answers. For ninety-five percent of my life, he'd been totally and utterly unfazed by anything. Mutinies at home, my teenage tantrums—if it didn't concern my mother in some way, he'd dealt with anything that came his way with ease.

"Yes, all of them," I said. "The only person who remembers her is Jonah. Jonah is a little cagey on the matter, although he did indicate that Mom was at the center of the trouble with Marlon, their old alpha. Any idea what happened?"

For a few seconds, only my father's even breaths traveled down the phone line. "Marlon made your mother his target, but don't for a second think she did anything to deserve it."

"I wouldn't."

"Sorry. Of course you wouldn't. But that doesn't matter. This is your journey and—"

"Come on, Dad." I rolled my eyes up to the ceiling, glad he couldn't see my childishness. "Give me something. The old *this-is-your-journey* spiel is wearing thin."

"I'm pretending I didn't hear that, for your sake, Kensington."

Ouch. He hardly ever used my full name.

"I made your mother a promise," he said. "One day, I would send you to Marlontown, where you would discover who you are for yourself."

"How, Dad? There's nothing here."

He grunted. "I refuse to believe that. Your mother would have taken precautions. When it came to you, she left nothing to chance."

Now it was my turn to sigh. This conversation had been a dead end before it had even started. Where Mom was concerned, Dad didn't compromise. The idea she'd sent me on a fool's errand never occurred to him.

"Okay, Dad. I'll keep looking."

"Good. Trust us, *Schatz*. You will find answers."

We said our goodbyes and hung up, surely with him as frustrated as me.

I made myself another coffee and checked my email—and my mood lifted. My friends had come through, and then some. Even though they'd found nothing on Cody, not even a DUI, Buck hadn't fared that well.

The werewolf might be a friend to Drake and a valued member of Jonah's pack, but what no one had told me was that he'd had a few run-ins with the law. Not once, but twice had he been investigated for inappropriate relationships with minors, specifically girls of fifteen. How had no one thought this was relevant?

With the human police involved, it didn't take great insight to surmise that Buck's groping hands had found human girls in those cases, but had this been a calculated step? If he'd laid a finger on a young wolf, Jonah would have expelled or even killed him. Werewolves did not misbehave or break pack rules. Ever.

But what if Raven had been the exception? What lengths would he have gone to in order to prevent anyone from finding out?

Yet despite the claims against him, he was never charged or convicted. Besides, Jonah's and Drake's trust in him did carry weight with me. Rap sheets only ever told part of the story. For all I knew, Buck was innocent.

The remaining emails in my inbox didn't bring me closer to a solution either. No university had heard of Raven. She hadn't been admitted to any hospital or shipped to any morgue. The hacker my assistant had hired on my behalf found limited camera surveillance to cover the Triangle, and his facial recognition software had brought no trace of Raven—not at bus stops, in stores, or motels.

She simply had disappeared.

That night, I slept only for a few hours. My dreams hopped from face to face, without rhyme or reason, and left me more tired than before I'd gone to bed. Dozing on the sofa, on the other hand, didn't help either, and I spent the hours between four and five a.m. trying to recapture the sensations Drake's kiss had conjured.

Coffee was the only thing that brought me back to a semblance of the old me.

Even so, I kept monitoring my email account.

My assistant had worked overtime, bless her, but looking into all of POOF's members would take a while, maybe even a few days.

After listening to my conversation with Cody again, I fell back onto the sofa and let out a scream. Leo had pegged him as a likely suspect, and I was slowly coming round to his way of thinking. Not that I'd dismissed Buck entirely.

At this moment in the investigation, my leads were threefold. My assistant could dig up some unusual activity or undisclosed criminal history on one of the environmentalists. A second visit to Cody could shine new light on my search. Or my visit to the lake could uncover a case-breaking clue as to Raven's whereabouts.

I checked my phone and sighed. Lounging on the sofa was getting me nowhere. I brushed aside my fatigue and started my exercise routine before getting back behind the laptop.

A taciturn Leo picked me up from home at twenty minutes to three, and we arrived at Jonah's just as Natalie waved goodbye to the driver of a minivan.

"Need my help?" I pointed my chin at the stairs.

"We have a ramp at the side." Leo led the way. "Jonah prides himself on being accessible to everyone."

No doubt this barb was aimed at Natalie, who—in his mind— would fail to change Jonah's mind, no matter what. Whatever he needed to tell himself to be okay with this human invasion of the werewolves' sanctuary was fine by me. I'd spent the entire morning combing through Buck's and Cody's social media accounts, and whatever the true difference between werewolf and human was, it was lost on me. My two prime suspects shared many friends, displayed similar political leanings, and had a morose streak.

Jonah, back in a suit, greeted Nat and me with deliberate courtesy, while Leo made himself scarce. Within minutes, Liza appeared to serve tea and thin chocolate cookies and, after gifting me a prolonged smile, she excused herself again.

One day I'd get her to tell me why she found me so fascinating.

"Kensi told me you're involved in the new project out by Dry River Farm." Jonah sat in his usual spot, with Nat in the chair to his left and opposite me.

Nat wore a white jumper that contrasted with her flushed cheeks. She sat straight in her chair and rested a hand on a file she'd brought from home.

"It's a wonderful project, but before I get involved, I wanted to ask you a few questions." She tapped her folder with her index finger. "You seem to be the leading voice rallying against the project."

Jonah frowned before speaking in a clear, measured voice. "I'm not at all against the project. The land on which you want to build is my only concern. It used to belong to a small group of people. As their only possession, it sustained them entirely for a long time before it was passed down through the generations to me. It is my responsibility to manage this land—or what's left of it—on behalf of that group's descendants."

Natalie slid her folder to the side. "That I know."

Jonah's eyes widened. "You do?"

"I did my homework." She brushed a streak of hair behind her ear. "I don't know what Kensi told you about me, but I have access to a large amount of historical data about this town and the people that live here."

"I see." He briefly glanced at me, and then turned his focus back on Nat. "Then you might know that Marlontown's people have seen their rights to use the forest curtailed for decades. In recent years, things have gotten worse. Since the *Kelo* decision, a judgement that gave Colorado the right to seize a person's property and give it to a privately owned pharmaceutical company, we've lost many private assets. Add that to disputes over ancient land lines…"

I brushed my crumbles from the table and deposited them on the cookie plate. "The Triangle's population has more than doubled over the past thirty years. It went from a place where everybody knew their neighbor to a place with a crime rate."

I, too, had done my homework on these towns.

"That's progress, isn't it?" Natalie balled her hands. 'The dark side of progress, mind you, but isn't that how societies evolve?"

Jonah spread his hands, palms down, on the table and gave a single bob of his head. "Do you live in a house or an apartment, Natalie?"

"A house."

"Does it have a garden?"

"Yes."

"How would you feel if the government ruled that you cannot have barbecues with your friends or that you must enter the kitchen through a window? We want to choose how we live in our own four walls and on our land."

She sucked in her bottom lip, gaze adrift, and then glanced up. "Who is *we*? How can you be so sure the descendants feel as strongly as you do?"

"Because I talk to them. We communicate every day." Jonah intertwined his fingers, his demeanor almost pleading now. "That's what happens in a close-knit community. Isn't that why *you* moved to our small town in the first place? For the community spirit?"

A shadow crawled over her expression. "I guess so."

They sat for a few seconds. The only sound was my chewing. And yet, their silence didn't create a stiff, unfriendly atmosphere. They held eye contact, and Jonah even coaxed a shy smile from her.

He shifted closer to her, his elbows propped on the table. "My fight is a fight for the community as a whole. Progress is necessary, but not to the detriment of those who were here first. For their sake, let's walk, not run."

He was almost the perfect politician. The way he'd turned the pack's sovereignty over territory into a matter for the whole town was masterful.

"Jonah's not the cult leader you were expecting, right?" I grinned at Nat.

Her face turned a bright red. "I can't believe you said that."

I laughed. "Yes, you can. It's why you like me. You said so yourself."

She shot him an anxious glance, which he calmed with a charming smile.

"Tell me." His gaze locked with hers, as if the two were the only ones in the room. "What would you do in my place?"

"I would do what you're doing." She ran a hand through her hair, before placing it near his.

"So where does that leave us?" He stared at her hand and licked his lips.

"Us?" Nat chuckled. "I don't—"

"I was referring to our disagreement."

If anything, Nat's shade of pink deepened while she shifted in her wheelchair. "In light of what I've learned, I can't in good conscience support the center now."

Her smile faded, as if the implications of her words only now dawned on her.

Jonah didn't look like he'd emerged victorious either. And why would he? Nat wasn't in charge of the project, and the project would still go ahead, only without her input.

"This isn't my business," I said by way of warning that I was going to stick my nose in it anyway. "But can't you help each other?"

"How?" Natalie sounded hopeful.

"Jonah isn't against the center. If he allowed it to be built on *his* land, the people running the project might welcome it, if the conditions are right. They could pay rent, and in that way he could continue to support the descendants. Meanwhile, the government would have no more reason to claim eminent domain."

"Kensi." His tone tapered to a point. "The rest of the…locals might have other ideas."

I straightened my jacket and my back. "No one would openly object, since it's a good cause. And explain that, if you work together on this, the newcomers may side with you in the future, too—against the government."

Natalie flashed a soft smile. "This solution won't return the land you've already lost, but people around here would be glad to get behind you on this project. I certainly would."

Whatever went through his mind involved calculations and theoretical conversations, no doubt. I wasn't naïve enough to think I'd suggested a solution for world peace, but maybe the two parts of the Triangle could find a way to become one whole.

"Yes." Jonah finally gave a pronounced nod. "Yes, I'd be okay with that."

Natalie's smile opened into a beam. "We could hold a street party and invite everyone who has questions. Your people and newcomers like myself. An informal get-together, without lawyers and red tape."

Nat and Jonah had gone from adversaries to peas in a pod at lightning speed.

Jonah noted down a few words on a pad before throwing his pen aside and taking Nat's hand. "I like that idea. Neighbors shouldn't be strangers. Would you help me organize it?"

Her face glowed from her pointy chin to her hairline. "Of course. But I don't know how much use I'll be." She dipped her chin at her chair.

"I would find your input useful." His pitch approached what was best described as a bedroom voice.

Cute.

But what the hell was I still doing here?

Jonah offered Natalie the last of the chocolate cookies, which she accepted. He didn't even ask me.

I got up and shoved the chair against the table's edge. "I'll go and find Drake. We have stuff to do."

"He's next door." His gaze traced the way Nat nibbled around the cookie's edges. "Thanks, Kensi."

"I imagine there will be lots to discuss if we want to make our project work." Natalie bowed her head.

"We should meet up regularly to discuss our progress. What day would work best for you?"

I lifted my hand in a wave neither he nor she saw. Whatever was going on between them, Jonah would need to be careful. As an alpha, he'd be acutely aware of the dangers of letting humans into our lives. Still, one way or another, a close friendship with a human would do *this* pack a world of good.

I entered the room next door. Drake sat in front of the TV, while images of a spewing volcano flashed across the screen. He'd folded his arms, so his biceps flexed at the sleeves of his T-shirt. Even in his relaxed state he struck an imposing figure. Some might consider bumping into him in the dark a scary proposition. For me, the notion unlocked all sorts of naughty possibilities.

"Hard at work, I see." I leaned against the doorframe and smiled, because I found it difficult not to.

He turned off the device and skulked toward me, using his werewolf grace to devastating effect. "Just waiting for you, smartass."

With lightning speed he pulled me into his arms and embroiled me in the sweetest kiss—quick, hard, yet passionate enough to make me realize I'd never have enough of him.

Whatever was in the air today, Jonah and Natalie weren't the only ones gripped by attraction.

Fourteen

D RAKE PULLED ONTO A SIDE road that led to a parking lot by the woods. "We're here. The lake's about twenty minutes that way."

One car, complete with child seats and a Baby On Board sticker was parked at the other side of the lot.

Drake killed the engine and reached into the glove compartment, with his head almost between my knees. Seeing his hair in my lap, guessing which way his mouth could wander any second… My legs loosened, opened a fraction, and I clawed at my seat, nails deep.

He pulled out a bottle of water and handed it to me.

I released the seat to accept the bottle, my fingers stiff.

He snapped the compartment's lid shut and sat back up. "Drink up. It's hot, and you're not used to the heat."

No kidding, dude.

I tipped back my head and gulped the water, so it might purge the naughty thoughts from my heart.

Leo's sedan pulled up next to Drake's truck. We'd almost left the house when Jonah's brain finally caught up and he asked what we had planned for today.

I explained quickly that a search of the lake area could hold vital clues. In all likelihood, we wouldn't find a thing, but we had to try. Jonah concurred and even suggested we hire a couple of helpers: Leo, who'd been taught survival and tracking skills by his father, and Buck, who had "the best nose in town."

Surely it was pure coincidence that Leo would not be able to chaperone Jonah's and Nat's discussions.

If two's company and three's a crowd, four was definitely a horde. Drake and I would have to keep our hands to ourselves, unless we wanted everyone to know about the shift in our relationship. Neither of us was ready to admit to anything yet. The question was, would Leo be fooled?

Drake, dressed in a casual T-shirt that didn't hide much of his ink, leaned against the bonnet of his truck, while Leo moved his weight from foot to foot. The sun was burning at a more pleasant rate today. In fact, it would have been the perfect day for a picnic.

After a few minutes, Leo's phone beeped.

He checked the message. "Buck's stuck in town. He'll be here in an hour."

"How about we get started?" Drake pushed himself off his vehicle. "He can join us when he gets here."

Leo and I exchanged a glance and nodded our approval.

The parking lot was a small plot of land with a parking sign. A few feet in, a typical nuclear family took a snack in a designated picnic area, complete with tables and benches. A human family, I suspected, since I detected no warmth between them and the two protectors.

The kids waved, and I waved back. Drake and Leo ignored them and stomped down a passage, which led onto a less traveled path snaking through the woods. The temperature here was significantly lower, only one of the many reasons I loved the forest.

"Are we walking randomly, or do you know where we're going?" I nudged aside a low-hanging branch.

"The photo was taken by the lake," Drake said. "Not the tourist part of it, but private land our pack hasn't yet returned to the humans. We call it Lake Marvin."

He bent low to force his bulk through two trees that stood close together, and made a sound that was half grump, half exertion.

Even though I was tall, I was half his width, so I slinked through without losing my step. "Are you saying Raven took Cody to a place where werewolves could be running around?"

"Looks like. Another reason for her to hide those pictures from her parents."

"This kind of reckless behavior could endanger the secret of our existence." Leo shook his head. "She could have got herself into real trouble."

Raven had disappeared, so one way or another, getting herself into trouble was exactly what she'd done.

A mesh fence stood in our way and warned away strangers with a *Do Not Enter* sign. Drake pushed open the gate, and we stepped through to the other side. A narrow dirt trail took us through the undergrowth.

I inhaled the familiar scent. With its soft grassy ground and tall, leafy trees, the forest was perfect for frolicking werewolves. The path widened and ended in a clearing—and a huge, glistening lake. The weather would have been perfect for a dip, but that wasn't in the cards for me. First, I wasn't going to run around naked with Drake or Leo in the picture. But there was a more primal reason for my hesitation.

Wild animals.

Germany's most dangerous creatures were adders—snakes whose bites were rarely fatal—wild boars and, of course, werewolves. I'd learned to avoid adders, and wild boars gave us a wide berth by nature. In other words, where I roamed, I was the sole predator even in my human shape, which made the Black Forest my ideal home.

America, on the other hand, was teeming with things that

wanted to kill me. Snakes, bears, spiders, crocs and alligators… Who knew what awaited me in that lake? Anacondas? Piranhas?

Drake pointed at a lone tree on the grass. "This looks like the one in the picture."

Even though the tree's perfect roundness wouldn't easily be confused with another tree, I retrieved the photos to double check. "You're right."

"Okay, so we have the spot." He took a careful look around the area. "Let's assume Raven and Cody met here that day. Maybe they argued. Then what?"

"He killed her?" Leo predictably suggested.

I pocketed the pictures again. "Maybe, or maybe she stayed behind for another reason."

"It's a nice place." Drake pushed his hands into his pockets. "Great for hanging around."

"I don't think so." Leo stepped forward and faced me. "The weather wasn't like it is today. Not exactly freezing, but look around. There are no benches."

"True." I nodded. "According to her file, she didn't own a car. And she wouldn't have run all the way back to Marlontown, right?"

"What are you getting at?" Drake asked.

"She could have been meeting someone else. Someone who promised to give her a ride home."

Drake sat on the ground and patted the grass to his right. "So this could be the place then."

"*The* place?" I joined him. "You think she's dead, too?"

"Drake's right." Leo sat to my right, his body a smidgen too close to mine. "Maybe it's time we seriously considered it."

Drake pulled up his knees and placed his arms on top. The abstract ink slung around his biceps, down to his elbows and beyond. Those were definitely good arms.

"Okay, let's think about this." He turned his head to me. "If she's alive, she was kidnapped, maybe by whomever she met that day, or she's run away."

"Running away is unlikely for a werewolf, but not impossible for a young woman at odds with her parents." I rubbed my chin. "So far, I haven't been able to find anything to support that, and believe me, I've looked."

"Living with Birdie and Pike couldn't have been easy, but she loved them." Drake grimaced. "*Loves*. Her friends are loyal and concerned. I don't see her splitting without telling anyone."

I gave a dry laugh. "Okay. You've crapped all over the happy options."

He looked out over the lake. "This isn't the first time I've thought about what might have happened to her. I didn't know about Cody or about this spot, but we turned the Triangle upside down. Checked into possible motives, train times, placed photos in the Gazette, offered reward money for information. Nothing."

"Okay." I lifted my shades up on my head. "Walk me through the suspects."

"As I said, I can't believe a wolf had anything to do with her disappearance. We have to look at humans." He caught my sharp glance and returned it. "I'm not one of those bigoted assholes that hate all humans, so don't get your panties in a twist, princess."

"Underwear under these pants? You're kidding, right?"

He'd be able to see every seam. Especially with a gaze as penetrating as his.

His eyes were so unusual. Pure silver with hardly any dark flecks. As if drawn by an artist. They went perfectly with the subtle flush in his cheeks.

"Cute." He wiped his mouth with the back of his hand.

"Anyway." Leo nudged my arm. "Considering Cody's admitted they routinely met here…"

Yet Drake held my gaze. Even in the shade of the tree, the heat made my pulse go faster. The temperatures didn't affect him, at least not on the outside. Not a hint of sweat had escaped his pores.

"Are you listening?" Humor touched Leo's voice.

"I'm listening." I turned my attention to the other protector. "So you think she could have been kidnapped?"

"A human would have a hard time kidnapping a werewolf." Drake groaned. "At some point, he or she would underestimate her strength. And I simply don't buy that one of us would have done anything like that."

"That leaves death." Leo's voice may have been fact-oriented, but the way he ran his hand through his hair cut deep.

He and Drake had known Raven since their school days and their jobs had made them responsible for her wellbeing. The possibility of death wasn't just a possibility of failure, but of a personal loss that might leave scars.

"Let's search the area around the lake, even if only to rule it out." I leaned back onto my arms, unable to meet either gaze.

The trees' leaves on the opposite bank of the lake reflected light in places, swallowed it in others, offering a range of greens in a mosaic-pattern.

"That's why we're here." Leo gave a sad smile. "What are we hoping to find?"

"Blood, drag marks, God forbid, maybe a body." My tone was clinical. If we were talking worst case, no point in sugar-coating it. "The killer, if there is one, could have dumped Raven in the lake."

Drake tore off a handful of grass, which he held out to be blown off by the breeze. "It's a natural lake. Real popular with fishers, and the currents are unpredictable. A body would have surfaced by now. And it's not like you can roll someone in at the shallow end. You'd need a boat."

I turned my head away from the lake. "The woods, then?"

He swiveled around and got onto all fours. He crawled close to me until his head blocked my view, and his breath grazed my face.

"Care to go for a run?" His voice burrowed deep into me.

The area between my legs went on alert, and I squirmed to calm it. There was no denying Drake was an attractive man.

"He didn't mean it that way." Leo sounded piqued. "He meant we should search in wolf form."

"Leo, you go that way." Drake pointed to his right. "Kensi and I will look over there." His finger shot to the left.

Before Leo could voice the objection that was forming on his face, I motioned for both of them to get away. "You two search the woods. I'm going to have a look around out here. If there was an attack, this is where it could have started."

Leo sat up on his knees and scowled.

Drake had asked me to run with him. Almost always, courting among werewolves began by running together. But if he'd been serious, why had he asked me in front of Leo?

Only one answer came to mind. Keeping our kiss secret was no longer his objective. Getting one over on his rival was.

"Whatever you say, princess. You're in charge, as you keep reminding me." Drake got to his feet and towered over me. "Be careful out here. The other side of the lake isn't private, and someone might see you shift."

"That's why I'll search in my human form." I waved him off. "Go on. We'll compare notes later."

Any warmth left his eyes. Arms crossed at his wrists, he slid off his T-shirt. Apparently it hadn't occurred to him his sculpted abs might leave me breathless. He kicked off his boots, dropped his jeans—

I almost cried out.

He turned his back to me and slipped out of his boxers.

That ass wasn't anyone's consolation prize.

He strode away, and I made an effort to catch every reflection of light off his body, every flex of his muscles. Mid-walk, he hunched to touch the ground with one hand, both hands, then his arched back dropped, and his tan skin turned into dark brown, shiny fur.

Such a smooth transition. I gritted my teeth and got to my feet, my body itching to join him, yet unable to do so. One day I'd succeed. One day I'd let my sleek wolf form transport me across bumpy terrain and through dense forest.

Drake glanced back at me once, before he sprinted off into the undergrowth.

Another wolf's head nudged me.

I shot Leo, resplendent in light-gray fur, an uncertain smile. "Thanks for helping us. There's a lot of land here, and without you, we wouldn't stand a chance."

He sniffed, like a mini-sneeze, and padded off in the other direction.

I breathed in the crisp scent of the lake and inched up to the water's edge. The breeze was stronger here, although not strong enough to blow away the sun's warmth. I picked up a flat stone and skipped it across the slightly rippled surface. It bounced once, twice, before disappearing into its depth.

The lake stretched into the distance and would make the perfect hiding place for a body, but Drake was right. Without a boat or a jetty in sight, hiding a body wouldn't be possible.

Eyes peeled for any disturbance in the ground, I returned to the tree and, from there, walked in ever-increasing circles, hoping I wouldn't find a clue. Because I hadn't given up hope of finding Raven alive.

Did she and I have more in common than looks? Our upbringing wouldn't have been so different. Mainly surrounded by our own kind, yet separate—she because of her parents' musical ambitions for her, and me because of my inability to shift.

A growl from behind jarred the tranquility. Drake dashed forth from the trees and transformed into his human self mid-run.

If I were struck blind right now, I'd be grateful to have at least once viewed absolute male perfection. Arms to sweep me up and never let go. A tattoo-free chest that wasn't ripped, but defined into a hard plate. And legs so powerful they shouldn't by right fit into pants. And then there was his dick. Even in its current state, it had no need to hide. It swung freely, supported by balls that were big enough to match his attitude.

"I found her." He breathed hard.

I strode toward him, heat rising in my cheeks, and met his gaze. He knew exactly where my attention had been.

"I said I found her." He picked up his clothes and got dressed.

"Raven?" A chill gripped me.

"Yes. At least I think it's her." He ran a hand through his hair. "Dammit. I knew it. But I was hoping, you know."

A layer of white veiled his tanned face.

Leo approached from behind. Panting, he picked his T-shirt off the ground to wipe his face. "What is it? Did you find something?"

"Drake thinks he's found Raven." I glanced past Leo's shoulder, whose physique was naturally lean.

"What? Where?" He pivoted his gaze and held up his hand to shield his eyes.

"Over there." Leo pointed behind him. "Leo, call Jonah and let him know. I'll show Kensi."

"Are you sure she needs to see a dead body?" Leo slid into his clothes, leaving his defined abs for last.

"Seriously?" I frowned at him. "Talk to Jonah."

His lips disappeared into a thin line, but he nodded. "I can't get any reception here. I'll be by the car."

"Okay. As for you, show me." I barely waited for Drake to get his boots on before I dashed off to where he'd broken from the trees.

He quickly took the lead. As the trees closed around us, the temperature dropped again, and the scent of damp earth combined with that of fallen leaves.

"Over there." Drake pointed to his right.

Among the fresh scent of the forest rose the odor of something moldy, something dead, like rotten cabbage, filled with feces and cheap perfume. I lifted my hand to my nose and coughed. With each step, the assault on my nostrils got worse, and my cough turned into gagging.

Drake also held his nose with his fingers and stopped at the bottom of a slope.

A divot ran through the ground, with moist earth scattered around it. In the middle, a gray-blue mottled arm lay uncovered, skin barely hanging on to the tendons underneath. A thin layer of wax gave the gruesome sight an otherworldly touch.

I turned away and retreated a few steps, heaving, but not vomiting.

Drake placed his large, warm hand on my back. "Are you okay?"

I took a deep breath, which only brought back the nausea, and I heaved some more.

"Here." He retrieved a wrapped candy from his pocket. "It's mint. It'll help."

"Maybe." I gagged. "If I stick it in my nose."

"Don't argue. Go on."

I slipped the candy in my mouth. Its bite carried into my airways, indeed making breathing that little bit easier.

I cast a glance back to where the body lay. "How do we know it's her?"

"We don't. Not for sure. I dug down as far as I could, or as much as I could stand. We have to call the cops." He slapped the tree trunk. "Fuck it."

I leaned against a tree, feeling the energy leave my body. Raven was no longer a stranger to me. In many ways, I might have known her better than her parents had. My chance to ask her about her music, about what she really wanted from life, was gone. Was this the end? The cops would identify her and maybe bring her parents peace, but what effort would they expend on getting answers? They'd take over my investigation and probably arrest Cody, guilty or not.

"Maybe we don't call the police." I wiped tears from my face.

Not tears of sadness, but a reaction to the nausea that still rattled my insides.

"Why not?"

"First, we should find out if it's her." I ducked past him and approached the hideous arm. "If we find something that ties back to Raven, like her sweater, it's up to us to get justice. No one has a more vested interest in solving this than us." Something shiny reflected the sparse light. I approached and kicked at the soil with my shoe.

Drake joined me. "What is it?"

I pointed with my toes, and he took a stick to unbury the item.

"It's the necklace. Raven's necklace." I shook my head. "The same one her mother wears."

"Shit." Drake wiped the back of his wrist across his forehead and eyes.

Why would someone do this? Raven had been so young. She didn't even have a chance to find herself yet. Who could she have possibly pissed off in her few years on this planet?

He and I exchanged a weighty glance. Someone had put that poor woman in this grave. Why?

"She wasn't buried deep. It's possible she was simply dumped in a hollow with earth shoveled on top." I crouched for a better vantage point. "I can't see any obvious wounds from here. Her death could have been an accident, but if so, why bury her *here*?" Saplings dotted the short sparse grass. I pointed further into the forest. "The trees grow denser back there. It would have been easier to hide a body there. Here, a werewolf was bound to stumble over her at some point. You found her within ten minutes."

Drake crossed his arm. "If you're human and you don't know about our sense of smell, you wouldn't have had reason to fear discovery."

"And this being private, werewolf land…"

"The killer probably assumed she'd never be found." He turned and kicked a tree. "Fuck."

I sidled up to his side and placed my hand on his arm. "I'm sorry. I really am."

He glanced away, but didn't shake off my touch. "Me too."

"Okay, so at this point, I'm inclined to believe a human might be responsible, which means Cody must be our prime suspect. But let's not rule anyone out. If we get the police involved, what are they going to find? A photo that shows Cody and Raven knew each other. Big whoop. They'll ruin his life by arresting him, but will never convict him, because being her boyfriend isn't a crime. Taking this to the cops is a lose-lose."

"Raven and her family are well liked. I doubt it would make it to trial." His voice was without emotion.

Old werewolf retribution had little to do with justice, but Jonah would be able to placate his pack by making the human disappear. It all came down to whether the alpha was a fair man— or a practical man.

"We could keep our find secret from the rest of the pack for now." I stepped away from the body, my stomach heavy with nausea. "Jonah promised answers by the full moon, which isn't for a while. Let's take the time to tie this to Cody directly, or an innocent man might be lynched."

"Innocent?" Drake brushed past me toward the body. "He doesn't sound innocent to me."

Yet he was kicking earth and leaves back onto the body and the pendant. Did that mean he was on-board?

"We'll keep working the case." I stared at the mound of earth, which now covered the grave. Yet the smell stuck to the back of my throat.

"I don't know." Drake returned to me and took my hands into his. "It's Jonah's decision."

I was too familiar with pack hierarchy to think this was a slam dunk for me. My only shot at holding onto this case was to convince the alpha to continue to trust me. After all, I'd made significant progress in only a few days.

"Drake?" I averted my head from the scene and briefly closed my eyes.

"Mm-hmm?"

"Do you have another peppermint for me?"

He handed me a candy, and I sucked greedily to get rid of the stench once and for all.

Drake led me back toward the fence and the parking lot. The family had gone, and so was their car.

Leo approached, his head drooping, his shoulders low. "Jonah told us to come in."

I nodded.

"Do you know if it's her?"

"Yes." I placed my hand on his arm and squeezed gently. "I'm sorry."

"You saw her?" Leo's chin pulled up and he glared at Drake.

"I kept my distance, but Drake is sure it's her." My smile probably did a poor job of hiding my white lie, but Leo didn't need to hear I'd been subjected to such a gruesome sight.

For all his talk about equality and respecting me, he was still a man, and a protector to boot.

"Shit." He spun around and leaned against his sedan, his hands on his head. "Okay. Let's tell the boss and then get drunk. I'm buying."

I smiled. "We'll see."

We got into our vehicles—Leo into his, and Drake and I into the pickup—and left the area with an understandable amount of haste. My time in Marlontown could be coming to a close. Drake and I might never get to explore our attraction. The personal quest Mom had sent me on might be a bust. But none of that mattered right now, because a young woman lay all alone in the woods, with the bears and the snakes and God knows what else.

FIFTEEN

T̶HE DRIVE TO JONAH'S PLACE was filled with thoughtful silence. Drake's face didn't give much away, although his broad shoulders seemed narrower and his movements less forceful.

Was Cody responsible for Raven's death? He'd never actually said Raven stayed behind to meet someone. If he was trying to divert suspicion from himself, why tell us about the lake in the first place? He'd appeared genuinely grief-stricken about Raven's disappearance, so much so he'd resorted to drinking. Or was the booze less symptom and more cause? Had he killed Raven because alcohol had shortened his fuse, and he'd run out of patience?

Leo's feelings about Cody had been clear. Hard to ignore the protector's opinion when they'd known each other most of his life.

Either way, before I turned Raven's boyfriend into puppy chow, I needed to be sure of his guilt.

The location of the body suggested the killer was a human, yet Raven had had the strength of a werewolf. Even though her trust in Cody would have put her at a disadvantage, it would have required luck for him to overwhelm her. For this reason alone I couldn't afford to discount another werewolf as potential suspect.

The Wild Pack knew only its own people, whereas I'd been exposed to the good and the bad throughout Germany and in many parts of Europe. Dark blood ran through the royal werewolf lines. Murders, rapes, kidnappings—if werewolves went bad, they went very, very bad. My mother was ample proof of that.

"We're here." Drake pulled into his parking space outside Jonah's house.

Keeping to the shade, I exited the truck.

"How are you doing?" he asked.

"Honestly, I have no idea. And you?"

He leaned against his vehicle and exhaled. "About the same."

"Should we wait for Leo?"

"Jonah would appreciate that." He drummed his fingers against the body of his truck. "This isn't going to be easy for him."

Leo's sedan arrived ten minutes after us. His face was flushed, with red veins radiation across his eyes. Had he cried? Not that I'd blame him. He too would have taken Raven's death personally.

"Nasty accident on the road. You must have just missed it." Leo gave a tired grin. "I thought for a moment they'd let you behind the steering wheel again."

"Funny." I smiled, but my mood wasn't light enough for banter.

Drake used his key to open the door and for once, allowed me to walk in front of him.

Jonah's large room looked more like an office today than it had when I first met him, with maps and papers covering about half the table surface.

Dressed in casual jeans and a shirt, he peered up from a document. "You're sure it's Raven you found?"

I fell into the chair opposite him, but he was too focused on Drake to comment on my minor digression.

"Yes." Drake stood a few feet away. He'd turned his toes out to spread his legs, and took long and slow breaths.

Leo entered from another room and greeted me with a silent nod. As he passed Jonah, he placed a comforting hand on his shoulder, a gesture the alpha acknowledged with a grateful look.

Then Jonah leaned back, without speaking, his gaze on Drake, whose figure occupied more space than usual.

Jonah was an effective leader, but I'd bet my last piece of gum that, if Drake wanted, he could be alpha of this pack. Without activating his dominance, he commanded the room by his sheer presence.

"We have reason to suspect Raven's death was deliberate." Drake's words sliced through the tension.

"She was killed on our land?" Jonah slowly rolled his pale fingers into a fist.

"Yes, in a shallow grave."

"Are you saying it was one of us?"

Drake shook his head with the precision of a machine. "We don't know that. A human could have done it."

"He means Cody, Raven's boyfriend." Leo uncrossed his arms and stepped close to the table. "He knew the place and often met her there."

"What do we know about Cody?" Jonah drank from a cup without spilling a drop.

His composure in the face of such absolute grief once again proved his ability to compartmentalize. Sadness was something alphas shared in private, if at all.

"Not much that would prove his guilt beyond a shadow of a doubt, but he's no doubt our prime suspect. As Leo said, Cody was Raven's *human* boyfriend." Drake shot a glance at me, as if this was my fault. "He met with her by the lake many times."

"He's a heavy drinker, too." Leo tugged on his earlobe. "I honestly don't know what she saw in him."

I coughed, and Jonah turned to me. *Yeah, dude. I'm still here.*

"Actually, we don't know whether the drinking started before or after Raven's disappearance." I sat upright and arranged my interlocked hands on the table. "The fact her body was found on werewolf land doesn't automatically mean it was a human either. If Raven's death had been unplanned, it would make sense to bury her on the spot rather than drag her body through town in a car. Getting rid of the scent of blood in the trunk is tricky."

Jonah's dominance shot out, wavered, and retreated. "None of my people would do this."

I lasered my gaze at the alpha. "With all due respect, you can't be that naïve. Marlon had too rough a reputation for you to dismiss all werewolves as angels."

He smoothed the sheet in front of him with his fist in two, three powerful strokes. "Marlon had his views, but he protected his pack. Whatever your private views on free packs, we engage in legitimate challenges, not cold-hearted murder."

"Fine, but what about my mother?" I took a jagged breath. "You must know she was killed at the hands of another werewolf. It happens."

He flexed his jaw and turned back to Drake. "Either way, what happened will be a matter for the human police."

"Because they've done such a bang-up job so far?" I clipped my tone. "We have no evidence that implicates Cody we could bring to the cops, and they might not find any. The law will have to let him go. What then?"

"Do you seriously need any more information?" Leo leaned into Jonah, but kept a wary eye on Drake. "If Cody is responsible, we must punish him according to *our* laws. It's the only way to appease the pack."

Jonah nodded slowly. "Yes, justice must be swift."

"Don't you want the real murderer brought to justice?" I got to my feet and widened my stance, the way Drake had. "And let's not forget, Cody's unexplained death or disappearance will raise questions too. Her parents will be questioned, and so will everyone who cared about her."

Jonah buried his nose between his steepled hands. The dot depicting seconds on the digital clock on the wall chased itself around the luminous dial face. "Kensi, could I ask you to wait in the room next door, please? This is a matter I must discuss with my protectors."

He was right. Even though I had a stake in this too, he had to do what was right for his pack. Fingers crossed he'd see my suggestion was what was right for the pack. I slowly got up and left the room with a final, pleading look at Drake.

They didn't say a word until I was out of earshot.

I entered an over-the-top dining room, with a long table seating roughly twenty people. Not nearly enough to host the Moon Festival for the entire pack, but longer than needed by Jonah alone. I pulled out a dark wooden chair and sat, tapping the table. Five days in, and I had achieved exactly zilch. Since I hadn't solved Raven's case, Jonah's support for my claim to the throne was anything but certain.

Not that it mattered, because in all likelihood, I'd never succeed my father anyway.

"Kensington?" a voice dragged me from my thoughts. Liza stepped into the room on soft soles.

I straightened against the back of my chair, keeping my expression smooth and free from emotion. She'd taken her sweet time, but I'd finally receive an answer to at least one mystery. Was she a fan of my work or did her interest in me have another reason?

Liza sat opposite me and took my hands. "I've been waiting to catch you alone for a while. Do you know who I am?"

"Yes. Your name's Liza." Despite my confident tone, I had the feeling this wasn't the right answer.

"I'm your mother's cousin."

I opened my mouth for all the questions waiting to tumble out, yet nothing came. Instead I sat frozen, the only sound that of my thumping heart.

"No one told you?" she asked.

"I don't think anyone knows." I squeezed her fingers, reassuring myself she was real. "I've been asking around, trying to find relatives, but Drake told me you were all gone."

"We are." Her gaze lost focus for a second. "My uncle, your father, ordered our pack to leave a long time ago. Right after your mother eloped with your father. When news reached me of her death, I alone returned to this wretched place."

Her aged beauty hid them well, but up close, the pains of the past were etched into every wrinkle.

"Why did you come back?" I shifted forward in my seat. "If you're the only one—"

"For you, Kensington." She brushed a streak of hair from my face and held my chin in the hollow of her palm. "I knew that one day, you would begin your journey of discovery, and I wanted to be here to set you on the right path, because Maarah couldn't."

"What is so important about this journey of discovery? According to Dad, Mom insisted I had to come here, but he never explained."

I bit my lip. Did Liza even know I wasn't able to shift? Maybe my shortcomings weren't genetic. If Liza discovered I wasn't worth her time, she might give up on me before she'd told me anything.

"Every woman in our tribe must take it, and it is her journey alone." Liza gently shook me by the chin. "It is your guide's responsibility to remind you that your existence carries deep roots. Until you understand those, you cannot know what kind of flower you're going to grow into."

"That's what I've been trying to do. Find out about my mother, how she lived, who she was."

"No, child. Your roots started long before your mother was born."

I scratched my forehead to hide my frown. "Meaning what?"

"When people are gone, they live on not just inside our hearts, but also outside, in our traditions. Traditions unite, give guidance, but mainly, they connect to the past."

"Like the Moon Festival."

"That's one example." She kinked her head as if searching for the right words. "Rituals provide spiritual guidance to all werewolves, including the Wild Pack and the Boroughs Pack. But in my pack, your mother's pack, rituals have a physical effect on us. We feel them, live by them, and let them guide us."

If my father had been vague in his explanations, Liza was downright cryptic.

"I see," I said, even though I didn't. "What's the name of *your* pack? Dad never told me."

She chuckled. "We have no name. We just are."

Her philosophies weren't helpful to me at all. "If you want me to look into traditions and rituals, where do I start? There are so many."

She got to her feet and raised a finger. "Our time is up. Jonah's looking for you."

With a tear-filled look, she yanked me against her chest. Her scent jolted my heart. Without conjuring a specific memory, it bathed me in the strongest feeling of home and belonging. And love.

"Kensi, can you come back?" Jonah shouted from the other room.

Liza dropped her embrace to let me turn toward the approaching steps.

Drake popped his head in. "Come on. Jonah's made a decision."

I nodded and reached for Liza's hand—which was gone. As silently as she'd appeared, she'd gone back into the kitchen or maybe her private rooms. One way or another, but before I returned to Chicago, she and I would sit together, and she'd tell me everything she knew of my mother. Her favorite food, her favorite jokes, even her favorite flower. Anything Liza could remember.

"You okay?" Drake asked.

No doubt my eyes were brimming, maybe my face was pale, but my heart was alive and strong. Liza was my blood, my family.

I'd finally found a link to my mother.

"Yeah, I'm good." I entered Jonah's office and steeled myself for his decision.

"Will you tell Kensi what you told me?" Jonah glanced at Drake, who was coming up behind me.

"Do I have to?" Drake flared his nostrils. "I said I don't want humans traipsing around Lake Marvin or digging into the pack's lives. Kensi's got us this far, so she deserves a shot to see this through."

"You said that?" I played up my genuine surprise by resting a hand on my chest.

Jonah surged to his feet, and an unhappy Leo scuttled out of his way.

"There you have it." Jonah fixed me with a stare. "Have another word with this Cody. The sooner we know if he's responsible, the sooner I'll know what to do next."

"Jonah?" Leo raised his hand. "I mean, I get why this is the best plan for now, but what about the others? Raven deserves a decent funeral. If word spreads—"

"It won't." Jonah lifted his chin. "Because we're not telling anyone. Not yet. Understood?"

Leo and Drake nodded.

Leo had proven himself a good protector, giving Jonah advice that showed he cared about the pack, but Drake was my hero in this. Whatever his reasons for taking my side, it was his opinion that had ultimately swayed Jonah. No doubt in my mind.

Even without Jonah's decision I would have continued my investigation. I'd already invested too much of myself to simply give up. Raven could have made a success out of her career in music, or maybe something off beat, like pottery. She could have become an environmental lawyer, or a mother with children. That was exactly the point, right there. Her path hadn't been decided yet, hadn't even begun.

Whoever killed her would face justice. I'd see to that.

I gave a small bow to show my respect to the alpha and, upon his dismissal, left the room. Drake's heavy steps followed me to the door and out to the truck. Despite the challenges he'd thrown at me, he'd shown faith in my ability. He deserved brownie points, or possibly another kiss.

A few steps from the pickup, I turned to him, sporting what I hoped was a kittenish smile. "Listen. Thank—"

"No, you listen." He came close. Very close. Breath-on-cheek close. "From now on, no more private excursions with Leo or anyone else, understood?"

So much for the warm fuzzies. "Where's this coming from?"

His dominance swept over me and forced me against the pickup's trunk, but the burn covering my skin didn't destroy my defenses. It only made them stronger. Not everything about his pheromones was pain. With his power came a sense of assuredness and of overwhelming confidence that he could handle anything.

"This is a murder now, and we'll be turning over rocks to find stuff that people don't want to be found." He poked my shoulder, while his low voice continued to shake my insides. "I'm responsible for your safety, so will you for once in your life listen to me?"

Would it be so bad to let myself drown in it? To let someone else take charge for once?

I took a deep breath.

Allowing another person to take the lead might not break me, but it wasn't in my nature to give up control. Drake's dominance had caught me off-balance. He'd found a crack in my armor and mercilessly exploited it. Our kiss had made me weak, if only for a moment, but *I* was in charge of my life.

Rather than become the whimpering wolf he expected, I leaned into his sphere, forcing him onto the back foot. "Who the fuck died and made you emperor?"

"Kensi. Be reasonable."

"I'm Princess Kensington of the Royal House vor Berg. You do not speak to me as if I'm someone else. Like I'm one of your subjects or submissives, or whatever the hell you call them."

I'd worked too hard to become what I was, *who* I was, to let a wannabe alpha steamroller me into submission.

His dominance wavered, but didn't weaken.

"Even if I weren't a princess, I'd still be the lead detective hired by your alpha. You..." I dabbed my finger at his chest. "...are my guard dog. Are we clear?"

"That's what you think of me?" His pupils contracted into dangerous pinpricks of black. "I could tell Jonah I've changed my mind. Let the cops handle the situation."

His dominance coiled around me and pushed the sweat onto my back faster than the sun's relentless heat.

"You know I'm your best chance of finding the killer." I slightly lifted onto my toes, shortening the height difference between us. "So save your threats."

His dominance flagged. He angled his body away and threw his hands in the air. "You didn't even know Raven. Why is solving this so important to you?"

The stress on my body lessened until, finally, his attack ceased. Yet the vacuum his power had left refused to fill. Somehow, he'd punched a hole in me, poured himself into it—and now he was gone.

Without uttering another word, I rounded the truck and slid onto the seat.

Why *was* I still here? My connection to Raven, imagined or not, was undeniable, but I was a realist and should know when to walk away from a case. Maybe my curiosity about my mother's past tethered me to this place. Liza had given me plenty of food for thought.

Or was it still that damned kiss?

Drake sat beside me, his hand on his keys, but showing no signs of starting the truck. "Why are you digging your heels in about this?"

"For crying out loud." I sprawled my hands flat onto my lap. "I want to see the case through. It's called having a work ethic."

"Is there another reason you want to stick around? The travelers, maybe?" Drake's voice had dissolved into silk and velvet and everything soft. "Or maybe a tall werewolf with a to-die-for smile?"

I stiffened, then slowly turned my head. "I don't feel that way about Leo."

He raised his eyebrows. "I walked into that one, didn't I?"

Rightly so. I was the first to admit I had a chip on my shoulder. Even though Drake might be honorable on a normal scale, werewolf men had given me plenty of reason to be cautious. As if to prove me right, Drake kept whipping out his dominance, treating me like a dainty maiden, and I was sick of his control issues.

Would I ever run like a wolf? Maybe not. Succeed my father to the German throne? Doubtful. But I was good at my job, and I'd be damned if I let Drake take the last ounce of pride from me.

"Can we visit Cody now?" I tapped the clock on his dashboard. "It's nearly seven."

Normally, I'd be stuffing my face with food at this time, but after our gruesome discovery, I had no appetite.

"Sure, let's avoid the elephant in the room and go talk to Cody instead." Drake smiled a tired smile.

"Dad had raised me to be independent from anyone, even himself. '*Faith is both given and earned,*' he'd say. '*One day, a man will try to steal your heart and demand your loyalty. Only you can decide if he succeeds.*'"

What Dad hadn't told me was that this man would be a competitive small-town hick who would use my traitorous feelings against me.

Still, the question remained. Did Drake deserve my trust?

Sixteen

"What if Cody's done a runner?" Drake furrowed his brows and turned the pickup smoothly into Cody's street.

The house looked sadder, somehow. Last time I was here, Raven had still been alive, at least in the way Schrödinger's Cat was. Now, the box was open, and with it, all hope was gone.

I shrugged. "We'll know in a minute."

"I shouldn't have taken my frustration out on you." Drake parked at the side of the road and switched off the engine. "Are we good?"

His gaze was glued to his dashboard, his expression unreadable. "We're good."

"Can you tell me what the hell happened? Between us?" He was biting his lip. The lip that, not long ago, had wielded its magic on mine.

That magic was gone. No matter how treacherous my feelings, too many things were working against us. Once Raven's death was solved, I'd return to Chicago, my future more uncertain than ever. Besides, he and I couldn't make it through a day without sparking off each other. Even if all he'd ever wanted from me was a fling, he was hard work—and something told me, he thought the same about me.

"Reality happened." I gave a bitter chuckle, gestured loosely with my fingers, then slumped my shoulders. "I guess we weren't thinking clearly when we kissed. Didn't consider how it would change the dynamics between us."

He opened his mouth again, then dropped his arms.

"Maybe we should act like it never happened?" My words hadn't been intended to form a question.

If Drake disagreed, if he turned to me and asked me to kiss him again, I might not have the strength to deny him.

"Yeah. Maybe." He got out of the pickup and slammed the door.

Case in point. My objective assessment of the situation had pissed him off, but what could I do? Change who I was? Even if I'd never know my inner wolf, Dad's alpha genes ran strong inside me. Things would always be done "my way." There was no "or."

We marched up the drive to Cody's house, and Drake rang the bell.

Cody opened the door and slid his gaze from Drake to me. "I thought you'd be back. At least you dropped Loser Leo." He slurred his words. "Come in. Come in."

Maybe the alcohol would loosen his tongue. It usually did mine.

His T-shirt, once white, now swam in a gray that no amount of laundry detergent could brighten. He padded on socks into the living room, where the reek of food clung to the curtains, mixed in with the smell of stale beer.

"How do you want to accuse me today?" He fell into his worn armchair and reached for a bottle from a knee-high table next to him.

I tightened my jacket around me and sat where I'd sat last time.

Drake leaned casually against the narrow bit of wall between two windows.

"I don't." I leaned forward. "I'm so sorry about Leo's behavior, Cody. How are you doing?"

He laughed and held up his bottle. "The way I've been doing since the day…" He sucked in air. "Since the day I left her behind."

"We haven't told the police about you, but you know they'll eventually put two and two together, right?" I kept my expression smooth and my tone soft. "They'll go through CCTV footage, ask your friends, canvass the shops. Someone will have seen you two together."

Cody shrugged. "Prob-ly."

"I can help."

He gave a bitter laugh. "Can you make her alive again?"

He was still convinced she was dead, and I didn't have the stomach to contradict him.

"You know the answer." I dropped my gaze.

"Then I ain't inter'sted." He closed his eyes, beer bottle balancing on his lap.

Drake gestured with his eyes to dig deeper. He was right. Softly, softly wasn't getting me anywhere. At least he didn't just take over.

"Leo suspects you were holding something back." I perched on the edge of the seat, forcing Cody to look at me. "Was he right?"

Cody's blood-shot eyes narrowed. "No, I fucking wasn't. Bitch."

Drake's dominance flooded the room, and I sent him a warning stare. Humans didn't sense dominance, but I wasn't that lucky. Drake crossed his arms, but let his power fizzle.

"I know you're angry." I focused back on Cody. "When was the last time you ate anything?"

Once again he raised the bottle. "Got all I need ra' here."

"Unless you want the cops on your doorstep, I suggest you start being helpful." I grabbed my knees to prevent myself from shaking sense into him.

His jaw tightened. He curled his fingers around the neck of his bottle, wringing it, or trying to, then shot to his feet. The bottle smashed against the table. Shards scattered through the room.

He raised the jagged remains above his head. His eyes gave away his intentions.

I threw myself sideways onto the sofa, just as he swiped his weapon down at me. Christ.

"Shi-it." His own momentum knocked him off-balance, and he wobbled.

Drake soared into view and overpowered Cody with his mass alone, as both fell to the floor. Cody had lost his enthusiasm for the fight and lay still underneath the protector's powerful body.

Idiots. Why did men have to be slaves to their testosterone? Violence wasn't just their first recourse, it was their *only* recourse.

I checked the floor around the two men for the bottle fragment. The last thing I needed was to leave a weapon lying around. It wasn't on the carpet, nor on the sofa.

My lungs turned to ice. Had Cody fallen on it?

"Are you okay? Guys?" I kneeled next to the two men and shook Drake by his shoulder, then prodded Cody.

Muffled gulps came from beneath Drake, like an old man in the last stages of pneumonia.

Cody was alive.

Trapped under a motionless body.

"Drake?" I whispered. Why wasn't he getting up? "Stop messing with me."

I leaned in to listen for his breath.

Silence.

He couldn't be hurt. Not Drake. He was too strong, too powerful to be harmed by a drunk human.

"Hey." I stroked his hair, my voice jittery. "Get up. Please. Please get up."

Cody grunted.

"Shut up," I shouted, before hovering close to Drake's ear. "Say something. Or you can shrug. Shrugging would be great." I briefly closed my eyes. "Please."

He moaned, and it was the most beautiful sound in the world. His head moved, then his shoulders, as he pushed himself onto his knees.

Blood soaked through his T-shirt, which sported a large tear. He ripped out the bottle fragment, leaving a gash that spidered high up on his chest. Damn, that looked deep.

"Hang on." I scrambled up and ran into the kitchen, then the bathroom, to find a towel, anything to stem the flow of blood.

Drake was strong, stronger than anyone I knew, and probably no stranger to injuries. He'd be okay.

Jeez, what a stupid thing to say. One wound wasn't exactly like another. What if this one was life threatening?

I kicked the radiator next to the empty bathroom shelf. Didn't Cody own anything that was clean? I sprinted back into the living room and took off my jacket, but its fabric was too stiff to serve as a bandage.

His expression distorted into a grimace, Drake swayed. Cody's gaze tracked his motions as if in a trance, but made no move to help.

I twirled on my feet. The curtains were filthy. The throw pillows—hell, *I* didn't even wanna touch them. Fuck it. With my back to Drake, I ripped off my top, put my jacket back on, buttoned up, and kneeled beside him.

"You'll be fine." I dabbed my vest against his chest. "Can you speak?"

He winced, but at least stopped swaying. "That hurts."

The bottle pieces lay between a kneeling Drake and Cody's sprawled body.

"Why do they sell beer in glass? I don't get it." I shook my head. "Soda, milk, fruit juice—plastic and cartons are good enough for them. But alcohol, which has a habit of turning men into idiots?

Sure, let's pour that stuff into glass so you can really smash each other's brains out."

Drake made a weird sound, and I eased my pressure against his wound.

A touch of pink returned to his cheeks, and I traced his jawline with my finger. My hand shook. *Seriously* shook. How easily a little scrap could have turned deadly. I willed my lungs to inflate, but they refused to obey. *Breathe, Kensi. And calm the fuck down.* A chest wound this close to the shoulder blade wasn't going to kill him, not even one this deep. But he would need to shift soon if he wanted to heal without a scar.

"I'm sorry." Cody's quiet gulps morphed into sobs. "I'm so sorry."

I rubbed comforting circles on Drake's head, kept him close by my body, ready to leap into action should Cody flip out again.

"This is all fucked up," Cody whispered. "God, I'm sorry."

I leaned past Drake toward the wretched figure lying prone on the floor. "Pull yourself together, man."

"Sorry. Oh God." His leg kicked out. "Raven."

The bastard couldn't even feel sorry for what he'd done to Drake, but maybe I was finally getting answers. "Did you hurt Raven, Cody? Is that why you're sorry?"

He violently shook his head. "Not me. No."

"Do you know who did?"

"You don't understand."

"Try me."

He rolled away from Drake, lifted his head from the floor and plonked it back down onto the rug. Tears streaked his face, and a red patch spread under his left eye.

"Someone followed us to the lake a few times." Snot flowed from his nose, which he sucked back in with one loud sniff. "That's what Raven said. She could hear better, see? She knew someone was watching us from the trees. I told her not to be para… para…"

"Paranoid?"

He gave an almost imperceptible nod. "The park was private, so I didn't think nothing of it, y'know? But maybe… What if she stayed behind to confront him?" He snuffled loudly. "If I'd been with her. I could have protected her."

"Who was watching you?" I shot a side-glance down at Drake, who sat still with his head against my chest. "Her parents? A stranger?"

"Someone she knows, is all she said." He rolled his eyes up toward the ceiling. "God, I should have believed her."

Even though the flow from Drake's wound had slowed, I kept my makeshift dressing in place. "Who was it? I need a name."

"She didn't say, did she?" He lowered his eyelids. "But he warned her not to see me anymore, she said, and that he got really weird about it. I thought she was playing with me. Trying to make me jealous."

"But it was a man. You're sure?"

"Yes, I told you." He held a hand over his eyes. "Can you leave? I don't know anything else."

"Are you okay to walk?" I gently removed the red-stained top from Drake's wound, which was no longer seeping.

"Yeah. I'm good."

I helped him to his feet. Even though he grimaced through the movement, he didn't stumble or look excessively pale.

"Do you want to go to the hospital?" My voice matched the tenseness in my shoulders.

He took hesitating steps. "I need to run, that's all."

His words helped unknot my shoulders.

"Okay. I'll drive." I held my hand out for his key.

"Yeah, that's not gonna happen." He lightly kicked Cody's leg. "See you, buddy. Get your life together, will you?"

We headed out the door into the falling darkness, his arm

draped over my shoulder. When we reached the pickup, I snatched his keys from his hand.

He growled. "We talked about this."

"*You* talked." I dragged him to the passenger side and dropped him in the seat. "I didn't agree. When are you going to get it through your thick head that I know what I'm doing?"

"When hell freezes over? When pigs learn to fly? When you're actually right?" He shrugged and instantly winced. "Take your pick. They're equally likely."

I sat behind the steering wheel, turned on the headlights, and adjusted the seat and mirrors. The truck purred to life. That's right. I knew how to bend machines to my will. With a little coaxing of the pedals, this could be a smooth ride.

But after Drake's condescending comments?

I tore away from the sidewalk, and then yanked the steering wheel around for a less than elegant turn. The front wheel crunched past the curb, and I nearly clipped a parked car.

Drake smacked against the door and pressed his hand against his injury. "Hell, do you even know how to drive?"

"I passed the test, but how much of it I remember will depend entirely on you and your behavior. Capisce?"

He gave a low rumble that could have been a chuckle, but was more likely a dissenting opinion.

Tough. Tonight, I was the one in charge. A temporary situation in his mind, no doubt, because Drake's stubbornness might just be more enduring than mine. He was annoying that way—and yet oddly adorable. Even though I found enjoyment in having the upper hand for once, the sooner he'd be back to challenging me for the lead, the better.

Seventeen

THE JOURNEY LED US THROUGH single-family homes and their lit windows into the pitch-black woods. Drake had his eyes mostly closed. Only now and again did he move and give directions.

His beautiful brick-built cottage lay nestled deep inside the forest, not a fence or paving in sight. A circular patch of dirt and earth served as a parking lot. But all this disappeared from view the second I turned off the headlights.

I gave my eyes a minute to adjust, then helped Drake out of the truck.

The living room had a homey feel, although those little touches—the throw pillows on the sofa, the curtains, and the paintings on the wall—could have done with modernization and the walls with a fresh coat of paint.

"My parents left this place to me. My brother got the other house." Drake held his breath and fell into an armchair.

"Can I get you anything? Gauze? Bandages?"

"Later maybe. I'm going to go for a run. The shift should heal the worst of it." He squinted up. "Wanna come?"

I awkwardly pointed toward the kitchen that I'd spied on my way in. "I'll make us food. Assuming I can find more than a package of ramen in your bachelor pad."

"Who says I'm a bachelor?"

"If you're not, maybe I should have a chat with your girlfriend about our kiss."

He heaved himself off the armchair and approached. That inch or two he had on me wasn't the only reason for his confidence. His self-assurance came from deep within, not just as part of his dominance, but a constant reminder of his power.

This *extra*, this *je-ne-sais-quoi,* was what I worked so hard to master in order to cover up my shortcomings, yet he wore it like an old sweater.

I held my ground, even managed to lift my chin.

He circled my hands around his neck and gifted me with a deep, sensual kiss that made my lids close and my insides gooey. He claimed my mouth with possessive determination, went so deep my lungs struggled for breath, and yet when he released me, I was seized by a feeling of loss.

"Only wanted to make sure you hadn't forgotten." He rolled back his voice to *sexy as hell*—and strode upright toward the door.

On his way, he pulled the T-shirt off his smooth, defined back and got to work on his belt in preparation for his shift.

Before he got to the good stuff, he was out of sight.

I placed two fingers against my lips. No, that wasn't a kiss I was likely to forget.

Was this flirtation of ours headed toward a crash landing? Sex lay in the cards, plain as day, but there was an outside chance our brains prevailed. Very, very far outside. Shoot. Who knew the protector who was supposed to shield me from trouble was the one getting me into it? Because neither Jonah nor my dad would be impressed with the two investigators sleeping together while on the job.

Drake's pots and pans hid in the cupboard near the stove, forks and knifes in the left drawer. Exactly where I'd have stored them. The drawer on the right contained an assortment of batteries, screws, and instruction manuals. While the pasta was boiling, I sneaked out into the hall, lined with photos of Drake and his friends—including an assortment of pretty women. Many. Different. Women. Some snuggled up to him in an embrace that indicated they'd been more than friends.

If my assumption was correct, he certainly had a type. Long dark hair, tall build, slim but not skinny. Would he add me to his wall, a pleasant reminder of *that woman he once knew*?

I shook myself loose and returned to the kitchen. A quick fling was the best way forward for us both. What was the alternative? He'd mend his ways, play second fiddle to my ego, and return to Chicago with me? I sat at the table, supporting my chin with my palm, and grinned. Not Drake. That man wasn't going to be anyone's *plus one*.

In fact, a one-and-done wasn't the worst idea. Our kisses hadn't gotten him out of my system, but a night with him surely would. Right?

The pasta and canned vegetable combo I made bubbled on the stove. Cooking had never been my strength, but my concoction offered a basic, filling meal, while salt, pepper and spices would make up for my shortcomings.

About twenty minutes after he'd left, Drake returned. His wound no longer seemed to trouble him, and he greeted me with a peck on my cheek.

"Help yourself." I pointed at the food, which I'd left on the counter to ensure he didn't think of me in an overly domestic context. "Did the run do the trick?"

He filled a plate, fell into a chair, and picked up his glass of water. "I'm nearly healed. I'll have a shower later, maybe put a bandage on to keep it clean, but it's all good."

I shoveled food into my mouth. "You've been a very brave boy."

Drake tipped his imaginary hat. "Why, thank you, ma'am."

Actually, the meal tasted okay. Then again, pasta was difficult to get wrong.

"Cody didn't get us anywhere, did he?" I pushed up my sleeves.

Since my top had served to mop up blood, I only sported a bra under my jacket. The cottage might be set deep in the woods, but the omission of an AC system had been a mistake.

Drake, once again seemingly unaffected by the heat, placed the glass back onto the table and folded his hands. "Not quite. Talking to Cody convinced me you're right. He didn't kill Raven."

"I'm right, you say?" I dropped my fork and smacked my flat palm against my heart. "Oh dear. Is it the fever? Are you that sick?"

The tip of his tongue made a brief appearance from between his lips. "You're prone to exaggerations. In any case, I bought his story. I didn't want to, but Cody's not hugely creative, if you catch my drift. I also believe Raven's claim that someone was following them."

"Someone Raven knew."

He heaved a sigh. "Yeah. Someone she knew."

"Like another wolf."

He snapped up his head, and his eyes appeared to flash, but in the end, he gave a browbeaten shrug. "Another wolf is a possibility. Yes."

"Are you going to tell Jonah?"

Drake speared the last of his pasta, slid the forkful into his mouth to chew, and at long last swallowed. "No. Not yet. Before I turn his view of the world upside down, I'd like to give him something that will ease the pain, you know? Like the killer on a platter."

I sipped water and regarded his pained expression, before taking another bite of pasta. "Do you have any ideas?"

"A suspect, you mean? Not her parents, if that's what you're thinking. Nothing on Earth could make those two kill their child. Raven's friends didn't have a motive either, at least not an obvious one."

He'd already come a long way with his insights. Could he be pushed further?

"I'm an outsider, so don't take anything I say personally. Okay?" I slid my empty plate away from me.

"I'll try." He sat hunched, but alert.

"Marlon might have started the campaign against the travelers for not being pure or whatever, but the rest of you are continuing his vision in a quiet way."

I scratched my arm, but the itch remained. No, not an itch.

Drake's dominance was seething and ready to break. "Now, why would I take your comment personally?"

"What I'm saying is you lot have a certain world view. I never said you've done anything wrong." I took a fortifying breath and softened my tone. "But Raven's choice of boyfriend could have pissed someone off, right?"

The prickle on my arm subsided.

"All right." His shoulders relaxed. "Say a dislike of humans might be a good motive for disapproving of Raven having a boyfriend, but why kill *her*? Why not kill Cody?"

I leaned back, deflated. "I don't know."

"There's something you don't know?" He sprawled his hand over his chest. "Oh my. Has my fever spread to you? Are you feeling all right?"

I kicked his shin under the table.

"Fuck." He winced and bent to the side to nurse his leg.

"Baby." But I didn't push my mocking any further. In fact, I hadn't even meant to kick as hard as I did.

"You know, you've bought into the going theory that the travelers were part human." He tapped his nose. "I have my own theory."

"Go on."

"Let's say, I've found intriguing references in my books that turn that thought onto its head."

"How?" I squinted. "Drop the vague clues and say what you have to say."

"What, no *please*?" He swiped a non-existent crumb off the table with force.

Ah. Bitchy McBitcherson had reared her ugly head again. "Sorry. My temper's a work in progress. But I know so little about my mother's pack, and you know so much."

His gruff expression softened into a smile. "Tell you what. Let me get a shower, and then we'll open a bottle of wine, and I'll tell you what I know. Okay?"

That sounded suspiciously like a date, yet I detected no predatory glint in his eyes, no ambiguity in his voice. Maybe he simply thought his revelations would be easier to bear with a generous supply of alcohol.

I crossed my arms and stretched out my legs. "Fine. Or, you know, thank you."

Yes, finishing school had truly paid off for me.

"Wine glasses are up there." He pointed to a corner of the kitchen. "And the wine's over there. I'll be quick."

He exited the room, leaving it to me to collect our plates. Typical. I placed the dishes onto the counter with an emphatic clang. I was his guest, so how come it was me doing the chores?

Because he was taking a shower and I wasn't. Because he was injured. Because for a second, I'd thought he had died, and that scare proved impossible to shake. Not everything Drake did had to do with keeping me in my place. Not everything was a battle. What was wrong with me? During my time in Chicago, I'd become a picture of calm and unflappableness. But a few days in the presence of werewolves, and I couldn't call a spade a spade without thinking, "Would this be the implement they'll use to beat me into submission?"

My suspicion wouldn't ruin this night for me. Maybe I'd learn about Mom, or maybe Drake and I would have sex in every room of this cabin. Who knew? No point spoiling an evening before it had begun. Gritting my teeth, I rinsed the plates and the pots, wiped the counters, and grabbed the wine and the glasses from the cabinet.

I was nearly out of the door when I turned back. Maybe it was petty, but I stalked back to the center of the kitchen and pulled the tablecloth to the side, so that one end hung lower.

There. My rebellion might be stupid, but it would not be crushed.

Hair still wet, Drake already sat on the small sofa—a pile of upholstered comfort—and paged through a book. The scent of shower gel that clung to his damp skin invited me to sit close.

He'd retrieved a pile of reading material on the history of the Triangle. "The few werewolf books that survived. This is what the three settlements looked like around the time your mother lived here."

The photos inside, more brown than gray, offered a view into the past. Women and gentlemen in fancy costumes strolled along busy roads, past tall cars we'd now reverently refer to as *automobiles*. Hundreds of these photos blended into one and took me back into the past.

What their idyll hid was that female werewolves still had a worth, like any commodity. At least now, human laws had penetrated our sheltered existence and guaranteed us a limited sense of equality.

Back then, in my mother's time, the idea that one day a female wolf would take the throne had been unthinkable. Yay for Dad, who'd never wavered in his support of my ambitions.

Shame the whole thing had been a lie.

"Looks human, you know." I pointed at a photo of a couple walking arm in arm.

"We're often so focused on what makes us different, on the wolf in us, that we forget that we are, at least in part, human." Drake slowly turned the pages.

His warm body rested against mine, our cozy togetherness helped along by worn springs and sloping sofa cushions.

"Living among humans has put me in touch with my humanity." I sipped from my wine glass and then held it tightly between my hands on my lap. "Humans are outward looking, always scouting for the greener grass. That's what really lies behind their wars and the violence, but it also makes them excel at the arts and sciences. Werewolves are inward looking."

"In what way?" He leaned forward to refill our glasses, but quickly resumed his spot by my side.

"We like to be alone or among our kind. Humans only ping on our radar when they encroach on our territory. It's not that we don't like them, but that we're simply not interested in them."

"I agree. Still, that doesn't explain your reluctance to use your dominance."

So that was his plan. Ply me with alcohol and find out my secrets?

I placed my wine glass on the dark wooden table only so that I could scoot to the side. "I have my reasons."

He breathed loudly through his nose. "I've hit a sore spot, haven't I?"

"Don't go there."

"You come across every bit the alpha you're going to be. And yet you never let loose. Don't you want to unleash your power sometimes? Watch others sit up and take notice?"

So he went there.

"I'm used to standing my ground without letting the wolf out." If I sounded brusque, it wasn't by accident.

"Bullshit. You're among wolves now, and your dominance is in your genes. I'm not saying you have to let it rip every hour of the day, but keeping it back should be more of a struggle than it is for you. Don't you worry that living away from your pack has made you *too* human?"

Drake's argument matched the whispers that buzzed around my father's advisors whenever I visited. *How can Kensi lead us if she doesn't understand us? Would she suppress our animal side so we'd be more like her?* Idiots. Stupid, ignorant, asshat idiots. Would I relinquish my ambitions to run free as a wolf just once? In a heartbeat.

Of course they didn't know the reasons, and neither did Drake. But while it was painful to be reminded of my inadequacy at home, listening to Drake berate me for something that wasn't my fault was torture. Of all people, he should accept me for who I was. Why didn't he open his eyes and look at me, the real me?

"No. I don't worry about being too human." I shot up from the sofa and picked up my phone from the table. "I'm all wolf and prefer to call my restraint *civilized behavior*."

"Where are you going?" Drake asked.

"It's getting late. I'm gonna call a cab."

He stared at the clock to his right, according to which it was after ten. "There are no cabs in the Triangle."

"Seriously?" I flung my hands up. "Fine, I'll take your car."

"First, it's a truck, not a car."

I rolled my eyes, making sure he saw me doing so. Being German, I didn't always pick the correct word, and trying clearly wasn't good enough for him. "I know, I know. A car is a car unless it's a pickup, in which case it's a truck, and yet a truck driver doesn't generally drive pickups. Who comes up with that stuff?"

"Not me. And second, no, you won't take my truck." He rose and stood pretty damn close to me. "You can stay here. I haven't told you about your mother's tribe yet."

"You've been dangling your knowledge in front of my face like a carrot for a while. I can wait a little longer. Besides, I'm tired." I glanced at the tiny sofa. "And I'm not going to sleep on that thing."

"Not what I had in mind."

His heart-stopping smile didn't affect my resolve. Not now. Not anymore.

I squared up to him, my body too drained for this shit. But that was the deal. Pissing contests never ended. Mark your territory. Scare off rivals.

"We kissed. That wasn't foreplay. It was a mistake. Let it go."

The atmosphere turned heavy with his dominance, and his jaw muscles rippled. "Tell me. What did I do wrong?"

I gave a grim chuckle, while keeping my discomfort under lock and key. "Nothing. And as fun as listening to you recite my shortcomings is, I prefer to get some shuteye."

"You kissed *me*. And I wasn't criticizing you. We were just talking."

His dominance fizzled and extinguished, but the hurt expression on his face was going to haunt me. Despite my words, he had to know I didn't mean it. The way he played me like a banjo, how could he doubt his effect on me?

I inhaled long and deeply, fighting to keep my trembling body in check. "Just because I do things differently doesn't give you the right to question my status. The free packs do plenty of crap I don't agree with, and you don't hear me telling you how things should be done."

"You're right." He placed his hand on my back and steered me back to the sofa. "Come on. Sit."

He topped up our glasses and handed me mine.

I took a huge gulp, as if the alcohol could wipe out the last few minutes. Drama wasn't something I usually indulged in, but around Drake, a new normal applied.

"Okay then." I moved, and my left knee touched his. He felt solid. Real. "Let's keep things pleasant and talk about my mother."

"I don't have much on her yet."

Seriously? Once again with the *later* routine?

He startled backward. "Don't look at me like that."

At least my glare still packed a wallop, even if my insides were more candy floss than candy ass.

"I'm not stalling, but I need to be sure." He raised my hands to his lips and kissed my fingertips. "I don't want to give us half-baked answers. I know how important your family's roots are. I was lucky to have known my parents. I promise, I'm not toying with you."

I sagged in my seat, slightly askew so as to study his face. Nothing in it tipped me off to a lie.

"Okay." I stiffened. "Can I ask what happened to your parents? You don't have to tell me, of course."

"They died under Marlon's rule. They were part of the group that stood up to him."

"I'm sorry."

He shrugged with a cool casualness that had to be fake. "That's what it was like back then. I never found out who killed them. That's the toughest part."

Probably why Raven's disappearance ate at him. He'd felt responsible for their death, just as he felt he'd let Raven down.

I squeezed his hand. "How old were you?"

"Barely out of my teens. My brother used to be a lawyer in Denver, but he moved back to look after me, he said. Not that I needed it, but we were both happier to be around each other. Jonah vowed to avenge my parents." He scoffed. "Tough when you don't know who did it, but he had my back all the way."

"And now you have his."

"Yeah."

At least I still had my dad. As self-absorbed as he was in his down time, and as busy as he was looking after the pack, at least he'd been around with advice and guidance.

"What did you find out about the travelers?" I stared at the books so as not to get side-tracked by his eyes.

"First things first. When we talk travelers, let's make sure they weren't real travelers. They shared neither customs nor rituals with any particular Roma tribe that I know of."

"Just a pack of transients, then?"

"No, not that either. They came to our woods to settle. Yes, they preferred living in forests rather than houses, but they wanted to make this their new home. Marlon was the reason they didn't."

"Okay. I get it." I finally looked at him again. "But you did discover something new, right?"

"I've translated the sentence on the campsite obelisk." He gave a triumphant grin. "It means *A wolf would not become a sheepdog.*"

"Aha. Does that mean anything to you?"

"It's an Estonian proverb." He let out a huge sigh. "I get the feeling my discovery is not getting the credit it deserves."

"Sorry." I placed my hand on his arm. "I thought that since they went to the trouble of chiseling it into a rock, it might have a special meaning."

"I think it does. It sounded familiar, and I've been going through my books, but haven't found anything yet. No excuses, I know." He raised his hands in a defensive gesture. "It's not like I've been busy, you know."

"I guess you've had a lot on your mind." I toned down my smile. "How are you doing? I know you're close to Raven's family. This must be killing you."

"I haven't processed it yet, I think." Drake moved his arm past my body and propped himself up against the back of the sofa, positioning his face an inch from mine. "My brain doesn't seem to work properly when you're around."

"That must suck."

He moved a strand of my hair aside with his nose. "Not so much."

And then his mouth was on my lips. His kiss was tender at first, asking for permission. I gave it and fell into his unyielding certainty that this was what we were meant to do.

He quickly laid claim to my tongue, coaxing and nudging it into surrender.

His hands multiplied as he gathered my hair in one, gripped my waist with the other, cupped my neck with the third. Warmth surged into every limb, dizzying what was left of my will. I took my fill of him, or tried to, but his clothes were a poor substitute for what I knew lurked beneath.

Drake dragged me to my feet, kissing, caressing, and crowded me across the living room, through the hall, and into a bedroom. He closed the door with a swift kick.

Who would sneak up on us out here in the woods? Yet his need for privacy was a total turn-on. He didn't want to share me with anyone, and to hell with reason.

"You can still stop this." I twisted out of his grasp and led him by the hand toward the bed.

The room was caught in a time loop. A teenager's poster of a rebellious rocker vied for attention with a grown-up's shelf of history books. A wooden box stood on his nightstand, its subtle earthy scent revealed it had been hand-carved recently. A sign, maybe, that Drake was good with his hands?

"I know this isn't the most romantic of settings." He swiped a couple of shirts and a book off his bed.

"I strike you as the romantic type?" I pushed him onto the mattress and straddled him.

"Romance comes in many flavors, princess."

"Don't call me princess." I bent over and pushed a kiss onto his mouth. Hot. Fierce. Demanding.

Even though it was *my* kiss, the feel of his lips and the softness of his tongue obliterated my sass. For one brief moment in time and space, I gave myself to his touch.

But even this small concession irked. From somewhere, I gathered the strength to extricate myself. He was wily, all right, with his panty-melting eyes and his oh-so-agile tongue, but I wasn't going to submit to him that easily. Or at all.

I cocked my head and winked. "How did you like that flavor?"

"Delicious. Let me get another taste."

He pushed my buttoned up jacket over my head and used my trapped arms to ease me back toward to him. The peppermint freshness that typically clung to him faded under his male scent—light, yet alive with vigor and intensity.

Could he smell me, too? Smell that I was ready for him?

Even though his lips remained soft, he called the shots. He switched between taking and giving, between bastard and gentleman. I'd been kissed more times than I'd care to remember, but not like this. Never like this.

He stroked my back, teased my spine, and with a swift flick, unclasped my bra.

Too much skill was in that motion. Too much practice. How many women had benefited from his dexterity before me? How many would once I was gone?

He nudged me, and I sat up. His gaze held a predatory glint. My bare breasts had become his prey. Even though I craved his touch, I stayed back. Kept my chest still. Would he hold them like a teenager, uncertain of their purpose? Or attack them with a starving mouth, hurrying me toward my climax with eager flicks of his tongue?

He reached out, hesitated, and cupped my breasts like two prized trophies.

I flattened my breath. Waited. My wide-open heart beating down the seconds.

He let go and, with a spin, twisted me back-first onto the mattress. His weight trapped me underneath him.

"What was that?" I gave a laugh that soared across the room as light and free as a feather.

The mattress still rocked by the time he had his mouth locked around my nipple. His tongue went in for the kill—and it was the sweetest of deaths. My nipple puckered to attention, my limbs lay still. I was boneless, entirely at his mercy. All I could do was let the waves of bliss roll over me.

He slipped his hands down to unbutton and unzip me.

When he lifted his head, he shot me a glance that was pure wolf. Dangerous. Dominant.

I knew not to toy with him then. Not until he eased off.

He rolled down my pants, taking my panties with them. His gaze burned a path into my flesh from my thighs up to my eyes.

"You're beautiful," he whispered. His flushed face had lost the shuttered look he typically carried with him like a shield.

"And you're still dressed."

He chuckled deep in his throat. "Feel like doing something about that?"

"Not sure my feelings have much to do with this, but sure." I jostled out from under him.

To hell with the women from his past. They weren't here today. I was, and I would make sure he wouldn't think of them tonight.

I started with his T-shirt, got side tracked by the solid plate of his chest and the ink on his arms, dedicated a second's pause to his tight stomach, before I zeroed in on his jeans.

He leaned back onto the bed, hands curled around two tufts of bunched-up blanket.

His zipper opened willingly to reveal his boxers. He was ready for me, too.

I placed my lips on his bulge and grazed him with my teeth.

He twitched.

"Everything working as it should, I see." I got rid of his remaining clothes, socks and all, and glided my hand over his lower stomach, charting the subtle ridges that spoke of sit-ups and discipline.

He propped his torso up on his elbows. Not a smidgen of shame at his nakedness, and no reason for it as far as I could see either.

"You're looking pleased with yourself, princess."

"Checking out the present I've unwrapped."

"And?"

"It's what I've always wanted." I fawned with a coquettish tilt of my head. "How did you know?"

"Oh yeah?" The huskiness in his voice cast my words in a different light.

I hadn't meant to say "always." He was my *right now*, and *always* had no place in his bed tonight.

He flipped me onto my back, and his mouth stopped my protest. His next kiss was as ferocious as his touch was gentle. My breasts, my ribs and hips vibrated under his grazing caresses, and just as tenderly, he slipped his hand between my legs.

I was already wet.

He teased me, tiptoed around the hot spots with precision, and finally slid his fingers into me.

I gripped his shoulder against the intrusion, but opened my legs. This taster of what was to come filled my body with tingles and shivers that cascaded and overlaid and drove me all but completely insane. I kissed the salt off his shoulder, coated myself in his sweat, in his scent.

He removed his fingers and positioned himself between my legs.

"Hang on." I traced his winding tattoo up his arm and then pushed him away by his chest.

He supported himself on his hands. "You change your mind?"

"I go on top."

"Excuse me?" His eyes narrowed.

My skin tightened as the onset of his dominance rippled like soap bubbles down my arms and spine. Harmless, yet so damn sexy.

"I. Go. On. Top."

"Not tonight." His words sprang forth like a steel spear. "I made plans."

"You're adorable when you're wrong." I bucked my hip and dislodged him, but he was too heavy to shake.

His dominance exploded over me, burned into me, commanded my body to submit.

My arms slacked, my neck relaxed. How could he want me still when my flesh was screaming?

"Shh-shh." His power surged across me, fixing me to the spot.

I gasped for breath, a shallow attempt, and his dominance entered me. Every ounce of his power leaked into my skin and found its way into my blood, yet it didn't hurt. Didn't frighten me. Merely filled the empty hole inside.

I held his head above mine and stared at him with a new calm. "I go on top, or this isn't going to happen."

"Why does it even matter?"

Why? Because I wasn't ready to submit, no matter what my treacherous body demanded of me. I was equal to him in every respect.

And I was *not* like one of his usual conquests.

"It matters." I kept my tone even, not in spite of his dominance, but because of it.

His dominance so deep inside me had woken my alpha urges. A borrowed power, but a renewed glimpse of what I could be. Of what and who I was.

I softened my tone. "Your choice."

He inflated his cheeks and exhaled through tight lips. "Knock yourself out."

"Seriously?"

He'd been in charge. Why give in now?

He rolled onto his back, flaunting his lick-worthy abs and broad chest. "Hey, when a beautiful woman asks to ride you, you don't say no."

"Is that your life's motto?"

If he mentioned his previous lovers, I'd punch him.

"That's every man's life motto, princess. An instinct we're born with." He beckoned me with a finger. "Come on then. This time you're getting your wish."

On my knees, I stalked toward him and climbed on top. "What exactly did you mean by 'this time'?"

A smile spread across his lips, and he withdrew his dominance, all except for the small pool within me. "I'm saying I'm yours."

The tremble in his voice fanned my desire. He meant he was mine *now*. For the next hour or so. Not in general. Right?

I scouted his face, as he scouted mine.

Drake knew the score. One night of fun, a way to pass the time. That was all this was.

And I was going to make it count.

My teasing motion didn't satisfy either of us. I needed more. As he said, for tonight, he was mine, and I'd be damned if I let this opportunity pass.

"Move up toward the back of the bed." I sat up to let him slide out.

He obeyed with a glance that didn't completely relinquish control.

We'd see about that.

After he'd stuffed two more pillows behind his back and rested almost in a sitting position, he winked. "Go on then. Blow my…mind."

Cocky son of a bitch.

I lowered myself onto his proud shaft with deliberate slowness, soaked in every stretch, every bump against my lining.

"That's what I'm talking about." His lids flickered as his shoulders pressed into the pillows.

I smiled sweetly. Driven by the power in my thighs, I rose, inch by inch, careful not to lose him.

He reached for me, but relaxed the second I began my next descent.

He felt large inside me, bigger than on my first move down.

The pressure he exerted against my muscles was exquisite, so much so I gave a satisfied moan.

I wasn't typically vocal during sex, but something told me he didn't mind the feedback.

On my next dip, I changed the angle by a fraction—and struck gold.

Damn.

"Hell, yeah," Drake mumbled.

His rough tone trickled down like syrup, and I repeated the motion, eyes closed, once again hitting the right spot.

I squeezed my hands onto his moist abs, drove up, then down. Up. Down.

Drake's grunts chased my moans. His mass ground against my raw insides, laid bare my nerves. They fired in quick succession, feeding a newly found addiction that forced me to go faster. Harder.

Drake was a drug I didn't want to purge from my system. The high was too intense, too beautiful to abandon. Slave to the sensation, I rode him with painstaking precision, turning every stroke into a masterpiece.

He slipped his hand into my wetness, caught my clit with the tip of his finger. All I could do was claw at his skin as he massaged me gently.

His length crowded into my center, fulfilled and distended it until nothing else mattered.

Despite my best intentions, I was no longer in control. Neither was Drake. A fire had grasped us, and we were clinging to each other for mere survival.

"You've no idea how good you feel." Drake flicked and teased me with his fingers, pushing me to ever increasing heights.

If he knew who I was, or what I wasn't, would he change his mind?

He grabbed my butt, and I moved my hip forward, descending onto him with a deep moan.

"Don't stop." He groaned with his mouth clamped to my breast. "Fuck. Don't ever stop."

A ball of pressure built inside, a coil that tensed with each stroke. Oh God.

I gripped his shoulders, rode him with untamed lust.

"Fucking—" He breathed the word through his teeth without relinquishing my nipple.

"Trying to," I whispered.

He laughed, gripped me tighter, and urged me down his length once again.

I deepened my strokes, while my core pumped hot with blood. The deep burn grew, intensified until it obliterated my reasoned thoughts. God, I wanted him for myself. Right now. Tomorrow. And every damn day after that.

I tipped back his head, forced my mouth onto his. At the moment of orgasm, he'd exhale his release into me. I'd safeguard his confession. Make it a part of me.

My muscles seized, and—oh hell yes—my core trembled. A spark ignited my flesh, adding to the inferno raging in every cell of my body, and I came with a deep moan.

Drake pulled me onto him once, twice more. His drawn-out grunt was the first piece of reality that pierced my bubble of bliss.

Unable to hold myself up any longer, I leaned into his neck and calmed my pounding heart with his earthy scent and his warmth.

He slid one hand behind his head and laughed. "That was a hell of a ride, princess."

He had no idea.

I stroked his soaked chest, moved the short hairs sticking to his face to the side, and kissed him. Not with passion, but because I had no words I wanted him to hear.

He'd listened to me come undone, but he'd never know of the inner turmoil he'd caused. My possessive digs at his other women, the loss of control, the depth of the pleasure he gave me... He'd never find out.

On the surface, my carefully crafted image remained largely intact. I'd been in charge. I hadn't submitted.

At least…on the surface.

EIGHTEEN

A TATTOOED ROCKER GIVING ME THE finger fell into focus first. Next, the frame in which the picture was mounted, then the rest of the wall. I moved my gaze to the gentle up and down of Drake's chest beneath me.

What now? Did I simply get up and act as if nothing happened? Or was I expected to slip out of the house and do the walk of shame?

I was no prude, so the fact that we'd had sex wasn't a problem. But I also wasn't a dreamer and, despite my mid-coital delusions, wasn't harboring ideas of happily ever afters. Drake, on the other hand, was an unknown. The photos in his hall had all but convinced me that he'd appreciate the one-and-done.

If it weren't for the use of the phrase "this time."

"This time" he'd let me go on top. Did he think I'd be his bed bunny for the duration of my stay?

The feel of his skin under my fingers, the pressure that had spread my walls with such delicious pain… No, the act itself wouldn't leave my memory for a while. His horizontal skills, no doubt acquired over many, many sexual encounters, only strengthened my belief that he'd be pragmatic about this.

"Are you going to speak at some point?" He pushed a strand of my hair back that wasn't even in the way.

"What's the time?" I lifted my head and glanced at his alarm clock. "It's nine already. We should get up."

"What for? There's not much to do today. Or did you dream up new leads?"

"I've indulged your notions about a human killer, but it's time to dip my toes into your world." I sat and rubbed my eyes before ruffling volume back into my flat hair. "First, I want to speak to Raven's friend."

"Sable?" He ran his hand from my shoulder down my breast to my stomach, sabotaging my concentration. "She lives in Florida with her husband now."

"Do they not have phones?"

"Now that you mention it, I think they do." His smile melted my professional demeanor into a swoon.

Not again. I'd had my night of fun. Why didn't it feel enough?

"Mind if I take a shower?" I rolled to the side and picked up my clothes.

"'Wham bam, thank you Drake' is all I get?" He shook his head. "All that hard work for nothing."

"What work?" I raised my eyebrows. "You just laid there."

"That's how you wanted it. Besides, I told you, next time—"

"Yeah, about that." I slipped into my pants using the blanket for cover. "It was great and all, but I'm here to do a job. There's not going to be a next time. You know that, right?"

If I sounded harsh, it was more for my benefit, but his expression hardened anyway.

He scoffed. "Calm down. I didn't ask you for a Moon Promise, princess."

"I didn't mean it like that." I eyed his solid shape, the symmetry of his face, the intricate symbols running down his arms. "What do your tattoos mean?"

He lifted his head and stared at his left bicep, as if seeing it for the first time, then fell back into his pillow. "Nothing. I had a couple of scars from my misspent youth, so my brother said to ink it over. Made sense when I became a protector." His gaze drifted, and he smiled. "I was told scars are scary, but tatts are mysterious. Women dig that."

"A woman told you that, right?"

"Are you saying she lied?"

"Who can say if she lied or not? I'd have to get to know her first."

He laughed. "Fair comment."

He rolled onto his front and crawled toward me until his head was in my lap. "Come back to bed."

I ran my fingers through his hair, soft despite its regimented appearance, and then wiggled out from under him.

Reality in his head had to look totally different than mine. In my world, cozy lie-ins with a man were reserved for mated women. And even though Drake ticked all the right boxes for a mate, I never asked him to fill in the questionnaire.

"Maybe later." I pressed my remaining clothes against my breast and got out of bed. "I expect breakfast when I'm done."

"Oh yeah?" His laughter faded as I hurried into the hall.

The bathroom had neither key nor lock, yet Drake didn't sneak in to lather shower gel over my skin with his generous hands, or to make every inch of me feel both clean and dirty at the same time. He'd never know, but I wouldn't have told him to stop.

So much for willpower.

I finished up with a necessary cold rinse, then dried myself and got dressed.

Drake's bathroom cabinet contained hair mousse, a comb, deodorant, toothpaste, and a single electric toothbrush.

I padded into the bedroom, which was empty now, and then into the kitchen. My wet hair fell loosely over the shoulders of my buttoned-up jacket. "No spare toothbrush. You'd think someone like you would be prepared."

Drake stood by the stove, frying up something that smelled fantastic. He was freshly showered and gave off the same scent as me, a mix of minty sharpness and soft fruit. The cabin didn't look large enough to offer a second bathroom, but then I hadn't yet ventured up the stairs.

"What do you mean, someone like me?" He stabbed at something in the pan as if only now trying to kill it.

"You know. A guy who likes the ladies."

"Who says I like the ladies?"

I chuckled and sat in one of the chairs. "Last night only gave me a glimpse of Drakeland, but I'm sure boys aren't allowed in."

He turned, no humor in his expression. "What makes you think I sleep around?"

"Nothing definitive." I blew air into my warming face. "We've known each other a few days, and we've already had sex."

He pushed the frying pan off the heat and focused his attention on me, arms crossed. "And that means I do this all the time?"

I pushed my jaw out. "I don't know. I assumed."

"You assumed." The monotony in his voice carved deeper than a note of hurt could have.

"Sorry." I moved around the chair's hard surface. "Isn't a reputation as a ladies' man every guy's dream?"

"Maybe for the men you date." He wheeled around and resumed making breakfast. "For the record, this isn't the city or royal court. We don't just screw anyone."

"I said I'm sorry. What do you want from me? How could I know you aren't the Triangle's answer to Casanova?" I glared at his back and pointed to my right. "There are fewer species of insects than you know women, judging by the pictures in your hall."

"They're friends, that's all. We're a small, tightly knit community, remember?"

For a while, the crackle of what I hoped were bacon and eggs drowned out his heavy silence.

"Any plan beside calling Sable?" he eventually asked.

"Think there's a way we can get a hold of Raven's case file?"

"One of the cops is a wolf. I've already told him to pass along whatever he can, but I don't expect to hear from him until tomorrow."

"Right. In that case, just Sable for now."

"As an aside, I've already done that. She knows nothing. Or am I now incompetent as well as a sex pest?"

I straightened the tablecloth. "Listen, I'm sorry about what I said. I don't know you, and I certainly don't know about your girlfriends and stuff."

"Right." He transferred his weight onto his right leg.

Why was he making this so difficult? Apologies didn't come easy, yet here I was, admitting my mistake. Didn't that count?

"I don't sleep with just anyone either, so who knows why I assumed you did." A lump in my throat made my confession even harder. "Anyway, the reason I'm such an ass this morning is that Raven deserves better than a half-baked investigation. I don't want to let her down."

Drake lifted the frying pan off the stove and slid food onto two plates he'd already laid out on the counter.

He was being the domestic god now.

"I get it." He picked up the two plates and arranged one in front of me.

"Good. Because I'm easily distracted." I inhaled the divine smell of fry-up heaven. Then I placed my elbows on either side of my plate and planted my chin in my interlocked hands. "And I find you highly distracting."

He lifted his eyebrows, but his mouth twitched into a little smile. "I know."

Touché.

He filled our cups with coffee then joined me at the table.

"What we do at night doesn't have to interfere with our day activity. And until we get a lead, the investigation is going nowhere."

I slathered a piece of bacon in runny yolk. "Agreed."

"The downtime should help me confirm my hunch about the Estonian proverb. You can speak to Sable. And if we find ourselves with time to spare…"

I sneaked a grin through my chewing motions. "It would be foolish not to work on improving our working partnership."

He pointed his fork at me. "That's all I'm saying."

For a few minutes we ate in silence. My ideas of professional conduct did not include getting involved with witnesses or fellow detectives. But if bending the rules meant I got to enjoy the, um, pleasures of Drake's company for a while longer, why resist?

I shoved the empty plate aside and licked my lips clean. "That was a good breakfast."

"A compliment?" He shook his head with fake sadness. "I have broken you."

I snorted. "As if. But they're rare, so take it."

"Okay."

"Is it too early to call Sable now?" I glanced around for a clock, but couldn't find one. "Where's the number?"

He stood and retrieved a small booklet from deep inside his messy drawer.

I blew a laughter-snort combo. "You have Sable's name in a little black book? If we hadn't established you're sexually pure, I'd call you a walking cliché."

"Smart ass. If I was sexually pure, you surely changed that last night. And this is an address book that happens to be black."

"Ever heard of smartphones?" I flicked through the pages. "What's Sable's last name?"

"Spencer. You really think she'll tell you stuff she hasn't told me?"

"She was Raven's best friend. Are you telling me she didn't

know about her boyfriends and crushes?" I blew a raspberry. "You clearly never had a BFF."

"Fine. Talk to her. Maybe she does know more. When you're done, there's someone I'd like you to meet."

I put the book down while holding the correct page open. "Who?"

"An old lady who was around when your mother still lived here. The new pack didn't mingle with anyone, but maybe she has a few good stories." His gaze traveled to my mouth.

I wiped my face but didn't detect any crumbs or dried egg. "What if this woman didn't like the newcomers, and I have to sit there for an hour, listening to her diss my mother?"

"I wouldn't suggest it if that was a possibility."

"Okay then. Yes. That might be interesting."

I held my hand out for my phone, which lay all the way over on the counter.

He squinted and let his dominance swell and ebb a few times.

I sweetened the deal with a "Please?"

He got up and fetched me my phone.

I nodded my thanks. "I'll tell Jonah how helpful you've been in my investigation."

"You're pushing your luck." Yet he ever so casually kissed my cheek and then stacked our plates on top of the dishwasher.

After I'd found Sable's number, I waited for ten rings until the answering service activated, and then hung up.

"Not leaving a message?" Drake asked.

"This is a conversation I don't want to have with a machine."

He rested against the dishwasher and crossed his arms. "I'll pop over to my brother's in a sec. That's where I keep the rest of my books. I'll drop you off at Greta's on the way. She's a hoot. You'll like her."

I got up. "I'll take your word for it. But before I do, I'd like to change and brush my teeth."

"Anything else, *your highness*?" He shook his head and gave a loud sigh.

I wasn't half as high maintenance as he made me out to be. "Maybe later."

He left the kitchen and returned a minute later carrying a packet of replacement toothbrush heads.

"Nice." I fumbled with the packaging until I'd freed one, and darted to the bathroom.

Once my mouth was minty fresh, I stepped into the hall and nearly collided with Drake.

He pushed a T-shirt into my face. "Wear that. It's clean."

"One of yours?" I frowned.

"Hardly. You'd get lost. No, this is my brother's."

I unfolded the fabric. It was too large, but it was better than wearing my jacket-over-bra again. I slipped the T-shirt over my head and smoothed it down to way below my ass.

"How do I look?" I twirled.

"Adorable." Drake pointed at my chest. "Worthy of your royal status."

I glanced down at the *Queen* logo across my chest. "Quite." Then I lifted my head. "Why—"

Drake's mouth claimed mine just as his solid grip claimed my body. He held onto the back of my head, burying his hand deep inside my hair. His other hand explored my waist. Then hip. Then butt.

I gasped, and his air filled my lungs with his taste.

How had he convinced me this was what I wanted? Because I did, more than anything. I wanted him, every inch of him—on me, around me, inside me.

With my arms tight in his grip, he hustled me across the room where we fell against a wall. His frame pressed against me, forcing my legs wide, and he slid his free hand under my T-shirt.

Hell, yes.

He chuckled into my neck.

"What's so funny?" I tugged on his shirt, scouting beneath to feel his skin against mine.

His fingers circled a spot on my arm. "I can feel your goosebumps."

"Maybe I'm cold."

He stopped the exploration of my body and stared. "It's ninety fucking degrees outside."

Making out, or being right? Not the toughest of choices. I yanked him back against me by his tight ass and traced the grain of his jeans with my nails.

His movements got slower the closer I got to his inseam.

I chuckled. "Look who's come out to play."

His hand found purchase inside the top of my pants and disappeared inside my panties where his fingertips slid down toward my apex.

I sucked in air.

He kept his hand still, breathing hard, his cheeks flushed. "Too much?"

"Not nearly."

Not ever.

He inched his way down toward the heat that was building between my legs.

My shoulders stiffened with expectation, my heart jigged and stopped, as if unsure what came next. I undid my button and zipper and held on to his hips.

His fingers found their target, and after two, three languid strokes, he'd built up enough lubrication to scout deeper. Once again, I was on fire, a heat only the feel of him inside me could quell.

I raked my hands across his curved, firm torso and—

There. His heart thumped against my palm.

Why did this feel so wondrous? It was a natural physical response. Yet I'd made it happen. Me.

I unzipped him and shoved his jeans down to his knees, then hooked my leg around his hip.

He yanked it higher around his waist, when an unfamiliar ringtone played in the distance.

Drake took a deep breath. "Don't move."

He slipped out of me and wiped his fingers against my panties on the way up.

"Seriously?" I asked.

He chuckled, pulled up his jeans, and headed to the table to answer the phone.

I clung to the wall, catching air, afraid a step would see me dropping to the floor like a lump of lead.

Drake talked quietly on the phone and threw me a glance that twisted my sanity. He'd had me in the palm of his capable hands, at the tip of his nimble tongue, and even from a distance he made my body hum with yearning.

This was bad. Strike that. This was a disaster. Forgetting about Raven's case wasn't going to be the problem. My work ethos would see to that. No matter if it took two days or weeks, I'd unmask her murderer eventually.

I pushed myself off the wall and, despite the morning heat, hugged myself against a chill. For the first time, I understood the *real* danger of working by his side. Because once my time here was up, would I still want to leave?

Nineteen

Greta *was* a hoot. From the pink wallpaper to the floral print of the curtains, her house radiated eccentricity. Statues of naked women adorned the fireplace which itself housed not a pile of wood, but a bookshelf.

Drake had dropped me off at around noon and left me with a kiss that made me walk up Greta's drive more prepared for another romp around the bedroom than a chat about my mother.

Despite her round shape, Greta wasn't lethargic or slow. When she wasn't offering me tea or cookies, she pulled photo albums from the shelf or rifled through a box of memorabilia.

She glanced up from a crate. "Your mother was a sweetheart, dear."

The diffused sunlight that came in through the narrow, yet high windows highlighted the white in her otherwise dark-gray hair.

"So you did know her?"

She got up, and her knees cracked. "Yes. She was a wisp of a thing. Shorter than you, but as thin. What is it with women nowadays? Are you not fed properly?"

I patted my stomach, which didn't bulge, but wasn't exactly framed by protruding bones either. "I eat plenty."

She returned to the sofa, and her lavender perfume spread around me.

"Let me see." She leaved through a stack of black and white photographs, then pulled one out. "Here it is."

The yellowed picture showed my mother in a gray or white dress. Her long hair fell over one shoulder, her mouth curved into a kittenish smile. Over the years, my memory of her face had wandered more and more out of focus. Now, she was always out of reach, too far away to hug, or to ask questions, like, "why did you leave me" or "why the hell can't I shift like a normal werewolf"?

"I can't remember her that clearly, but this picture brings it all back." I gently stroked the photo's smooth surface. "Dad has her pictures on his nightstand, in the living room, even in the throne room."

"She was cherished by her people, too." Greta's voice fluttered. "It's important to be loved. It gives your life purpose."

Or heartache.

I hid my doubts in my matter-of-fact tone. "My mother's father was their leader?"

"He spoke for them and made decisions that concerned his family, but community problems were solved by the elders of all the families together." She giggled. "I sometimes snuck up to their camp to visit her cousin."

"Why were the travelers so bent out of shape when my mother hooked up with my dad?"

"I'm afraid I can't help you with that." She fluffed a throw pillow, while her gaze drifted to the wall behind me.

She yanked her focus back to me. "But I can tell you her life left a mark on our community that can be seen to this day."

I sat straight. "Marlon? I was told he singled her out. Had she done something that upset him?"

"It wasn't like that." She leaned forward and placed her bony hand on my arm. "When the new pack appeared, Marlon wooed your mother relentlessly, but she didn't want anything to do with him. Neither did her father, and he fiercely rejected Marlon's advances. Even laughed at him for suggesting such a mating."

"How did Marlon take the refusal?"

"Not well." Her grip on my arm intensified. "He was humiliated, and his hatred of the travelers ultimately led him to commit unspeakable acts in the name of racial purity."

"Quite the legacy for my mother," I mumbled and stared once again at her young, happy face. "But if he ultimately made his attacks about race, how did he explain making a move on my mother in the first place?"

"He claimed he never intended to go through with his *charade*. That he'd always intended to dangle a Moon Promise in front of her nose, only to drop her before the mating."

I averted my gaze. Whether Marlon had put on an act to save face or not, it took a cruel mind to devise a plan like that.

"So, um." I cleared my throat. "Did Marlon have proof that the travelers were racially impure?"

"Oh, I don't think he really thought that. They kept to themselves, so who knows how many of them were werewolves or how strong their genes were. To him, truth was flexible."

They had certainly liked their privacy. Without Drake's knowledge of the woods, I'd have gotten lost searching for the camp. And even if I had tracked down their communal clearing by chance, finding their tents and caravans and huts would have been ten times harder.

"Did the travelers refute Marlon's claims that they were racially impure?" I locked my teeth together. "Did they have evidence they weren't?"

"I doubt they worried about what others thought. They didn't involve themselves in our world. Marlon started a campaign against them, and when they didn't defend themselves, Marlon's own pack did." She interlaced her hands.

The travelers pack may not have cared about Marlon's accusations, but I couldn't say the same about me. How human was I? If my mother was fifty-fifty, I calculated my chances of finding my wolf one day at 75%. Any less, and my dreams of succeeding my dad to the crown were close to zero. Not without an alpha male by my side.

Greta pushed the delicate china cup toward me. "You look pale, dear. Drink something."

I did, with the enthusiasm of an automaton.

The stuffy atmosphere of Greta's home served as a reminder that I hadn't gotten much sleep the night before. Not that I regretted a single minute of my time with Drake. In fact, considering the mood I was in now, I'd gladly snuggle back up in his arms to block out reality.

"Have a cookie." Greta smiled. "And listen. This is ancient history. No travelers were killed."

"But things didn't go back to normal for *your* pack, did they?"

"Not quite. As I said, a rift opened in our community, one that took a while to close again."

"Now the travelers are gone." I took a shaky breath.

Only Liza remained. She could tell me what I needed to know. If I confided in her, would she keep my secret? If she already knew, did she have a cure?

"We were too focused on our differences to pay attention to them. Neighbors warred with neighbors. School friends attacked each other. It was absolute chaos. Not even a state visit from the future German king, your father, brought a halt to the violence. He stuck around for a while, though. God knows what he must have thought of our petty hatred." Greta shook her head. "How he met your mother, I don't know."

Maybe he'd needed a break and sought refuge in the woods. It's what I would have done. And there, between the trees, a slim brunette challenged and ensorcelled him, and he, her. They'd have met at twilight, walked hand in hand until, in the end, and he slipped quietly away with her.

An Oscar-worthy story it may be, but the romance angle was too on-the-nose for me. Dad on the other hand was a sucker for cheese and soppy love stories, so that's probably exactly what happened.

And like every tragic love story, her father forbade her from marrying an outsider. Was it possible my grandfather's refusal had nothing to do with my mother's choice, and everything with exercising his power over her?

I blew a strand of hair out of my face. "Do you know why my mother's father, my grandfather, objected to Marlon's advances?"

"We wondered about that, my Bertie and I." She glanced at a photo on the wall behind me.

A younger version of her had her head tilted onto the shoulder of a handsome man with a stiff posture. Maybe he'd been a military man. Werewolf age was difficult to guess, but he could have even served with the last American king.

"Bertie thought it was a racism of a different type. The travelers wanted her to mate with a wolf of their own line. Someone who spoke their language and understood their ways."

"Is that what *you* think?"

"I didn't like your grandfather, but he sensed that Marlon was a bad lot." She gave a determined nod. "That's what I think."

The doorbell rang. Once again, Greta moved with the speed of an arrow.

"Hi Greta." Drake's voice liquefied my insides. "I'm here to pick up the princess."

"What a shame." Greta led him in by her hand. "Sure I can't get you any tea or cookies?"

He entered the room and threw me a glance that transported me back into the bedroom.

"I'm good, Greta." He dazzled her with a smile and proved no woman was immune to his charm. "We must go."

Face flushed, I got to my feet. Did he have news about the proverb already? Or had the case file finally come in? Or was it as tough for him as it was for me to spend any more time not being together?

"I appreciate you speaking with me, Greta." I lightly touched her arm.

"My pleasure, dear. Hang on." She darted to the low coffee table and picked up a picture. "Maybe you'll want to keep this?"

It was the photo of my mother. "Are you sure?"

"Yes, I want you to have it." Her glance once again sought comfort from Bertie's photo. "We all have memories we treasure."

She patted my hand, yanked me into a tight lavender-soaked embrace, and then let me and Drake head out into the sunshine.

We headed to the truck and got in.

"Did you know my grandfather wasn't the alpha of the traveling pack? He was only a spokesperson. It was exactly like you said. Each family lived their own life, each with their own alpha. Like real wolves."

Drake turned to me. "What do you mean, like real wolves?"

"You know, like real wolves in the wild. They live in families and only get together to hunt and stuff. You knew that having one leader for a large number of people is a human concept, right?"

"No. I didn't. But that makes sense. It all fits together."

"In what way?"

He turned the key and drove off. "Patience, princess. My research is coming along, but history can't be rushed."

"Tease." I settled into a comfortable position and closed my eyes against the perfectly aimed flow of air. "Any news from your cop friend?"

"No. We're a small community. I'm not even sure we have our own lab. This isn't the city."

"No, it's not." I smiled a private smile.

Everything was different here. The pace, the people, the burgers. And dammit, if I wasn't getting used to it.

"Good, honest living." Drake set his jaw. "You can go hiking, kayaking, fishing, mountain biking, climbing, horseback riding. Let's not mention you can run free whenever you want. You don't have those luxuries in Chicago."

"I'm sold. You forget I come from a small place myself. Chicago is great, but I do miss the woods."

"So why do you live there?"

He steered away from the smooth town roads onto a stretch of crumbly asphalt. His gaze was locked on the road before him, but every so often, he directed it at me.

What did he see? The spoiled brat he met a few days ago, or his lover?

I rolled my head away from him. "I have to live somewhere. Being a cop wasn't my thing. I'm not good at taking orders."

"No kidding."

"But I do like mysteries and solving crime. I took a course and hooked up with a P.I. in Chicago, and two years ago, I set up for myself."

"You could have moved to a smaller place."

"You have much work for P.I.s around your parts?"

He turned onto the unpaved trail that led to his house in the woods. "Vegetable theft, vandalism, the occasional break-ins. But if that's too tame for you, I could rob the bank or start a protection racket with the human shops."

"Shoot. Now you've told me who committed, um, will commit, the robbery and the protection racket. Not much of a mystery left." The pickup jetted across a dip in the road, and I slammed my hand against the door for support.

He maneuvered around another hole and pulled up in front of his house. "You'd have to arrest me."

"I couldn't turn *you* in." I fluttered my lashes.

He placed his left arm on the steering wheel and leaned over. "How do you feel about handcuffs?"

"I feel very positive about them, but I must warn you."

"Yeah?" He casually brushed a finger across my collar bone.

"I might not let you take them off." My voice was hoarse, the words barely a whisper.

He kissed me, long and hard.

Somehow we made it into the house. Somehow we found the bedroom. The rest became a blur. Hands begot moans that turned into screams, and each time I rode him harder than the time before, and each time I came more spectacularly than the time before.

We finally came up for air at five in the afternoon, when our phones rang and vibrated in alternation.

Drake gave in first. "Hello."

I lay sprawled across his body, wet, breathing hard, and satisfied to my core. The bed's blanket was nowhere in sight. Maybe it had dropped to the floor on his side, maybe on mine, or maybe it cowered under the bed, sticky with our fluids and in fear of the ferocity with which Drake and I had fed off each other.

"Nothing." Drake tiptoed the fingers of his free hand down my spine toward my ass.

Who cared about blankets? The last vestiges of insecurity had left me hours ago, after we'd included a few acrobatic moves into our routine I wouldn't have attempted with another lover, but with Drake... I don't know. It was fun.

More amazingly, I came every time. The first one should have been a fluke, like beginner's luck, but nope, Drake knew what got me going and what he didn't know, he took the time to learn. He'd mapped out my hot spots in his brain and wasn't too shy to exploit them.

I now paid for every orgasm with muscles that had turned to custard. Christ. Anyone who still had the strength to hold a cigarette after sex had never had sex with Drake. Of that I was damn sure.

"Okay." Drake lifted his head to kiss my hair. "I'll speak to you tomorrow."

And every time, he'd let me be on top without making a fuss.

He finished the call and put the cell back on his nightstand. "That was my brother."

"Does he need you?"

"Just checking in."

"That's nice. So, what's next for us?"

"Hell, princess. Give me a minute."

I slapped his chest and laughed. "I was referring to the case. What's our next step? It feels weird to lay around with nothing to do."

"Sable will be in town tomorrow. Until then, we have to find other ways of keeping busy."

Once I'd finally left a message for Raven's friend, she'd called me back while I'd been wrapped around Drake's body. Luckily, she'd spoken onto my messaging service.

"Aw, look at you." I patted his face. "Every day you think more like a real detective."

"Yeah? Could I cut it in big bad Chicago?"

I lifted my head so he could see me roll my eyes.

"A yokel like you?" I waved him off and returned my head to its spot on his chest, right over his heart. "You don't want to live there. It's loud and dirty, and full of humans."

His fingers stopped their march across my skin.

"What's wrong?" I asked.

He rolled me onto my back and lay on his side, head propped up on his elbow. "What is this to you? Us. What does this mean to you?"

More than you'll ever know.

I softened my voice. "I enjoy being with you. You make me laugh."

He exhaled sharply. "That's it?"

"What do you want to hear?"

"The truth. For once, will you drop your defenses and let me in?"

How could I bare my soul when doing so would see him running for the hills? "I'm not lying. I admit, some things are difficult for me to talk about, and there are things I can't tell you at all, but I'm not lying. I like you. A lot."

He opened his mouth, maybe to speak, maybe to snap for air, but I squeezed his lips shut before he'd uttered a sound. "Let's not ruin this."

He swiped away my hand. "I want more. This isn't a fling for me. I want you."

I sat. "That's a pretty thought, but it's not practical. My business is in Chicago, and you belong with Jonah."

"If I have to, I'll follow you to Chicago, even all the way to Germany."

I twisted away from him and pulled my knees to my chest. "I'm destined to rule a pack that can't stand me. The backstabbing and machinations at court never cease. Why would I want to wish that kind of future on anyone, most of all you?"

"I didn't know you felt so…lost about your future." He traced my spine with his fingers. "Here I thought you had it all figured out."

"That's what I want you to think." I chuckled grimly.

"I'll be by your side."

"*You* want to be king?"

Drake had the power to rule a royal pack, no doubt, but did he have the stomach for it? Until now, he'd chosen the easy lane by allowing Jonah to bear the burden of leadership.

"I don't *want* to be king." He splayed his palm against my back. "But if that's what I have to do to be with you, it's a small price to pay."

Was he serious? Were we really talking about this? While I'd been pushing away thoughts of a future without him, he'd been working on ways we could be together.

But then there was this insurmountable obstacle, the reason this would never work. I wasn't a real werewolf, not like he deserved. Maybe one day that would change, maybe it wouldn't, but I couldn't string along a guy like him on a *maybe*.

My skin went cold, and not because of the AC. I lay back down and found my spot on his chest as easily as I'd find the off key on my remote control.

He wrapped his arms tightly around me and kissed my head. "What are you thinking?"

"Way too much to answer that question."

"Don't you want to be with me?"

"Want? Yes. Should I? There's much you don't know about me, or me about you. How do I know that once we're mated, you won't go all alpha on me and start pushing me around?"

"You think I'd do that?"

"Not a bit. But my point is, I don't know."

He dropped his arms onto the mattress, taking his warmth from me. "Is that why you've been holding back? Because you don't trust me?"

I lifted my head. "When have I not trusted you?"

"You've never run with me. I don't just ask anyone, you know, but every time, you find an excuse."

"I don't like running, so what?"

"You don't like running, you don't use your dominance. It's like you try so hard to be human." He pushed me aside and sat up. "Is that why you don't want to be with me? Because I'm not human?"

"What?" I shook my head. "That's idiotic."

"Then why?"

Was I ready to tell him the truth? The future of my kingdom rested on my secret. If word got out that I was a dud, challengers from far and wide would petition my dad and the Council to set aside my claim.

Drake might handle the secret. Maybe he didn't even mind that I was a poor excuse for an alpha-to-be. But his loyalty was to Jonah, and this wasn't something he could keep from his alpha.

And then Jonah would have my dad by the balls.

I liked Jonah, I really did. And as for Drake, it was too late to deny my feelings for him. But my dad was all I had. As sparse as he was in terms of affection, he believed in me, trusted me, and in his own way, he loved me.

"This is pointless." I scooted to the edge of the bed and picked up my clothes. "I need to get home."

"Away from me, you mean."

"Yes." I stuffed my head through the T-shirt's neck hole and buttoned up my jeans. Whatever Drake's expression, I didn't want to see it.

"I'm not taking you home. We need to talk about this."

Drake's phone rang.

"Kensi, don't over analyze—"

"Answer the damn phone." I shot to my feet and left the room to find my boots.

I returned a minute later to a thunder-faced reception. Even with his cell glued to his ears, he'd somehow put his clothes on.

"You can't be serious." Drake stared daggers at me. "No, I get it. Thanks, buddy. I owe you."

He hung up.

"Was that you cop friend?" I pointed with my chin at the phone.

"What?" He glanced up. "No. That was Jonah. The cops found Raven's body."

A bitter taste crossed my tongue, and I grimaced. "What happened? How?"

"Buck told them." Drake took two steps to the side, glanced

around, then took a deep breath. "He texted Jonah, apologized. He said he felt Raven deserved a funeral."

I frowned. "How did he even know we'd found her? He didn't turn up to the search, did he?"

Drake stared at me for a second. "Shit. Did he kill her?"

My heartbeat picked up. Had we solved it? Had Raven's killer finally made a mistake?

Drake pressed my phone into my hand and twirled me around. "Let's go."

"To question Buck?"

"He's dropped off the face of the Earth." Drake looked at me. "I'll find him, either way."

"Not without me."

He held my head between his hands. "If Buck's gone into hiding, I'll find him. I used to hunt drifters, remember? You have things to do here. Talk to Sable. Find out everything you can about Buck's movements. Leo will help, if you need him."

Damn, his plan made sense. Drake knew the area and had experience finding people who didn't want to be found.

I slowly nodded. "Fine."

"Good." He angled my head so as to trap my gaze. "Just don't get too comfortable around Leo. You and I aren't done by a long way."

Twenty

THE OUTSIDE TEMPERATURE HAD DROPPED, at least in part due to the wall of trees flanking Drake's home. A more peaceful surrounding was hard to imagine, yet its tranquility had been disturbed by our fight.

Drake fumbled with his steering wheel, put the truck in gear and guided the pickup along the path. Despite his words, our fling was over. It's what I wanted, what I needed to happen, yet nothing had prepared me for the dull ache inside.

We skipped and rolled over bumps and holes in the dirt road, until ten minutes later, Drake pulled up outside my home.

He turned off the truck and sat silently.

"Keep me informed, will you?" I mellowed my tone to make it sound less like an order.

"You too." Then he leaned over, face up, and kissed me.

I was in no position to deny him. His pull on me was too damn strong.

He held my face tenderly, stroking my nerve endings which fired in my brain, my spine, and deep in my core. I wiggled to diffuse the building tension inside while his large hands, not nearly as rough as one would have guessed, caressed my waist under the T-shirt.

"Wow," I whispered.

He chuckled. "Yeah?"

I slowly pushed back from him. At this point, we were only torturing ourselves.

"Try not to get into trouble." He raked some of my hair behind my ear and kissed my neck.

"I haven't so far."

"Because I've been by your side."

I got out the truck and laughed. "You keep telling yourself that."

He honked and drove off, while I watched his pickup turn into another road. The cloudless sky was a blue too artificial to be real, as if someone had scrambled to finish a painting with whatever materials they had at hand. Despite the heat, I clutched my jacket tightly against my chest, then marched up the path and opened the door.

Inside, nothing ticked or rustled. Not even the AC made its presence known, even though its flow of cooling air gave me shivers. I picked up a yoghurt and entered the living-room, where Raven's case file mocked me from the table.

The sharp lines of the furniture lacked the lived-in comfort of Drake's place, but without much persuasion from me, my legs carried me to the angular chair that stood in the corner, the forgotten orphan of the living room.

I sat. Leaned forward, arms pressed against my stomach. Had I made a mistake? I'd advised Jonah to keep Raven's death a secret. No one even suspected we'd found her before the cops did, but that only made me look incompetent. Of course I could argue that my advances had forced the discovery, but nothing about the case had been clean. Jonah's gratitude, which I'd built my future on, might no longer materialize. How could he possibly support me now? Either he admitted he'd denied Raven a timely funeral, or he'd hired an incompetent investigator.

All that paled, however, in light of the real issue. One of their own, one of Jonah's trusted people, had done the unthinkable.

Had I done my due diligence on Buck? His troubles with young women were well documented, but I didn't even mention them to Drake. Never pushed him on the truth about his pack member. Too focused had I been on Drake's eyes, his mouth, his everything, to follow the breadcrumbs. Now Buck was in the wind.

Maybe I could salvage this. If I did as Drake had asked, tracked Buck's movements, I'd find the proof Jonah needed. He'd be redeemed in his pack's eyes, and maybe I'd redeem myself in the process.

Although my motivation for finding the truth was personal, my staff, both permanent and contracted, required money to get their butts in gear, and I dipped deep into my own pocket to get the best out of them. While I dissected Buck's friendships and pestered Andy and the other POOF members for more information, my hackers hacked, my police contacts dug, and my assistant followed leads at her end. Soon, a disappointing picture formed.

No one had heard from or seen Buck since he'd sent the message to Jonah. No credit card transactions, video footage or witness statements nudged my investigation forward. He'd been at POOF HQ when he got Jonah's message to help with the search. After that—not to be glib—*poof*. He'd disappeared. Jonah assured me the entire community had been asked to keep an eye out for Buck's truck. Again, the results were a disappointing squat.

By morning, nothing had changed, except I'd discovered that waking up without Drake by my side sucked big time. But we both had our roles to play. Mine was going to involve a face-to-face with

Sable. If she knew Raven as well as I hoped, she could provide insight into Buck's motives.

Because I had no idea why he'd killed Raven, or why he'd tell the police where to find her, or even why he'd confess to tipping off the cops. Buck hadn't struck me as stupid. Had overwhelming guilt driven him to come clean? In that case, Raven's death might have been an accident to begin with.

Despite the sad news, Sable agreed to keep our appointment. She was keen to help in any way, she assured me, so around noon, with my USB recorder fully charged, I entered the BBQ joint where I'd previously met up with Natalie.

Once again, the summer heat failed to spoil anyone's appetites, and lots of hungry mouths had turned up to be fed.

Sable wasn't what I expected. Instead of meeting Leo's Lolita, I found myself shaking the hand of a sophisticated woman with the confidence that came from having achieved a certain modicum of success. Her suit was tailored for the season, with a light fabric that flattered her figure. Her makeup complemented her subtle chic.

I dabbed at my face, which felt moist despite my grease-proof foundation. Since I didn't have a mother or a slew of girlfriends to guide me, growing up surrounded by men had left me trailing in many respects. Making the best of my looks was only one example.

"How are you holding up?" I asked once the server had taken our order. "I'm sorry I couldn't bring Raven back alive."

Sable considered me through clear, blue eyes. "From what I hear, she died months ago. There's nothing you could have done."

She was consoling me. Yeah, Sable was a class act.

"But it's hard," she said. "We'd always meet up when I visited. To think I'll never see her again, yeah, that stings."

"I can imagine." I waited a second to let a mother calm her noisy child. "What can you tell me about Cody, Raven's boyfriend?"

"Nothing." Sable leaned back and lifted her hands off the table while her food was placed in front of her. "Raven and I were close once, but after school, we lost each other a little bit. I got to pursue my dreams, whereas she…"

"She wasn't allowed to." I picked up my greasy double-bacon burger and bit off a huge chunk.

My usually disciplined diet had taken a severe knock since I arrived. In the absence of regular meals, my diet had largely consisted of cookies, fast food and caffeine.

Sable removed the top bun from her burger and picked at the remains with a fork. "You've met her parents then?"

"Yeah. Good people but strict."

"Exactly. All of Raven's dreams ended the day her father told her she was going to work in the bakery with him." She put down her fork and gave me a wide-eyed look. "I gotta wonder, would she still be alive if she'd attended music school?"

"How do you feel about Raven dating a human?"

"Cody?" She shrugged. "I'm surprised. From what I remember, he wasn't her type. To be honest, I thought she was only into werewolves."

"What was her type?" I raised my voice to make myself heard over a discussion in the booth behind us.

Sable cocked her head for a second and licked her ruby lips. "Earthen. Basic. Cody had always been a poser, but maybe he'd changed."

I frowned. "Do you know if Raven and Buck ever hit it off?"

She dropped her fork and covered her mouth with her hand. "You're kidding. Right?"

I lifted my eyebrows. "Not a bit. I'm wondering if she could have been seeing anyone else."

"On the side? Definitely not Buck. Don't get me wrong. He's helpful, but you always get the feeling he's looking at your breasts from behind those sunglasses. You know?"

She hadn't dismissed the idea of Raven two-timing Cody.

As I suspected, Sable knew a different side to Raven. "You don't like him?"

"I don't know. Jonah relies on him, so you don't want to speak out of turn, but between us, no." She lightly touched her napkin to the corner of her mouth. "Creepy Crawley Bug, is what Raven called him. When her brother was still alive, Buck was always hanging around our group. Hanging out, but never belonging."

Somehow, that made me sad for Buck. Trying so hard to find friends, only for two clueless teenage girls to ridicule him.

Then again, he probably killed Raven, so I wasn't going to waste a lot of time feeling sorry for the man.

"If Buck wasn't Raven's type, who might have been?" I nudged the plate away and patted my bulging stomach.

"As I said, she liked reliable guys. Solid." Sable used her napkin to collect the crumbs from the table. "Someone who wouldn't hurt her. Mister Perfect, if you believe in such a thing."

"Does anyone?" I coughed the second I said it, because what used to be true now sounded hollow.

"Don't tell anyone, but when we were younger, we crushed on Drake and Leo." Sable laughed, her head tilted back. "We spent hours devising plans to ensnare them into our happy endings. Who can blame us? Protectors are strong and hulky, and of course influential. Who wouldn't get with that?"

There she was, the flirtatious Sable Leo had talked about. She owned every syllable of her words, without a hint of helpless woman I so often saw in my own kind.

I grinned. "I hear ya."

"I crushed on Leo big time." She raised her right hand to show off a sparkly ring. "But I married a protector of another pack. Major, he's called. It was love at first sight. We nearly took the Moon Promise, mainly because his parents advised us that we should, but in the end we opted for a modern wedding. We wanted to celebrate with friends and family, not sneak off into the woods by ourselves."

"Good for you." I eyed her ring. Expensive cars I understood. Also a nice pair of boots or a condo with a killer view, but jewelry had never been my thing. "So, um, you were into Leo, but not Drake?"

I balled my hand around a grease-covered napkin. If she gave the wrong answer, how could I still look Drake in the eyes? As long as I remained in the Triangle, he was supposed to be *my* fling.

"You find it's usually an either or with Leo and Drake." She patted her chest. "I was camp Leo."

The breath I'd been holding broke free, and a smile returned to my face.

"Oh, I must go. Sorry." She snapped her fingers for the check. "By the way, Raven was into Drake."

My heart stopped for a moment. "She was?"

"Yes." She looked at me with knowing eyes. "But if you're thinking he was her mystery man, no way."

She shook her head with determination, and each motion dialed back my panic level. Raven and I had had a lot in common, and a similar taste in men shouldn't have been a surprise.

"Okay," I said. "Good to know."

Sable held out her credit card to the server, then leaned toward me. "Raven wasn't stupid. She and Drake were completely mismatched. That became crystal clear when they dated. Total car crash."

The rattle of the diner and the punters' voices closed around me into a ball of noise. Drake and Raven. Could Sable be right? But he would have told me. Someone would have mentioned it. Her parents. Or Jonah. Leo would have said something for sure.

While I went through the motions of thanking Sable, I felt the tremble in my hand, heard the jitter in my voice, yet was unable to get a grip. Despite my years of talking to people with secrets, this one had slipped through undetected. Why not tell me, though? To get me into bed?

Outside the diner, I found a bench and sat, because my legs

refused to operate. The town blurred before my eyes. For Drake's sake I wished that sex was his only reason for pulling the wool over my eyes. Because if it wasn't, if he had a different motive, I might have just uncovered another suspect in Raven's killing.

TWENTY-ONE

"JONAH'S ASKING TO SEE YOU," Leo said over the phone. "Where are you?"

I blinked to clear my vision, letting the parked vehicles and hedges form a picture. "Joe's BBQ."

"I know the place. Be right there."

For a while I continued to stare at my cell phone. If Jonah wanted to speak to me, something was up. Had Drake found Buck? If so, my job here may be done. Right now, I'd be okay with that outcome. I'd been looking for a way to disconnect from Drake, and Sable had delivered it.

He'd withheld vital information from me. If Buck hadn't messaged Jonah and confessed to talking to the cops, Drake would be my prime suspect. But Buck had known where the body was buried. What's more, Drake wasn't the murdering type. He certainly wouldn't harm his best friend's sister.

Leo rolled into the parking lot ten minutes later. I climbed into the sedan and gave him a sad smile. The energy for more enthusiasm simply wasn't in me right now.

"What's so urgent?" I pressed deep into the seat. "Everything okay?"

"Jonah is going to tell you himself, but everything isn't okay." His voice sounded strangled.

In my self-absorption, I hadn't even noticed his hunched shoulders and tense jaw. A fine investigator I made.

"You can tell me." I lifted my smile a little.

He exhaled sharply. "Jonah's world is falling apart, so please, let me be the one person he can still rely on."

"I assume Drake hasn't been much help with this whole Buck situation. Have you heard from him?"

Because I hadn't.

"You could say that again." He gave a bitter laugh, quickly wiped away by a somber expression. "And no, he hasn't been in touch."

I stared at the pretty buildings that made up the Triangle. Hadn't I predicted eerie secrets lurked behind that perfect appearance?

"I talked to Sable today." I fumbled with the map holder inside the door. "She told me that Drake and Raven once dated. Did you know that?"

Even with my gaze averted I felt his sideways glance.

"No. Wow." He shook his head. "When?"

"A while ago. Still, you would have thought he'd mention it."

"Probably thought Jonah wouldn't let him near the investigation." His tone dipped. "Sounds about right."

The last few minutes of the drive remained silent, made less awkward only by the pensive song of a singer whose name I couldn't recall.

Once Leo had parked next to the empty spot where Drake usually kept his pickup, we went inside. Jonah's voice traveled the distance to the entrance—and he was pissed. I didn't blame him. The mess he was trying to clean up was partly mine. I was the one who'd insisted on keeping Raven's death a secret. I was the one who'd failed to suspect Buck despite his record.

"You'd better wait here." Leo raised a warning hand, reflected in the hall mirrors like a bad omen, and stepped away.

"Hang on." I pulled him back by the hem of his T-shirt. "Is Liza here? I need to speak with her."

If Jonah was about to kick me out of his town, this might be my last chance to gather first-hand memories about my mother.

"Who?" Leo frowned. "No, Liza's no longer employed here. Handed in her notice and left just when Jonah needs all the support he can get."

Leo hurried into Jonah's office while his alpha was still mid-rant.

I fell against an empty spot of wall and bumped my head against the hard surface. Why had Liza left? What kind of guide deserted her charge before passing on any information? Without her, my so-called personal journey was over, at least as far as this town was concerned. I could check out the rituals Liza had pushed so hard in Wildbach, where the Royal Library held more werewolf-centric books than Natalie's.

Leo appeared and beckoned me with his hand. Jonah was no longer shouting, which I took as a good sign, yet I steeled myself for a formidable display of dominance.

"Have a seat," Jonah demanded.

I slowly approached the table, crammed with paper, coffee or tea mugs, and a cell phone. "If this is about—"

"Sit down." His haggard face hung pale over pulsating jaw bones as he stood in front of me.

Being the alpha was a blast when things were going well, but right now, I didn't envy him his position.

"Early today, the police found Buck's body." Jonah supported his arms on the table and fixed his gaze on me. "Have you heard from Drake?"

"What?" A rush of noise pumped inside my ears. "No. Why?"

"Drake is close to Raven's family. If he's on a revenge trip..." He pushed himself up and paced along the length of the table and back again. "I'm supposed to be the alpha and I've lost control. One of mine is killed right under my nose by someone I considered loyal, and now one of my protectors has gone rogue."

"Maybe it was an accident, and Drake didn't mean to do it." I straightened, even though my body wanted to shrink and disappear into a hole. "Or more likely, it wasn't Drake at all."

"Then where the fuck is he?"

If only I knew. I missed his solid presence. If he were here now, he'd bring order to chaos, calm Jonah the hell down, and start tackling the issues.

Worse, wherever he was hunting, he was alone. Either he was still tracking Buck, or he had Buck's killer in his sights. Suspects were plentiful.

Raven's father could have taken revenge. Despite being significantly older than Buck, Pike would have years of experience, his natural werewolf power and the might of his wrath. A lethal combination.

Cody, too, would have been motivated to take Buck out, although a human pitched against a werewolf would have resulted in a different outcome.

Not that Jonah seemed in the right frame of mind to listen to reason, at least not until he settled down.

"If Drake really did kill Buck, didn't he have good reason?" I tried to overshadow my pleading tone with a confident posture. "I'm not saying he should have undermined your authority, but a slip like that is understandable, right?"

Drake didn't slip up, and that alone was proof enough he hadn't taken out Buck.

Leo's face was shuttered, making it clear I should expect no help from him. No matter what happened, he'd take Jonah's side, even if it meant throwing Drake out with the trash.

"At this point we know jack." Jonah ran his hand through his hair, while his eyes darted around the room. "I'm not condemning his actions, but why hasn't he checked in? Yesterday he messaged me to say he thinks Buck killed Raven, but offered no proof. Today? Not a word from him."

"Buck had no way of knowing where the body was buried." I kept my chin up, keeping my shakes under lock and key. "Only the three of us and the murderer were familiar with the precise location. Not even you knew enough, except that she was buried in the woods by Lake Marvin."

"Okay. That makes sense." He looked at me. "Why did Drake go after him by himself? Leo could have helped him bring Buck in safely."

"For once, his swift departure had nothing to do with a lack of confidence in Leo's skills." I smiled at Leo. "Drake figured Buck would have gone into hiding. After all, no one had seen him for a while. Drake's training as a hunter just kicked in. We agreed I'd work above ground, talk to Sable, interview the people who knew Buck, while Drake would work underground."

Of course we'd also decided to keep in touch, which Drake had so far failed to do.

"What's the point?" Leo asked. "You just said, Buck had to be the killer. Why would you still be working the case?"

"Because legally, we have nothing. A well-founded suspicion is circumstantial at best." I tapped the table. "I don't close a case unless I have proof."

"Buck would have never seen the inside of a court room." Leo's grim expression shadowed his face. "Jonah would have passed judgement, and Drake or I would have executed it."

"No, Kensi is right." Jonah fell into his chair, as if his legs could no longer carry their burden. "I'd have asked for proof before sentencing one of my own to death. I still can't believe Buck killed Raven. Why?"

"I spent a lot of time pondering that." I crossed my legs at the ankles and leaned forward to place a comforting hand on Jonah's arm. An impudence at any other time, but it simply wasn't in me to ignore his emotional struggle. "Did you know the cops have received a couple of complaints about Buck's behavior toward young women?"

"Human women who led Buck on and then cried assault when he showed interest." Jonah's brows furrowed. "We looked into that. These women made up the whole thing just to get him into trouble."

I scratched my temple. "What if—"

"I'm not saying this because they are human and Buck is a werewolf. They'd planned the whole thing. Drake found evidence to that effect, presented it to me, and we threatened to go public unless they withdrew their allegations. They would have been in serious trouble, but Buck just wanted the sorry affair kept quiet."

Once again, Buck was revealed as a victim. The taunts, the cruelty he had to endure, the pain would have scarred him. Too many times I'd been teased with an offer of friendship, only to end up locked in a closet or left stranded on a highway. Why did people have nothing better to do than punish others only so they could feel better about themselves?

"Creepy Crawley Bug is what Raven used to call Buck." I covered my mouth, overcome by a sense of kinship with the man I'd hardly known. "Do you think he could have killed Raven in a fit of rage? It would explain a lot. He'd have thought he could outrun his mistake, but when I turned up and started digging—at the exact spot where he'd left her—he knew the game was up. Feeling guilty, he disappeared. At least Raven would find peace now. She'd get a funeral, and her friends and family could finally mourn her."

Jonah crossed his arms and chewed his bottom lip.

Leo stepped forward. "And when we didn't announce our discovery, Buck forced the issue and called the police himself."

Jonah slowly rose from his chair. "It's possible. Hell, I don't know if I should feel sorry for the guy or hate him for what he's done."

The cell phone on his desk rang, the vibrations running up my arms and giving me goosebumps.

He raised a finger and answered. "Yes."

Leo and I exchanged glances, but neither of us was willing to give voice to our thoughts. Not that I'd be able anyway. My investigations were usually clear-cut. Someone had gone missing—I tracked them down. A company was hacked—I kept a nerd squad on retainer for exactly that purpose.

I should have known that throwing werewolves into the mix would ruin my success rate. Had my presence in town even been a positive thing? Raven was no longer missing thanks to me, but my sleuthing had led to a second death. Drake had disappeared, and so had Liza, and I had no clue how Jonah rated my performance.

"Christ, are you sure?" Jonah once again sagged into his chair, his face grayer than before. "Fuck."

I leaned forward. It looked like the crap fest wasn't over yet.

"Keep me apprised." Jonah slammed the phone onto the table and buried his face in his hands. "Fuck."

Despite burning with curiosity, I sat still and quiet. The alpha was on the edge of an explosion, and I had no desire to get caught up in the blast.

Jonah finally looked up and gave a bitter laugh. "That was Orson."

"He's working as a police officer with the humans." Leo leaned in and kept his voice quiet, clearly eager not to set the alpha off either.

A chill rose in me, paralyzing me from the waist up. My mouth dried, my heart slowed, and my arms lay heavy on the table, unable to move. Had the cops arrested Drake over Buck's murder? No. Not possible. Because if they had, we'd forever be apart, and that wasn't an option I was physically able to handle.

"The police have made progress in Raven's case. They've just finished interviewing Sable."

My eyes widened, about the only parts of my body that still functioned. Sable would have relayed our earlier conversation and pointed the cops to Cody.

"Did either of you know that Raven once dated Drake?"

I jerked back, my mouth open.

"Kensi told me in the car." Leo shrugged. "She only just found out today."

"Unfortunately, Drake is now on the cops' radar." Jonah shook his head. "You couldn't make it up. One punch in the nuts after another."

"Cody will be their prime focus for now," I said. "While they're investigating him, we should try to find Drake."

"What do you think we've been doing all day?" Jonah glared at me, then turned his gaze on Leo. "Take her home. There's nothing we can do but wait."

"I can help." I got to my feet. "Please. Let me be useful."

Jonah shook his head. "Go home. I'll let you know when we have news."

Before I made the mistake of opening my mouth again, Leo placed his hand on my shoulder and led me out of the room.

"We have people out looking for Drake," he said.

"What's going to happen when the cops reach the conclusion that Cody isn't responsible for Raven's death?"

"If that happens, and I'm not sure they will discount him any time soon, they will look into Drake, dismiss him from their investigation, then tread water until the case goes cold again." He patted my back. "Don't worry."

I gave a dry chuckle, but had no counter-argument. Leo's reasoning was sound. The sooner Drake realized he was better with his pack than as a lone wolf, he'd return.

My chest clamped around my heart, and I inhaled a choked breath. Once Drake was back, I'd chew him out, yell at him—and then never allow him to leave me again.

Twenty-Two

Back home, I did my best not to ping on Jonah's shit-meter again. The alpha had too many worries for me to add my uncertainties. Instead, I re-read my notes, organized them into neat folders for my files, even played back my conversations with Buck and Sable.

My procedure wasn't to blame. Every step I took had been the right one, and my omissions wouldn't have made a difference. Then how had everything gone so wrong?

I opened my Garry Rodgers crime novel, normally a sure-fire way to keep me occupied, but my ability to focus was shot.

After one-hundred sit-ups, a five-mile run followed by a hundred squats, my hardcore workout routine had officially failed to quieten my mind. Physically, I craved Drake's presence. Emotionally… No, I wasn't yet ready to engage with my feelings.

Before I called it a night, I spoke to Jonah, who had no news.

Drake's voice, captured on my recorder, lulled me into a sleep that consisted of sporadic bouts of weird dreams, blissful emptiness and sweat-drenched awakenings. By six o'clock I couldn't stand the not knowing anymore. I got up and raced downstairs to boot up my laptop.

My inbox didn't bring illumination, and Jonah hadn't been in touch either. I knew better than to wake a sleeping alpha, so I doubled my morning exercise routine and then took a shower.

By eight, I started calling people. A tearful Sable recalled her conversation with the police. Her main worry was that she'd got Drake into trouble, even though she made it clear he'd never have hurt Raven. I assured her they'd never suspect him, and she eventually calmed down.

Pike wasn't what I'd call forthcoming on the phone. Without Drake's dominant presence, the distraught father had the nerve to call me incompetent. It was the human police who'd ultimately discovered his daughter, not the hot-shot investigator Jonah had hired.

Natalie hadn't seen Drake, and since I didn't want to alarm her, I kept our conversation short.

The list of contact numbers Buck had given me kept my phone busy for the next hour. Drake's brother, still out of action with a fractured leg, threatened to leap into the woods himself to lead the search. A well-meant sentiment but difficult to implement. A simple shift merely sped up the healing process, but was unable to cure such a serious injury in one swoop.

By mid-morning, I was out of names, numbers and patience.

My phone rang at lunchtime.

"Jonah, do you have any news?"

The sigh from the other end of the line proved his load hadn't lightened yet. "I hear you've been calling around, looking for Drake."

"Of course. If I knew the woods better, I'd be out there myself."

"Jeez, Kensi, you're riling up my pack. As if mourning two of their own isn't bad enough, you've now announced to the world that their protector has disappeared."

I grimaced. "I hadn't considered that. My bad."

"Forget it." Another deep sigh. Not a good sign. "There's worse news. The cops tracked down a witness who saw Drake and Raven arguing days before she disappeared."

I shot to my feet and folded my free arm across my chest for warmth. "What's that supposed to prove?"

"It's enough to make the cops want to speak to him, but guess what? He's gone."

"He's not fleeing, though. He's just, I don't know, hiding out, tracking Buck's real killer."

"A few hours ago, the cops executed a search warrant on Drake's cabin. They found evidence."

"Evidence of what?"

"That he killed Raven."

"Raven. No." Forced by a thump of my heart, I moved back. "That's ridiculous. He didn't. He couldn't have."

"I don't want to believe it either, but the police are convinced they have enough to arrest him."

"But Buck did it." My voice had lowered to a whimper.

"I don't even know what's true anymore." Jonah gave a quiet groan, maybe even with his phone away from his mouth, but still loud enough to be picked up by me. "If Drake hadn't taken matters into his own hands, we could have avoided this mess."

No more words came to me. Drake hadn't done this. Impossible. He wasn't the silent brooding type of books and make-believe, but a real guy, an unbelievably hot real guy, who, despite his impulse to dominate, had shown vulnerability—because I wouldn't. A guy like that wasn't a killer.

Or had sex with Drake turned my head so much, he'd become a blind spot to my common sense?

"I think it's best if you went home. My pack is fractured, and you're not helping the healing process."

"I'm not leaving." I set my jaw. "This is ridiculous. Processing evidence takes time. The police can't possibly have settled on a suspect so soon."

Jonah's growl might have been scary in person, accompanied by a heavy dose of dominance, but over the phone it lacked weight. "This is my territory, and you're here with my permission. Consider that permission withdrawn. Your presence will disrupt my efforts to calm the pack. Don't make me call your dad again."

He would, too. "And tell him how you put me in danger?"

His second growl left a better impression. No argument would change his mind now. That wasn't to say I was beaten yet.

"Fine." I punched the wall. "You win."

"Leo will be with you shortly. He'll take you to the airport."

Jonah hung up.

My throat ached, and I rubbed small circles over it.

Even if Drake had lied about dating Raven, that didn't mean he'd killed anyone—not Buck, and definitely not his best friend's sister. Besides, he'd been as involved in the investigation into Raven's disappearance as I had. Finding her body had shaken him to the core, of that I was sure.

All of that could have been a ploy, of course. He'd been eager to boot Leo off the investigation and keep me close, maybe for the purpose of steering my inquiries away from the truth. And why claim he hadn't talked to Raven in a long time? Was the witness mistaken or did he have an agenda?

No, I wasn't going there. Too many questions were lacking answers. What proof did the cops really have? Had Drake left evidence behind in the woods, like footprints or candy wrappers? Maybe it would help if I gave the police a heavily redacted truth. My reputation was such that it shouldn't take me long to convince them that anything Drake had dropped had been due to the discovery of the body, not to murder.

Except in reality, it had been Drake alone who'd found the body.

Quickly.

Very quickly.

I dialed his number, and it went straight to voice mail. "Um,

Drake. Call me. The police think you killed Raven, but I know you didn't. And we can find the real killer if we work together." I let the noise of the recorder run another few seconds, then added, "I just need to know you're okay. Please call."

I disconnected and scoffed at my weakness. Was he even still interested in me? Had our link been real?

Jeez, I used to be a level-headed investigator in the human world, but the Wild Pack had thrown me out of kilter. Up was down. Good was bad. And a man who was so wrong felt so right.

Outside, kids played on the street, making a hell of a racket. Life went on for those who weren't caught up in this nightmare.

The plan that had implanted itself in my head was growing by the second, and step one involved keeping up appearances. I dashed up the stairs, splashed my face with cold water, and then began to pack. My underwear, and towels went in the bottom as an unfolded heap. I exchanged my T-shirt for a strappy vest and checked the contents of my jacket pockets. Everything from my recorder had been backed up to the Cloud and subsequently deleted from the device, except for Drake's calming voice, his flirtations, his smoky whispers.

The bell rang.

"Hi. It's me." Leo followed up with a couple of knocks.

I stared at my suitcase and smoothed my jacket.

"Kensi. Open up."

I rolled my neck and crossed the spotless hardwood floor. Leaving this place at this time hurt, but Jonah's word was to be obeyed. Ish.

"Good. You're ready." Leo stared at my tote. "Let's go."

This time he reacted fast. Without giving me a chance to grip the handle, he heaved my suitcase down the path to his trunk. We climbed into our seats in silence.

Leo's simple black T-shirt was a little tight, but he had the physique to pull it off. He was a werewolf protector, *the* werewolf protector now, and flaunted strength was what the community needed.

Good old, reliable Leo. He'd made my stay interesting and often provided light relief, especially in those early days when my relationship with Drake was stuck in its teething phase. His occasional lack of backbone had simplified life and now gave me hope that he'd forgive me for what I had devised.

Because of course I wasn't getting on any plane. Jonah could kick me out of his house, exile me from Marlontown, but not all of the Triangle belonged to him.

I tipped down my sunglasses and stared into the hazy mid-afternoon sun that cast its unforgiving heat across the landscape.

Over the last few days, I'd become accustomed to the rocky roads and double-sized portions and the smells that filled the air: the unpleasant wafts from the cows on the farm closest to Jonah's home. The mingling aromas of pizza and burger and garlic from the food joints in Denville. The forest's earthy and floral bouquet. And Drake's unique scent, this mix of peppermint and lemon that did crazy things to my stomach and mind.

Leo held his head straight, his gaze fixed on the road. Not many cars hurried to get out of town, and he took full advantage of the empty roads. A loud rock tune forced its way through the noise from the engine.

Soon, Marlontown lay far behind us. And with it, the woods that brought not only my mom and my dad together, but also Dad and Jonah.

Back then, a friendship was forged. A peace was born.

A peace that may be broken the second I disobeyed Jonah's order to leave, but I'd have to deal with the fallout later—after I'd found Drake and unmasked the real killer, be it Buck, Cody, or the alpha himself.

My mission had changed, but I was going to prevail. After all, I had a man to acquit. *My* man.

If only I had help. Key to operation Save Drake was a certain human librarian. Natalie wouldn't throw Drake to the wolves, so-to-speak. Not without hard evidence. Of course, doing anything without clueing her in on our animal nature came with its own problems.

I glanced at Leo's face. His smile was gone, and not a hint of his flirtatious side peeked out. He and Drake had their problems, but not even he could have predicted this turn of events.

I put on a brave smile and made it water-tight. "No news then?"

"Everyone knows, or thinks they know, that Drake killed Raven and Buck. Jonah has hired the best drifter hunters in the country to track him down and bring him back for trial."

Hunters were the last resort, but what choice did Jonah have?

"What did the cops say?" I asked. "The whole thing makes no sense."

Leo's jaw clenched tightly.

I turned the volume down. "What evidence could make them close in on Drake so quickly?"

"First, there was a shoeprint they'd found next to Raven's body. It matched one of his boots."

"A shoeprint alone isn't going to convict him. Besides, I can easily explain that with the truth."

"The witness statement and correct shoe size were enough for a warrant. When they searched Drake's house, they found jewelry Raven wore the day she disappeared. He kept it as a trophy or something." He rolled his head to the side to regard me briefly. "Lucky escape for you, eh?"

"Jewelry like what? A ring?"

"A necklace. Birdie recognized it immediately."

I pressed my fist into my thigh. Too early to get excited. "A necklace with a blue pendant? The same one her mother had?"

"Yes. Why? What is it?"

"Turn around. Now." I pointed to the rear of the sedan and gripped his steering wheel.

He slammed on the brakes, and we jerked forward.

"What the hell are you doing?" His dominance lassoed around me, but fluctuated with the skidding of the wheels.

"Drake is innocent. I knew it. We have to tell the cops."

He recovered control both over himself and the car. "Kensi—"

"Hear me out. I know the necklace you mentioned. Raven was wearing it when we found her. I saw it."

"You said you didn't go anywhere near the body."

Always the protector.

"Focus, man." I slapped his shoulder. "Don't you get it? Drake didn't take it as a trophy. I bet Buck retrieved it from her grave and hid it in Drake's house before he called the police." I smacked his arm again.

"I don't know. Once we give the police Buck as our suspect, guess who they'll name as their main suspect?"

"One disaster at a time." I glanced over my shoulder. "Why aren't you turning around? We have to tell the police."

His fingers tightened around the steering wheel. "How are you going to explain seeing the necklace on her body? If you admit that you found her, you'll get in trouble."

"We're talking about Drake's life." I tapped the steering wheel again. "Go. Drive."

"Your funeral." Leo turned the car around and drove back the way we came. Back toward the Triangle.

"I knew he didn't do it. You know?" I sought confirmation from Leo.

His face remained unreadable.

"What's wrong? You're still not convinced?"

"Let's wait and see what the police think. He's not out of the woods yet."

I clamped my hands between my legs to stop them from shaking. "Yeah. You're right. This is too important to mess up now."

This development was merely a first step in exonerating Drake. After all, the police might assume that he'd retrieved the necklace as a memento *after* my initial discovery.

The way back took longer. Each minute dragged. My throat had dried up, my heart raced up and down my body. If only I had solid proof Buck was the real killer. Drake had been framed, of that I was sure.

Not many humans could have known Drake would make a good suspect. As Raven's confidant, Cody might have known she'd once dated Drake, but would he have the balls, let alone the wherewithal, to frame his old school buddy?

Leo turned from the road into town onto a narrow dirt road into the woods. The trees stood to attention, their branches pointed the way.

"Where the hell did they build the police station?" I asked.

"It's a new building, and they didn't want to place it amid the old buildings. You know what humans are like."

I pressed deep into my seat, my brain now running hot and not interested in another debate about annoying humans.

If Raven's killer was a werewolf, who'd have the stones to take on a protector? After all, Drake's dominance came in two flavors: strong, and one hundred percent concentrated whoop-ass.

Another dominant wolf, maybe? An alpha or…another protector?

I snapped my face toward Leo, then, belatedly, smoothed my features. Could he be the killer? The notion alone seemed preposterous. What possible motive did he have?

My breathing turned flat, and I sat ramrod-straight so as not to appear spooked.

"You know, don't you?" Leo's knuckles turned white.

Was it too late? Had he read my mind?

The path forked, and Leo turned right, deeper into the woods.

There would be no police station waiting for me out here. Not this far from town.

"Know what?" I asked, trying to sound normal.

His jaw flexed and relaxed, over and over. Any second now, he would stop the car. Would he do to me what he'd done to Raven? Was his face the last face I was going to see?

Or had I lost it completely and allowed paranoia to kidnap my mind?

The real question, though, could I take the risk? If he turned on me, I stood no chance. In human form, he outweighed me. In wolf form, he'd tear me to pieces.

I tensed my muscles and yanked at the steering wheel, sending Leo's sedan soaring into the trees.

TWENTY-THREE

THE SEDAN VEERED. THE TIRE struck something hard, and Leo's vehicle leaped to the right.

"Shit." Leo counter-steered, but not fast enough.

I squared my shoulders against the seat, my head flat on the head restraint.

A white wall hit my face and disappeared in a fraction of a second. The impact jolted my bones from my body.

For a moment I sat, stunned. The smell of explosives singed the air. My nose stung, my vision blurred. I took a deep breath, but something was in my throat. A cough wracked my aching chest, my aching everything.

A dark shape moved to my left.

Frame by frame, reality re-entered my consciousness.

Leo.

Killer.

Shit.

Within a second, I'd undone my seatbelt and pushed against the door. Something blocked it, so I rammed my shoulder against it. A sharp pain shot through my arm and into my leg, but at least the door opened.

Run. Don't think.

I scrambled away from the totaled sedan. Through the woods. Back the way we'd come.

My lungs stung with each short breath. Had I done the right thing? Was my suspicion even correct? Trees surrounded me, dizzying tall trees in every direction, and I zigzagged with only my arms as buffers.

A log stuck up from the ground and tripped me. I tussled up. Pushed harder. The faster I ran, the darker and colder it got. I kept the road to my right, close enough to jump in front of a car. Not that I was likely to find one out here.

How long before Leo was *compos mentis*? How long until I would die?

I ripped my phone out of my jacket, dialed a nine. Tripped. Fell. Got up. Pressed the next number.

Thuds drummed behind me, building to a crescendo. A force knocked into my back. My cell flew from my hand as I went sprawling onto my front.

A sharp pain stole my vision.

"Let me go." I rallied onto my back, propping myself up.

I wasn't going to go without a fight. Not me. I kicked out.

"Shit." Leo's spit hit my face.

I swung my arm and somehow got off the ground. My fist connected with his stomach but only grazed it. Running had made no difference.

But my father's lessons would save me. Judo, aikido, fencing. I hadn't endured torture after torture to be beaten now.

Leo swung me against a tree, chest first. My face scraped across the sharp bark. Then his arm curled around my neck from behind and squeezed.

I let out a muffled cry that died on my lips. Kicked his leg. Slapped at his hand. Scratched until I drew blood.

"Shh. Nearly over," Leo whispered.

His tone was soft, comforting.

But I didn't want to be comforted. I wasn't done. Drake was innocent, and he needed me to prove it. All it took was a lucky punch, a good kick, and I'd be free.

I strained against his hold, rammed the heels of my boots into his shin.

He yelled out, squeezed harder.

My throat closed. The pressure in my head built, blocking my ears. In front, a branch reached for me. But the trees couldn't save me. Powerless, they waved.

I snapped for oxygen, it was gone. My lungs didn't inflate.

No air.

No police.

My muscles burned, and I slackened in Leo's grip. This was it. My last moment. At least I didn't have to see his face.

I dropped my arms and looked into the woods. At least I was going to die in my happy place.

A cramp seized my leg, and I kicked out. Then I opened my eyes, inhaled sharply.

I could breathe again. Safe.

Or maybe not. I sat in a kitchen of sparse décor, the kind one might describe as rustic out of kindness. A phone lay on the table. I pushed with my legs to get up, but a nylon cord wrapped around my arms and torso. Similar restraints wound around my legs. Someone had tied me up. Not someone. Leo.

I wiggled in the chair, but with its metal frame, it seemed too robust to break, even if I slammed it against something.

Leo hadn't even been careless enough to leave knives lying around.

"You're awake." He entered the kitchen and propped himself up by the counter to the right of the tall fridge.

"What's going on?" I kept my voice measured.

I understood why he'd attacked me. But I hadn't a clue why I was still alive.

"You were done. So close to being safe." He pinched his index finger and thumb together. "But you wouldn't listen. Had to keep on drilling. Now the police will never know of Drake's innocence."

I glared. "They will, once I get out of here."

He crossed his arms. "Maybe you're going to be his latest victim. I mean, you look like Raven."

"Why did you do it? Kill her? What could she possibly have done that would justify it?"

"You know what she did."

"I have no earthly idea." I took deep breaths, stretched against my restraints without letting the effort show on my face, but the cord didn't loosen.

"She was going to elope with Cody. Leave her parents behind. Leave *me* behind. For what? To have mutts with him?"

"He's not a catch, sure, but it was her life. No one's controlling your life, are they?"

Leo spat on the ground, or certainly made it look that way. "Mutts don't ask to be born, but Raven knew better. She should have listened."

"This is insane. I know you. You're better than this."

"I didn't set out to kill her." His top lip moved and briefly revealed his teeth. "I tried to reason with her, reminded her that dating a human was going to hurt her parents, but she didn't listen."

"See, I knew it had to have been an accident. Let me go, and we'll find a solution together."

"I don't want to hurt you, believe me. But the way Jonah's handling the crisis was an eye opener. He's useless."

I raised my eyebrows. "This is about power?"

"No. It wasn't supposed to be." He steered his gaze onto the ground where he scraped the floor with the toes of his shoe. "But now we've reached a point. Lines are drawn. If you aren't with me…"

My breath came more evenly. Leo was deluded, no doubt, but I wasn't going to tell him that. "I totally agree. Jonah didn't handle this the way an alpha should. Not the way you would have."

He glanced up, his eyes moist. "Exactly. At first, Raven's… disappearance even had a positive effect on the pack, you know? I used it to remind everyone that we needed to stick together. Then Drake found the body, and I knew the moment Buck got his nose on the ground, he'd smell me."

I jerked up my head. "Are you saying you killed Buck?"

"I kinda had to." His shoulders slumped. "I told him not to come to the lake and to meet me on the way instead. Unfortunately, I didn't have time to bury his body."

I strained so hard, the ties ate into my forearms. "When he was discovered, you needed a new scapegoat."

"You were the one who told me about Drake dating Raven." He spread his hands out to his sides to support himself on the counter. "I'd gone back for Raven's necklace so I could plant it on Buck later, but Drake would work just as well."

"You were spot on. It's looking bad for him."

Flecks of light bounced across the creamy-white floor. Colorful utensils completed the tasteful decor. It seemed inconceivable that someone as damaged as Leo could have gone shopping for tiles to create a home for himself. It was possible he hadn't always been this way. Maybe killing Raven had triggered a dark streak in him.

"At least with him out of the picture and Jonah weak, I can bring order to the pack again." Leo cocked his head. "I'd hoped you'd be by my side."

"Really?" My eyebrows shot up. "I mean, my father is the one with ties to Jonah. Your alpha has made it clear he doesn't want me in his town."

"Our town. If you're willing."

Would Leo believe my charade? I'd have to be careful not to lay it on too thick.

"It beats waiting another century before I get my chance to take my father's throne." I sighed. "I don't know. Could I even trust you?"

"I told you I didn't intend to kill Raven, and Buck, well, he was collateral damage."

I waved him off with a swipe of my chin. "I didn't mean that. I meant, could I trust you to be a fair alpha, and not to push me aside if I disagree with you?"

"It's a serious offer." He stepped forward and crouched. "You're more progressive than I am, which will help us modernize, and I remember the old values, which will strengthen our base."

"We can turn this dark time into something positive."

"Exactly." A smile formed on his lips, and he ran his thumb down my neck.

"Give the Wild Pack the stability it needs."

His hand tightened around my throat as his expression twisted into something feral. "You think I'm stupid?"

My breaths came in short bursts. "Of course not. I'm serious."

"Oh, please." He straightened, and in the process pushed me back with sufficient strength to make my chair wobble. "I know about you and Drake."

"He and I made a mistake. You know me. You know how much I hate show-offs like him who flaunt their dominance like a cheap cologne."

Leo crossed his arms. Regarded me through shrewd eyes. Then twisted and left the kitchen.

Why was I even still alive? Maybe he still hoped my desire to join him in his madness was genuine.

Someone rapped on the door.

"Kensi, Leo, are you here?" Drake shouted. "Are you two okay?"

I twisted on the chair, but didn't scream out for him. Leo had to have heard him, and if so, Drake was in danger.

"Where the hell are you?" Drake punched the door again.

Leo returned and looked at me through wide eyes.

I shook my head. "Let's not tell him we're here."

"Why not?" He opened a drawer and took out a knife. "I'll have to deal with him sooner or later."

"You don't have to do that."

He winked at me and ambled to the door.

"Run, Drake!" I shouted at the top of my volume. "Get out of here."

Had he heard me? He'd stopped knocking, which I took as a good sign.

I used my feet and body weight to move myself and the chair toward the drawer Leo had left half open.

A scuffle erupted in the hall, or rather a full-on beating. Drake was stronger than Leo, no doubt, but Leo had a knife and surprise on his side.

With renewed energy, I wedged my sore teeth behind the drawer's corner and dragged it out. The sharp edge cut into my lip, but this might be my only chance to get ready.

How had Drake found us? If he'd followed Leo, he must have had a reason. For all I knew, he wasn't alone and had brought the cavalry. But judging by recent events, my luck would swing the other way.

The knives were wedged too far up into the drawer, but a pair of scissors could be within my reach, provided I could bend that way. I lifted myself up, with the chair glued to my butt, and stuck my face inside, using my mouth to scout for the scissors. The metal loop and blades felt cold against my skin, and once I'd closed my teeth around them, I lifted them out.

Great. Now what? How did I get my tool from up here to down there?

A penguin couldn't have been less elegant as I shifted my arms a little and slid my hands toward my lap. Next, I tipped my chair back against the cabinet and let go of the scissors. Their weight dropped first onto my stomach and then my legs. I wriggled and jerked until my palm finally closed around the loops.

I applied the scissors to the ties, but with my hand still secured, I couldn't get proper purchase. A twist of my fingers opened them enough for me to press one blade against the plastic cord. Spies made this look easy on TV, when in fact, the up-and-down movement tired the wrist, with very little gain to show for your trouble.

The sounds outside fell few and far between, but Drake was still alive.

A dull thump froze my lungs.

"What a beauty." Leo's triumph came out of nowhere.

Frantically, I pushed the drawer shut with my back and hopped back to my spot, in the nick of time.

Leo popped his head in. "Looks like you backed a loser."

Blood trickled from his mouth and ran from a wound on his head. Something was wrong with one of his eyes, too, because one lid hung lower than the other.

"Is…is he alive? You can't kill him yet. Too many bodies will make your pack suspicious." My words toppled over one another.

"Of course he's alive. Can't blame your death on a dead man, can I?"

He limped off, dragging something heavy with him. A door opened, and the sound faded.

Still alive. Still alive. Still alive.

As each syllable ran through my mind, I sawed up and down, up and down, and slowly, my efforts were paying off. Not long ago, I'd half-suspected Drake of being a killer. Now he lay unconscious, at Leo's mercy.

His own fault, of course. Probably used his stupid phone app to track me, then ran into the wreck of Leo's car and came looking for us. If there wasn't a lesson in this for him, he was a hopeless case, which I'd be sure to tell him the minute we were out of danger.

I intensified my sawing motion, stretched my shoulders and arms to increase the pressure, until finally, the cord snapped. A few more wiggles, and the restraints fell away. Red streaks wound around my wrists and arms, which pulsed with a dull ache. I snipped open the cord around my legs and shot to my feet to pick up a solid frying pan.

My hands shook, and I took a measured breath. Could I really bash in Leo's head? What if I misjudged my own power, and rather than knocking him out, I caved in his skull? I'd be in the same situation Leo had found himself in when he killed Raven.

Steps alerted me to Leo's return. "I wonder how Drake found us."

I took a big swing and bashed the frying pan into his shins. He dropped to his knee, and I smashed my weapon into his back.

His body sagged to the ground, but he wasn't out yet. Instead, he whimpered and tried to push back up.

I bunched my lips, stepped back. Why wasn't he unconscious yet?

Leo glanced up at me, his mouth open. "Why?"

A leaden hum buzzed through my chest. "Oh God, I'm so, so sorry."

Another firm smack, and Leo's body sprawled on the kitchen tiles.

I tied the plastic cord remnants around his arm and body, wrapped duct tape I discovered in one of his drawers around his legs, and picked up the cell phone from the table.

"Jonah? It's Kensi."

"Are you at the airport? Where's Leo?"

"Unconscious by my feet. He killed Raven. Her and Buck. It was him all along. He kidnapped me. His cabin—"

A sharp pain against my right knee made me suck in air. Leo kicked out again, foot high, and knocked the phone from my hand. I reached for the frying pan, but his reaction was faster. His foot shot up again and smacked it from my grip. It flew up and fell onto his thigh.

His scream of pain was beautiful. I'd felt bad about hurting him, but even my sympathy had limits.

I dashed to the phone. Its display was cracked, but I pushed the buttons anyway. The lights didn't come on.

Damn.

For now, the cord around Leo's legs and hands limited his movements, but he was nearly on his feet now.

I opened the cupboard doors, grabbed a saucepan, and pummeled his frame with it until he slumped back down.

"You're gonna pay for that." He wheezed.

"We'll see." I reached back and planted my fist on his nose, which gave a satisfying crunch.

His eyes glazed over and his facial muscles sagged.

I straightened and rolled my neck. Good thing Drake had softened him up. Otherwise Leo would have made an easy meal out of me. My years of training hadn't prepared me for the reality of a fight. Frying pans and pots didn't glide through the air the way a sword did, and real-life pain hurt worse, too.

At least Drake could shift his injuries away, and the sooner the better. I dashed out of the kitchen and scouted the hallway for a telephone. Nothing. Maybe Leo had built this place for the solitude. If so, what were the chances Jonah had the address?

I yanked open one door after another—but one was locked.

Despite lacking the dominance of a werewolf, at least I had the strength. The second my sore shoulder crashed against the light-brown wood, the lock splintered and the door slid open. Wooden stairs led into a separate room that had been built at a lower level than the rest of the house, yet not so deep it qualified as a basement.

Wide, short windows, grimy from neglect, let in sparse sunlight, which reflected off the dust particles. Wooden shelves lined one wall and the floor, stone with a thick layer of dirt, was strewn with tools.

"Drake?" I whispered.

What if he couldn't answer because he was dead? Leo could have lied. He'd done much worse already.

"Drake?" I raised my voice.

A moan sounded from the back. A moan so laden with pain, it tore at my heart. I skipped the last two steps and dashed to Drake's crumpled form. Pounded to within an inch of his life, he lay slumped on his back on the dirty floor. A bloody gash glistened through a tear in his T-shirt.

Leo had stabbed him, because he couldn't have beaten him in a fair fight.

"Can you walk?" I squeezed Drake's arm. "We have to go."

His eyelids snapped open, but no understanding lay in those red-veined eyes.

I placed my hand against his cheek, which was cold and damp, much like this room. "Can you hear me? We need to leave."

I ripped his T-shirt, rolled it up and pressed it against his chest wound.

Still alive. Still alive. Still alive.

"Come on." I prodded him gently. "Move. Please,"

He groaned and nudged his head to the side.

I stroked his cheek, deflated. He was in no state to go anywhere. Leo had made sure of that. His best chance was for me to get help. I'd stick to the road, so that if Jonah was on the way, I could flag him down.

But how could I leave Drake behind? His cold skin needed warmth, his bruised face gentle kisses.

"You need to shift." My words spread through the room without making any difference.

Drake gurgled, struggled for breath.

"Sh-sh. It's okay." I rested his head against my chest.

My whispers seemed to soothe him, and his inhalations grew lighter and more regular.

But this wasn't getting me anywhere. Go or stay? It had to be one or the other.

"Shift, dammit. Shift now." If I had dominance, I could have compelled his change into wolf form, weak as he was.

Drake didn't even move.

I rested my chin on his hair, which was matted to his head. "I'm sorry I've been so difficult. I have so much to tell you, things I tried to keep secret. But you deserve to know."

A moan. Quiet, but a sign he was listening, of hope.

I caressed his cheek, rough with stubble. He probably hadn't shaved since he'd gone on the run.

No more dithering. Without help, Drake wouldn't make it. I searched his pockets, but he didn't have his phone on him. Maybe he'd left it in his car. I took his keys and carefully placed him onto the ground. "I promise I'll be right back. Just…don't go anywhere."

I ran up the stairs when an ominous scrape forced me back into a corner.

Twenty-Four

Leo limped toward me, one step after the other, grimacing each time his weight shifted. His hand wrapped around the red-stained knife he'd stuck into Drake earlier.

"Thought you were all clever, didn't you?" He propped an arm against the wall and briefly closed his eyes.

I raced back toward Drake and crouched. "Come on. We're out of time."

A miraculous recovery would have been well-timed right now, but as predicted, that wasn't how things were working out for me in this goddamn town.

I lunged to the shelf on my right, curled my fingers around a metal rod that stuck out of a bucket, and moved forward, putting a buffer zone between me and Drake.

Leo's eyebrows lifted by a fraction. "You really think you got a shot at getting out of here alive?"

"I was raised to be an alpha, with all the training that entails." I swished the rod through the air, which already felt more comfortable in my hand than the heavy frying pan.

Leo halted his approach, but only for a second. "Your bravado is sexy, though. We could have created something wonderful together, you and I."

"I'd have eaten you alive, buddy. Not that you ever stood a chance, not with Jonah and Drake around. But that's your real problem, isn't it? Always the bridesmaid, never the guy in charge. You'll always be the alpha that wasn't."

His facial muscles hardened, and he pointed his blade in my direction. "I wanted this to be as painless as possible for you. I changed my mind."

My werewolf force would give me a lot of bang per swing, but Leo's genes also made him harder to injure. Harder, but not impossible. I feigned up, then slammed the bottom of the rod against his shins, where the frying pan had struck him during round one.

He hissed out a stream of air and bent his knees.

I spun the rod and tapped its end against his left shoulder, immediately followed by his right elbow.

He sagged, stepped back.

The rod was heavier than the sticks I'd trained with in my youth, but that only meant a more lasting impact.

"Not bad for a girl." He thrust his knife toward my chest.

I sashayed out of his reach and kicked him in the stomach.

He fell back, tripped over a small pile of tools on the floor.

A whole cache of weapons that could hurt me. Swell.

"Come on then." I grinned and beckoned with my free hand. "Afraid of a woman now, are we?"

If I got him angry enough, he might not see the arsenal by his feet.

He slid his T-shirt over his head as his eyes narrowed and grew dark. His mouth bowed forward, his forehead reclined, and fur sprouted between his eyes.

Crap. A shift wouldn't just heal him, it would also mean the end of the road for me.

He stepped out of his pants.

I dove forward and slammed my rod full-force into his skull.

He opened his snout wide and let out a bark, revealing his teeth. His dominance wrapped around me like barbed wire, whipping my arms. I bashed him again, but none of my blows could take him down mid-shift. His skin would close up quickly, again and again, until he'd fully changed.

The hammer, screwdrivers and spanners lay useless on the floor. The rod in my hand was already the best weapon around, and it hardly made a difference anymore. Still, I applied my full might to bash my metal stick into his furry back, onto his skull, across his snout.

His pained howl chilled my blood. I brought my weapon down again, my energy wiped now. A breath, that was all I needed. Just a quick break.

But my time was up. Leo's head rotated and his legs transformed into powerful hindquarters.

The fully formed wolf lunged at me, mouth withdrawn into a snarl.

I swung back and struck. The rod scraped against the ground, grazed paws that looked far too lethal.

Leo's teeth caught my skin, just barely, but enough to leave a trace of fire in their wake.

"This wasn't your plan, remember?" I shoved him away with my hand and spun to keep my neck safe.

He bounced off the ground and leaped again.

I hopped to the side, opening a gap between us. "No one will believe that Drake tore me apart, you idiot. Jonah will never buy that."

Leo's mouth opened, but as much as he wanted to exchange insults, that privilege was mine alone.

"Let's finish this." I blew my hair from my face. Watched his body. His eyes. "Come on, you gray sack of fur. Let's play Come on."

He snapped for me. His mouth might not be able to form words, but his eyes said it all. That guy was pissed, and his dominance finally became painful.

But pain was relative. After Jonah and Drake, it took more than a moderately powerful wolf to throw me off my game. I motored my rod through the air, keeping him at bay, away from Drake. Nothing else mattered. Sweat soaked through my top into my jacket. My face and limbs ached with a dull thud. How long until my arms grew too tired to lift? How long until Leo got his opening?

A growl behind me disturbed my rhythm.

Leo didn't take his chance. Instead, his gaze drifted past me to the furry shape that slinked out from the shadows and stood, a little taller than Leo, next to me.

Drake's dominance was devastating.

Leo hunched back.

I slammed the rod into his flank.

He whimpered and retreated. His instincts were telling him to leave Drake alone, to not push his luck.

The burning stings that peppered my skin left a mark on me, too. I took a deep breath, flexed my hand muscles to stop my weapon from slipping from my grasp. Yet some part of me, the wolf part, recognized the flavor of Drake's power. He'd unfolded his alpha might into me before, and this time, it infused me with his strength to compensate for a lack of my own.

Leo lowered his head, but within a few seconds, his human reasoning overcame his animal instinct. His pelt bristled, and with his tail as straight as a baseball bat, he lunged at Drake.

The two snapped and tore into each other, so fast, with such devastating power, their shapes became a frenzy of fur and canines. I flattened myself against the shelf and kept my weapon raised against my chest. After all, I might still need it. Drake's injuries had been serious. If he flagged, it would be my turn again to fight.

If my dad had picked a wife who'd been a full werewolf, I could have shifted. Stand head and tail by Drake's side. Let my dominance force Leo into submission.

But he'd lacked foresight. It was his fault Drake was bleeding, limping, fighting to save us even though he could hardly stand.

Despite being at a disadvantage, Drake caught Leo by the neck, teeth buried deep. His rumbling growl fed his dominance, and I had no choice but to channel more into me, or risk being wholly overcome by it.

He had the upper hand, but his strength was waning. He shot me a glance, swiveled it between my face and the metal bar in my hand.

I tightened my grip and took a deep breath. Then I nodded.

He intensified his bite, forcing a high-squealed whine from Leo, then withdrew.

Leo stood still for a precious second, long enough to let my weapon connect with his skull.

He whirled around, but his focus was off, allowing me to land another blow.

He swayed on his legs—yet didn't go down.

"Come on," I shouted, exasperated. "What the hell does it take to put you out of your misery, you stupid wolf?"

I swished the bar again, and this time, Leo ducked out from under it.

Drake leaped, once again buried his teeth in Leo's fur.

A rumble sounded outside the door, then the door swung open, and two more wolves darted down the stairs.

TWENTY-FIVE

RAKE RETREATED TO MY SIDE, panting, yet watchful. Leo barked, hackles up, but the spark was out. The two wolves knocked into him with their chests and shoulders.

I crouched, not yet ready to yield my weapon, and patted Drake. "We did it." I blew a kiss onto his forehead.

He pressed his head against my shoulder, and we rested, waiting for Leo's ultimate submission.

One of the wolves had Leo in a muzzle-bite, forcing his nose toward the ground and holding it there.

"Everyone all right?" Jonah skipped down the stairs, his face still gray but more determined than ever.

"I think so." I squeezed Drake and let out a jagged breath.

Jonah stood tall before Leo and shot out his dominance with so much precision, I only caught a few stray pheromones.

"You're done, Leo. You've forfeited your life." Jonah's voice held no sorrow for the loss of a friend, but all the pride and conviction of an alpha. "Was it worth it?"

I got to my feet. "You need him alive."

Jonah lasered me with his gaze. "Excuse me?"

His dominance radiated in my direction, and yet it barely affected me. Drake's power still hummed inside me, making me all but immune. I dusted off my own alpha urges and straightened to my full height.

"The police think Drake killed Raven, and Buck's death is also unsolved." I limped toward him. "If we want to clear Drake's name, we have to give them the real killer."

"A werewolf in a human prison? They might get suspicious when he doesn't age." Jonah's jaw flexed, but he nodded anyway. "We'll work it out. Come on, guys. Take him away."

While I followed Jonah and the three wolves out, Drake stayed glued to my side, also limping, but alive.

Still alive.

Outside the cabin, two cars had parked behind Drake's pick-up. Natalie waved from the passenger seat of one of them.

I returned the greeting with an uncertain hand movement. "Um. Jonah. Did you know Nat's sitting in your car?"

He gave a weak smile. "Oh no. How did that happen?"

I lifted my head and eyebrows, begging for an explanation.

"When you said you were at Leo's, I got Channing over there to check out his home." Jonah pointed at one of the wolves who guarded Leo relentlessly. "You weren't there. Clearly, Leo owned, or at least had access to, another place, and who better than the local librarian to help out?"

"How are you going to explain this to her?" I gestured at the four wolves. "She isn't stupid, you know."

He gave a sheepish smile that spread into a full-on, high-beam grin. "That much has dawned on me. I don't know. Maybe I'll hit her with the truth and see where we go from there."

"Are you serious?"

The playfulness died on his lips. "What choice do I have now?"

Drake, still bloody, prodded my thigh with his snout. If I had to guess, I'd say he was eager to get back to his human shape. And even though he had few inhibitions, showing his package to Nat might be a step too far, even for him.

"I get it. Things change." I rubbed my eyes, worn and tired. "I just wish change could come without so much personal loss. Raven. Leo. Especially Buck. I wish I'd taken the chance to get to know him."

"He won't be forgotten." Jonah placed a hand behind my neck and pulled me closer so we stood forehead to forehead. "Thank you. For everything."

This intimacy was usually reserved for loved ones, and my heart swelled. I lowered my eyes, a deliberate sign of respect for an alpha who was dealing with his pack issues in a way that made me optimistic about their future.

Drake nudged my leg, and we separated.

"Hang on." Jonah opened the trunk of his car and threw me a pair of jeans, a shirt and a pair of shoes. "For Drake."

I squashed the clothes under my left arm and slipped two fingers into the breast pocket of my jacket to retrieve my USB.

"It's got a built-in recorder." I pressed a few buttons, then played a snippet of my earlier conversation with Leo. "Play the recording to your pack. They'll be so pissed, Leo will confess if it means not having to face their wrath."

"Thank you." Jonah raised a hand as a goodbye. "I'll see you at the Moon Festival."

Drake poked my hip with his nose.

The afternoon had whipped up a breeze, offering fresh air that cleared my lungs. I walked back toward the cabin, favoring my injured leg. Drake lapped at my heels, surprisingly sprightly after his fight.

He'd shifted into his birthday suit by the time I'd laid out his clothes across the kitchen table.

The sooner we got out of this place, the sooner I'd forget about this nightmare. My job was done. Despite the pain and rollercoaster adventure ride of the past two days, I couldn't fault my actions as far as the case went, and damn it, I wouldn't fault my decisions in as far as they related to Drake either.

"Do you want me to leave so you can get dressed?" Despite my words, I lifted myself atop the counter and dangled my legs.

He gestured down along his body. "I wouldn't want to deprive your royal eyes, *princess*."

From my seated position, I checked his fierce legs and the beautiful landscape of his abs for wounds. "You're too kind."

"What, you're not telling me off for calling you princess? You must have been worried about me."

"I'm giving you a one-time pass, but mind your tongue."

Drake stalked toward me, jeans buttoned up, T-shirt clutched in his hand. "I hoped minding my tongue would be your job now."

He kissed me, long and deep. Brushing my hand across the artwork on his arm, I inhaled his tangy sweetness. His shoulders flexed under my brazen hands, his skin radiated warmth.

He wrapped my good leg around his waist and yanked my butt toward him. Perched on the edge of the counter, I grazed the softness of his hair at the back of his head, the rough terrain of his chin and neck, the satin smoothness of his chest.

Our lips parted, yet we remained locked in our entwined state, unwilling to lose the heat that curled between us.

"We should go," I whispered.

"You're right." His breath grazed my cheek. "The sooner we get my charges dropped: the sooner we get to—"

"Talk." I tracked his jaw with my thumb.

"Talk. Sure." He stepped out of my embrace. "You took the word right out of my mouth."

Deprived of their purpose, my arms dangled uselessly by my side. "Thank you for helping me save you."

He tilted back his head and let out a deep laugh. "I simply

couldn't allow you to carry the weight of my death. I'm just sorry you got hurt. That's on me."

I placed my hand over the dull thumping inside my knee. "I heal fast. And you did keep me safe. Alive is safe."

He hopped onto the counter in the space next to me and pushed his tongue against the inside of his cheek. "Let's talk about the elephant in the room."

If only there were an elephant in the room. Even a squirrel would have provided sufficient distraction.

He covered my hand with his, both now flat between us. "Is it possible you don't possess any physical dominance?"

My ears rang with the echo of his words.

I glanced at his fingers, big-knuckled yet capable of so much tenderness. "It's possible."

"And you can't shift?" His voice coaxed me with its velvet pitch.

The area between my chin and throat tightened to make swallowing difficult. Not too long ago, I would have told him anything he wanted, if only he survived. Now, reality had set in. My father's warnings. The future his advisors had painted for our pack should my secret get out.

The corners of my mouth trembled, and I bowed my head. "No."

"Okay. Wow." Drake removed his hand from mine, leaving a chill that drilled into my bones.

"Not yet." My face, my voice, everything was back under my control, even the arrogant chin-lift I practiced so often. "My father is sure my wolf will break out soon."

Drake took a hold of my hand again, except this time he wrapped his fingers all the way around it. "For what it's worth, I agree with your father."

"You do? Why?"

He tilted my face toward him with his hand and fixed his eyes on mine. "Because of who your mother was. You've confirmed what I suspected about her, and what the books hinted at."

"Hit me." I shuttered my face against any emotional leakage. "Whatever the truth, I can take it."

He caressed my cheek, before tapping the tip of my nose. "First, let's go talk to the police."

He slid off the counter, arranged himself back between my legs, and lifted me off before placing me on the ground.

Putting weight on my leg lit the flame in my knee again, and I strode across the hard floor so he wouldn't see my pain. "Let's get this over with."

Drake was well enough to drive. We rescued my tote and laptop from Leo's wrecked car and, an hour later, I gave my statement in a drab room that smelled of vomit and bleach.

The station chief was a fan. I'd made a point of praising the police in bringing the Socialite Strangler to justice, and he eventually let me off with a strong reprimand for not reporting finding Raven's body. Drake had a tougher time ahead of him.

I could be patient if I had no choice, and by eight o'clock, Drake was free. As he left the station and walked toward me, my chest tightened in a good way.

"Hi." I placed my arms around his neck and didn't wait for his reply.

My kiss was a confession of sorts. Words, tone of voice, they expressed my thoughts well enough, but only my lips could do justice to my feelings, and I didn't hold back. In his arms, I melted.

Dad warned me the heart made decisions more quickly and resolutely than the brain, but then he was biased, of course. My parents had been together mere days before they took the Moon Promise, when their love was fresh and at its peak. In the years following their decision, the magic of the ritual made sure their feelings for each other never waned.

I'd witnessed the aftermath, though, and made sure to stay clear of emotional entanglements. Until now. Today, my brain lay defeated, quiet, accepting, but was my heart reliable?

Drake tightened his embrace. "Ready to go? If I ever see a police officer again, it'll be too soon."

We walked to his pickup and got in.

"How come you didn't tell me you dated Raven?" The words tumbled from my chest and lightened a load. "Sable told me."

"Sable must have misread the situation." He chuckled. "We didn't date. But Raven and I had been close, and once I realized she was getting attached, I retreated. God, I had no idea how to handle the situation. Maybe I pushed her toward Cody, toward her death. I'll never know."

"If you look hard enough, you can find guilt in everyone, but don't forget to lay blame only where it belongs."

"Still…"

"Witnesses saw you with her before her death."

His face ran the gamut of expressions and settled on a forlorn look. "We ran into each other and I could tell immediately something was troubling her. Maybe the prospect of leaving her parents for Cody. She refused to say, didn't mention Cody, and maybe I pushed a little too hard."

"She was a grown woman," I said. "Young, but entitled to make her own decisions."

"Yeah."

We passed the next few minutes of our drive with a series of pointed looks and fleeting touches. Every now and then, his lips twitched into something akin to a smile.

"So. What have you found out about my mother?" I opened the glovebox lid and took out a bottle he kept stored there. "Give me at least an idea of what to expect."

"You're impatient."

"I'm totally patient. I just don't like waiting."

"Remember the text on the boulder?"

I swigged water and nodded at the same time.

"I found the same line in a book about werewolf origins."

I wiped my mouth with the back of my hand. "Meaning what?"

Drake turned into a small lane I recognized as the one that took us to his cottage. "We're home."

I crossed my arms with enough force that the water sloshed inside the bottle. "You think you're so mysterious, but really, you're nothing but a tease."

He laughed.

As we entered the dirt circle in front of Drake's house, the moon was already on the rise, plump but not yet round, as it geared up for the coming full moon.

Drake parked up, and we got out. While he went up on the porch to unlock the door, I lingered.

Tall, slim trees rose from the long grass, nothing like the dense undergrowth where Leo had hidden Raven's body.

"If I die, I want to be buried in a place like this." I gestured around me.

He skipped back down the steps. "Before you consider the afterlife, how about you enjoy the present?" He placed his hand on the back of my neck and gathered me against his chest

Here I remained for a few minutes, until he led me into the house. Tonight wasn't going to be about control, or about dominance. All I wanted was what I'd wanted all along: to be me.

TWENTY-SIX

ON DRAKE'S SUGGESTION, I CHANGED into something *more comfortable,* although he'd probably hoped for more than my washed-out pajama pants and a cami. Five minutes later, I joined him in his living room, which unlike me was dressed to impress. He'd lit a candle at one end of the table, and its light flickered over a bowl of chocolates, a bottle of wine, and the accompanying glasses. An old stereo, only a generation removed from a Bakelite wireless, whispered songs of romance and love.

The snide comment on my tongue, ready for deployment, didn't roll off it. He'd turned the room into a cliché, and my heart gave a double beat.

He dragged his gaze across my baggy bottoms and the graying strappy top.

The silk PJs would have made a more attractive picture. Certainly more enticing than an outfit that looked like last week's dirty laundry. What had I been thinking?

Either way, the evening was going to end in sex. The certainty of it was woven into the atmosphere, like an inevitable law of nature, and neither of us had the inclination to stop it. But we were no longer two passing ships. We'd weathered storms and sought refuge in each other. That meant something.

If only I knew what.

I grabbed my left elbow with my right hand and pivoted toward the sofa. "Trying to keep your eyes on the prize."

His nostrils flared and his hungry stare burrowed into me. "Oh, I am."

I slumped into the upholstery and quickly crossed my legs, because the familiar pucker in the area between them was already four steps ahead of us. "I meant I'm doing whatever I can to keep your mind on your news about the travelers."

He joined me on the sofa, a healthy three inches of space between us.

"It's not an easy story to digest. Read?" He gently slapped my thigh as if gearing up for a day's work, but left it there, warming my flesh, his fingers tantalizingly close to my apex.

I picked up the book from the table and wriggled in my seat, suddenly aware of my clammy back. With the curtains drawn tight, the room's heat had nowhere to go but into my head.

Drake angled his body toward me and pulled his knee up to place it between us. "This is a theory, and in many ways absurd, but it fits. It explains why your father asked you not to reveal what you're doing here, why your mother's departure caused uproar in her pack, and why you can't shift. Yet."

"Go on."

"I believe your mother's pack was the last of the original werewolves, the ones that started it all."

"The First Ones?" I curled my fingers so the edge of the book cut deep into my flesh. "How is that possible?"

"The First Ones left, at least in part, for Europe many centuries ago. We know that your mother's pack returned from Europe. Then there's the proverb, which basically means 'A real wolf will never be domesticated.' The travelers believed in this motto and kept their distance from humans—even from second-generation werewolves like your father."

"That's why my grandfather didn't approve of Marlon or my dad." My stomach rattled like a washing machine on steroids. All this time I'd thought my mother's line was more human than wolf.

Drake caressed my arm using tender strokes of his thumb. "Like Marlon, the travelers wanted to keep their bloodline clean. Your mother and father's romance put the future of their tribe at risk. According to eyewitness accounts from that time, only six or seven grown females belonged to the pack, and out of these, only two were unmated."

I watched the comforting strokes he made with his hand. "Hardly enough to sustain a population."

"Exactly. Every female werewolf was precious. They ran from Europe to the woods of Colorado, but civilization found them anyway. Once your mother left, their survival became dire, and I suspect they moved further into the mountains. Away from humans and other werewolves."

"Liza came back." I closed his opening mouth with my fingers. "Jonah's Liza and my mother's cousin. She came back to guide me on some personal quest the women in her pack undertook. Something to do with their old rituals and customs. Sadly, she left without giving me details."

"All First women have to go on a journey to discover their wolf."

"Can't say I've had much luck yet." I leaned my shoulder against the back of the sofa. "Assuming I buy this, how does that explain why I can't shift? If my mother was genetically close to the First Ones, shouldn't I take to being a wolf like kids take to dirt?"

He leaned in and kissed me. The kind of kiss that was made up of a fleeting contact between our lips, but would stay in my mind for years to come.

"Much about the First Ones hasn't made it into the books, but we do know that it was the Moon Promise that forced the first shift." He curled a lock of my hair around his finger, his mouth only an inch away. "Even now, that pact has power. Especially on you."

I stiffened, at once entranced by his gaze and paralyzed by his words.

His hand gripped the back of my neck. "You won't shift until you promise your future to a wolf under the full moon."

My vision zoomed in on his lips, then pivoted, blurred, turned upside down. I tore myself away from his face and took a deep swig of wine. "The Moon Promise is archaic and evil. It's why Dad can't move on with his life even after all these years."

"I assume your parents had little choice. Without the Moon Promise, your mother wouldn't have been able to shift and display dominance, but she needed both to rule by your father's side."

There it was. My mother's life explained. The mystery gone. This was what Dad wanted me to understand.

All the while I'd been consumed by the possibility I might be too human. At one point, I'd assumed there might be a psychological defect. Not once had I considered…this.

Shit, this was insane.

I opened the book and let the pages cascade through my fingers, an oddly calming sensation. "My mother never got a chance to stand on her own two feet. The minute she got out from under her father's control, she had to bind herself to my dad. That sucks."

Drake tucked a strand of my hair behind my ear. "She entered into the Moon Promise because she loved your dad. If she hadn't, the ritual wouldn't have worked."

The sparse candlelight softened Drake's features. Most times, he was sexy, or annoying, or both. Right now, he was beautiful.

"What is it?" His lips twitched.

"Your eyes."

"I have two. They're gray."

I rewarded his attempt to cheer me up with a weak smile. "Sometimes they look like mercury. Right now, they're storm clouds."

"I don't speak female. Is that good or bad?"

"I like the way they run through all the shades of the spectrum. It's definitely hot."

He waggled his eyebrows. "Through all fifty shades of gray, you mean?"

"Yeah." My smile quickly waned. "So I have to take a Moon Promise before I…"

"Yes."

The chocolates stood untouched on the table, a travesty, yet amid the twirling and wrenching inside my stomach, they wouldn't stay long.

My dreams of being the single ruling alpha of my pack—shattered.

Ten minutes ago, my attitude verged on the line between what-the-heck and who-cares? Wine, chocolates—I was allowed to enjoy romance without appearing weak or dependent. But in my case, romance might lead to commitment, and then to much worse.

Drake's revelation, if true, meant I was strong by genes, but weak by birth. No one saw my DNA, but my shortcomings were all too plain.

"It isn't fair." My tone wavered. "I always hoped I'd one day run free, as I'm meant to, but no one warned me the trade-off would be to give up my freedom and submit to a male."

"Loving someone doesn't mean you submit to them." Drake pressed the heel of his hand against his temple. "The Moon Promise isn't about conflict between men and women, but about a compromise. The First Woman gave up some of her human freedoms, like the First Man gave up some of his. Each gained from the other. Voluntary submission, not enforced subjugation. What's a little compromise compared to eternal love?"

"Eternal love is dangerous. When one dies—"

"The love remains. Your father still mourns your mother, but does he regret committing his future to her?"

I blinked down the heat behind my eyes. "No."

Drake lifted my chin with the crook of his finger. "Don't you want to feel the wind rushing through your fur, to run free, or put idiots in their place through your dominance? Don't you want to be the alpha you were born to be?"

"More than anything."

"Then…" He shrugged as if the solution was so obvious an idiot would grasp it.

The problem wasn't "getting it." The problem was accepting it.

"Have you met alpha-capable males?" I scoffed. "They're idiots. Interested in power and intrigue and putting women in their place. Submission, subjugation—they don't care about semantics."

"No offense taken."

I shot him a lop-sided grin. "Sorry, I didn't mean you. Or, you know what, actually I do. From the minute we met, you were in my face."

"It's a pretty face."

"You know what I mean." But heat flooded my cheeks regardless.

He stroked my arm. "We found a balance, didn't we? We haven't argued in, what, at least twenty minutes. Maybe that means something. And next week *is* the full moon."

I tilted my head, emboldened by his transparent hint. "Oh really? What, are you applying for the position?"

"Of being your mate? I don't know. Do you offer medical?"

"If you mean bruises when you piss me off and pull your alpha crap on *me*, then sure."

"Fair enough."

I grinned, but under his unchanging look, my smile faltered. "Hang on, are we really talking about this?"

"You know I've fallen for you, don't you?"

Christ almighty, my heart skipped. A right old lurch into my throat with enough force to jiggle my brain. Worse, a rush of giddiness shot straight into my head to join the quake.

We'd been flirting for a while, sure, and he had saved my life, and I his, but was that love? Hardly. My need to remain close by his side, was *that* love? Or the way his dominance had filled and protected me. Was *that* love?

He massaged my hand, keeping his gaze level, waiting, expecting.

I opened my mouth, inhaled sharply. "I didn't know."

"How could you not? I'm a simple, straight-forward guy."

He was certainly that. And his confession wasn't a total shock. Many times, I'd wondered, hoped…

"I'm not good with this." I wiggled my free hand from me to him. "Relationships. Feelings."

"Considering you grew up having to find new ways to prove yourself every day, I'm not surprised. But you don't have to prove yourself to me." He curled his hand around my neck and drew me close. "And I'm not trying to make you do anything. I merely wanted to get it out there."

He blew against my ear, his scent filled my nose and mouth, and somehow his presence even affected my breathing, which became fast and shallow.

"My mate will one day rule the German pack alongside me." I rested my head against his to soak him into me. "You'd have to move. Leave Jonah."

I really said that. As if this were real, as if Drake and I would actually—

"My German needs polishing, but I'll go wherever you go. I'll do anything if it means you'll finally be mine." He claimed my mouth in one swift, passionate move.

His kiss nearly snatched all thought from my head, but I found the strength to turn away. The striped throw pillow I picked up would have made a useful temporary wall, but instead of shoving it between us, I pressed it into my lap and clung to it. Could I be happy belonging to someone?

My whole life, I'd fought for my independence. Giving it up felt like…giving up.

I glanced up at the glistening lips of the man who'd won me with his strength and slayed me with his compassion. Could I abandon this important part of myself for him? The part that had kept me fighting for my rightful place in my pack?

"Where's your head, princess?"

My heart seemed an ill-equipped organ to make such a life-changing decision.

His lips stretched into a wide smile. "It's because I said you were going to be mine, isn't it?"

I closed my eyes and leaned into him again, wrapping myself in his scent. "How did you know?"

He playfully bit my earlobe. "I might not be able to predict what you're going to do at any given minute, but you're not as mysterious as you think."

"I don't know if I should be insulted."

"I'm saying I want to spend the rest of my life with you, feeling the way I do now. You know, head over heels, pounding heart…"

I checked. It was thumping a steady rhythm under my palm, just as he said. "What you're suggesting, that's not an easy decision to make."

"I'm used to life on my terms, too, and handing the keys over to someone else terrifies me. And one day moving to a different country to help you rule a pack? Scares the shit out of me. But you know what's worse? Not being with you."

The Moon Promise, we learned as children, was a mutual pact. A two-way street. How could I have overlooked that? If I went through with this, Drake was going to be my mate, my life and my soul.

At long last, a genuine smile worked its way onto my lips. "You'd be mine. Interesting. Very interesting."

He chuckled. "I bleed heart for you, and you go on a power trip. Figures."

I kissed his cheek. "You're right. I'm in love with you.

Remember that, because I'll be too self-absorbed to say it as often as you deserve."

"I'll remind you." He took my hand. "Is that a yes?"

Oh jeez. It all came down to one question. Could I imagine life without him?

I glanced at the candle, for no reason other than to avoid looking at him. "That's a yes."

TWENTY-SEVEN

MY HANDS WERE CLAMMY, AND I couldn't remember the last time I'd taken a free breath, unencumbered by tight lungs. Tonight, the full moon was going to change my life.

Once we'd made the decision to commit, we didn't have sex. Instead, we talked. Really talked. About how losing Raven had hurt him. About what a good guy Buck had been—needy, yes, but also helpful. About the changes that lay ahead. And then I'd spent the night, and every night for the past week, in his arms.

Just the two of us, stripped bare of all pretenses. No more werewolf games. No challenges. No sex.

How we'd survived was a miracle.

By day, I threw myself into the preparations for the Moon Festival, which was slated for three days after the full moon. That was the sacrifice I made in order to keep my mind off Drake's naked chest. Jonah's gratitude went unspoken, but not unnoticed. The little things he did made his feelings clear enough, like the way he confided in me about his growing affection for Natalie, or the fact that he added my name to the Moon Festival committee's call sheet.

All mysteries had been solved. Liza had sent me on my journey in the most cryptic way, and she'd been right not to elaborate. My way forward lay mapped out in front of me, designed by my own hand. One day, I might do the same for my daughter. Would I run into Liza again? Maybe. Maybe not. Either way, she'd done her part. Wherever she was, I hoped she'd find happiness, too.

As for me, the wait to start my new life was finally over.

We'd kept busy today, Drake and I. We'd cooked a meal together, took a walk through my mother's old camp, and did about a hundred other things that didn't involve the words *moon* or *promise*.

By nine o'clock, I was jittery as hell and an emotional wreck. Drake took my hand and gave me that look that just about obliterated my thoughts. "The moon's ripe, and so are we."

Clutching a blanket in his free hand, he led me out of the cottage and into the woods.

"You know what?" I stumbled after him. "I didn't tell my dad. Doesn't he deserve to hear the good news? This decision will affect him, too."

"Call him tomorrow. Now quit stalling."

Darkness shrouded the world, save for the silver moonbeams that cast weak shadows around us. The temperature had dropped to a tolerable level, but the most stunning aspect of this location, one I'd failed to appreciate before, was the scent around us. The soft, satisfying fragrance of freshly carved wood piggybacked onto the herbal tang of cut grass.

A smell more like home couldn't be found on this planet.

"Where are we going?" I kept pace with Drake, not without sneaking a glance at his ass.

I'd developed a mild obsession with it—no surprise after our self-imposed celibacy—but it wasn't the only part of his body I wanted to sink my teeth into. And before the night was out, I'd do exactly that.

We headed to a large patch of grass surrounded by a circle of trees.

Here, he spread the blanket and grinned. That guy didn't have cold feet in the least.

I glanced at the picnic blanket that wasn't going to be used for any picnic. "So we're doing this, huh?"

He kissed me, sensually and languidly, exploiting my temporary loss of reason to rid me of my clothes. Then he removed his. A mere formality without seduction. Naked, we stood in each other's arms and let the breeze caress us.

"Last chance," he whispered. "We can wait if this is happening too soon for you. There will be more full moons after tonight."

The feel of his skin under my palm calmed and excited me in equal measures. "I'd considered finding someone, someone I didn't hate, one day, but that wasn't supposed to happen for a long time. You messed up my plan."

He rested his arms on my shoulder and regarded me with an air of mischief. "I bet it was a good plan. You probably have a diagram on the wall of your office."

"It's color coded, too."

"But now that I'm here..." He tilted his head.

"Yes. Now that you're here..."

We stood, separate in our nakedness but united in our decision.

He gently nudged me back to look at me. "Don't be scared, 'kay?"

"Who says I'm scared?"

Actually, the tremble in my voice said it pretty clearly.

Drake tightened his jaw, and then leaned forward until our foreheads touched. "Sweet Kensi. My love is yours, and with it, my future. I will foreswear all others, from now until eternity. You are my true and rightful mate forever, and this I swear by the moon."

The wind didn't blow. The trees didn't rustle. Where was the resistance against his words? The objections to keep him at arm's length?

None remained. For the first time in my life, my doubts were silent.

"Sweet Drake. My love is yours, and with it, my future. I will foreswear all others, from now until eternity. You are my true and rightful mate forever." I inhaled deeply, not to play for time, but to make sure my voice wouldn't break. "And this I swear by the moon."

Our breaths came strong, fast.

He straightened, and traced my lips with his thumb. "You're shivering."

Understatement. I was a walking rattle. My entire body had turned into a cabinet assembly kit without the screws. "You're surprised? This is a big deal. Plus, it's actually a little cold, when only this morning it was over a hundred degrees. Oh, and I'm naked."

"That you are." He lowered himself onto the blanket and beckoned for me to join him. "Now stop panicking. And you'll get used to the weather around here. It changes faster than your moods."

I kneeled by his side and shoved him. "Your seduction technique sucks."

He kissed me gently, while at the same time, reclining me onto my back. The touch of his lips and the play of his tongue took away the shakes and infused me with an entirely different energy.

Then he cupped my face with his hands. "Are you going to take over again tonight, or are you going to trust me?"

"Trust you with what?"

"Your heart." He slid one hand down my body and observed its journey along my curves. "Don't get me wrong. I love it when you're in charge. It's none of the work and twice the reward. But I don't want you to use sex to put up walls between us."

"I won't." I slung my hands around his neck and coaxed him fully on top of me. "See?"

His frame didn't only warm my skin, it also pushed heat into spots that lay far, far deeper.

For another moment, we kissed and nothing else. Our hands

didn't wander, our legs didn't move. This moment was all about his weight on me, the feel of his mouth, and about teasing wet kisses that made my core vibrate.

He parted my lips, paved the way for his tongue. Flashes of lightning coursed through me, and it was at that moment that the full impact of our decision dawned on me. This bliss, this unerring knowledge that my world was in kilter and I'd never want for love or affection again, would be inscribed into my soul. More permanent than the tattoo on Drake's arm. My obstinacy, my neuroses, my guilty pleasures—he'd uncover each in time, just as I'd learn his quirks, in the glow of eternal love.

When we separated, Drake's eyes, almost entirely silver tonight, watched. Not watched, communicated. And his unspoken words made the heat pool into my cheeks. His next kiss was fluid, a tender touch that sent a flutter through my stomach. It flipped a switch that made my legs open, and he swiftly arranged himself between them.

He was primed, ready to go, yet he slid his hand along my breast, my waist, my hip with languid certainty. Our fingers scouted each other's shapes, each bump and each kink receiving special attention.

I was getting wetter by the minute, but wasn't prepared to beg for him.

Yet.

"Say when you're ready, princess."

Even at this stage, hard as a rock, he remained attentive. Nudging, not pushing. Suggesting, not forcing.

My skin hummed under his exploration, and my hips squirmed for him.

A crack ripped through the air. I froze. "What was that?"

"The woods." He smiled. "You've lived in the city for too long."

The tension flowed from my shoulders. "Yeah. Guess I'll have to get used to living in the woods again."

"Don't worry. I'll turn you into a yokel like me in no time." He peppered soft kisses across my neck.

I sighed, but in a way to let him know I was relishing his attention. Drake had learned my secret spots, and he used his knowledge with lethal precision. His hands grazed where lightness sent a shiver down my back. Rubbed where pressure brought stars to my eyes.

Finally, my body melted into an ocean of lava, hungry to claim him. My need for my mate tipped into a yearning that shook my soul.

I seized his shoulder, buried my hand in his hair, slid my heel up along his leg. My need for him was too great, too urgent to leave the pace up to him. I wanted him now. No more delays. He drew me closer, skin against skin, feeding off my mouth with a hunger that wouldn't be sated. Never again would we go our separate ways. We'd spend every free moment in our embrace, where the firmness of his chest made my heart gallop, and the feel of his length promised a bliss no other man could.

"I'm ready," I whispered. And I so was. The heat between my legs pulsed like a beacon, guiding him.

"Thank God." He grabbed my knee, slid his shaft along my wet nub, then drove into me.

The force with which he entered me stopped my lungs. My mouth opened for a moan. Within the flicker of a flame, he'd slid out and pumped back in.

So fast. No reaction time. Mind blown.

"You're testing my sanity." I breathed in his scent, all freshness and sweat and arousal.

"Sanity's overrated." He kept me between his elbows and used his legs and butt to thrust back in, probing, searching.

A delicious thump here, a teasing blow there kept me in a state of constant arousal. No let-up. No break. Move after move, he honed in on my spot.

Another near miss, and I prodded his hip, shifted aside. I had to get on top, guide him—

A moan ripped through my lungs. And another, as he struck bull's eye again.

"Found it then?" He chuckled.

I arched my back. "Ye-es."

He built up a new rhythm, unhurried now, calculated, and with devastating aim.

"Don't stop." My voice quivered. "God. Don't stop."

I dug my nails into his back, couldn't let go. This was better. Oh hell. Much better than calling the shots.

"You've no idea how this feels." His voice was labored, his forehead wet.

"Yes, I do." I wiped his brow, while waves of bliss melted my lower half. "If only I'd known…"

He gave a triumphant grin and bent my knees sideways to open me further.

His girth spread my walls, bumped my spot, while his length massaged my clit, until I was a sweaty, trembling mess. The exquisite ache in my core toyed with my sense of self, as nothing I'd ever known existed anymore. Just he and I, under the full moon. I snapped for air, clenched my thighs around him, drew him into me until his balls squished against me. If I could, I'd take them in, too, anything to have him fill me to the brink.

He firmed his hand around my thigh. "My show, so take it easy."

"Are you freaking kidding me?" But I relaxed against the sensations until I was awash with the whirl of breathless anticipation. Any minute now, I'd die the sweetest of deaths, or would bear witness to something truly religious.

The tingles rushed into the deepest reaches of my mind. I lifted my head for a kiss. He rocked his hips, gave me nothing I wanted yet all I needed, when finally, we reached perfect sync. He moved his mouth across my body to my breast. Sparks fired on the surface of my skin, in the deepest cells of my core. The to and fro left room for nothing but the staggering heights he pushed me to.

"Oh mm-hmm," I mumbled repeatedly, too far out of my mind to even form words.

Sway by sway, the tension amplified until finally, loudly, almost painfully, I came undone. I rode my orgasm with my legs locked around him. Seconds became moments. More thuds thrust into me, and Drake's shoulders tautened under my hands. He grunted deep, once, twice, then all but collapsed on top of me, spent.

The breeze licked the parts of my skin that weren't protected by him. The cool air dried my face and brought oxygen to my overworked lungs.

At long last, I slid my rubbery legs onto the ground and spread my arms as my muscles turned to water.

Drake lifted his head. "Still alive?"

I mm-hmm-ed. "That was quite something."

"Hell yeah. Can I assume the country lad pleased the princess?"

"Are you kidding? Your moves should be patented. You'd make a killing."

"How about we keep them our secret?" The tenderness in his voice nearly brought me to tears.

This surge of emotion, this love I felt for him, was alien and yet familiar. Shit. I was totally whipped.

I wrapped my arms around him and held him tight. "By the way, I see you more as the stable boy."

"Whatever gets you off." He buried his nose and chin in the crook of my neck.

My mate. Drake of all people was my mate.

Who'd have thought?

TWENTY-EIGHT

WE LAY UNDER THE TREES' canopy, the swollen moon high above us, legs and arms intertwined. Our sweat-soaked bodies still trembled from exertion.

I placed my hand on his chest. "They say the only time a man thinks clearly are the five minutes after he comes. The one time he's not scheming to get a woman into bed. So how about it? Are you regretting taking the Moon Promise?"

His heart pounded with force. Good. I had no intention of losing him to a heart murmur. Or ever.

His eyes shimmered almost as bright as the moon. "With my thoughts clear, I promise you I'm not. I love you." His expression shifted into pensive. "Of course the next time I say these words, I'll be trying to get you into bed again."

"Not the worst prospect, but here's the small print." I patted his cheek. "If I agree to have sex with you more or less whenever you want, you'd better work your ass off to make me enjoy it."

"For someone who's subjugated herself, you have a pretty big mouth."

"Submitted. Voluntarily. Temporarily." I grinned. "Besides, isn't a big mouth an asset in a woman?"

"I hope it will turn out in my favor, yes."

We interlocked hands and let the breeze tickle our bodies. I'd never had sex outside before. Going by this occasion, it wouldn't be the last time. Being one with nature had intensified my link with Drake. The freedom and total abandon of our joining built into a physical and mental climax like no other.

I swiveled my head to the moon. "I feel more connected to you, but physically, nothing has changed. What if it didn't work?" I closed my eyes. "What if you've promised your future to a useless dud?"

"You'll never be useless to me. If nothing happens, then nothing happens. But give it time. I don't know if the shift is meant to be immediate. Maybe you have to wait until the next full moon."

I blew a raspberry. "Waiting sucks."

"You know you can never tell anyone you're a direct descendant of the First Ones. If other werewolves hear about this, they might try to get to you."

"Why?"

"To make babies with you."

"I'm mated to you now."

"And I'll protect you any way I know how." He placed his hands over my mouth. "Even if you are perfectly capable of kicking ass yourself, I know." His *kicking ass* came as a poor imitation of my voice.

My stomach rumbled without sound and tightened into a dense ball. I should have had a few of the chocolates Drake kept around the house for me.

Man might live off air and love alone, but woman won't. At least not this one.

"What about Jonah? Shouldn't he know?"

"Definitely not."

"He's your alpha. Your friend." I dug the heel of my hand into my stomach, pushing the cramp down.

"And I wish him all the best and will serve him as a protector until we leave. But *you* are my mate."

Pain exploded in my core, forcing me into a ball. Black and white flashes burst before my eyes as an unbearable burn decimated my nervous system.

"Kensi?" Drake's muffled voice barely grazed me.

My throat twisted, my tongue swelled to twice its size. I turned onto the side to force myself onto my hands and knees, but my knees were gone.

How? Dreams disappeared, chocolates did, but knees?

Another wave of agony rippled through me. I moaned, too weak for a scream.

"Let it happen, Kensi. Breathe. Come on."

Why the fuck was he so calm?

"Help me." But my words weren't words. More a yap or a whine.

"Breathe, baby. That's all you have to do. Nature will take care of the rest."

Drake seemed confident, so I breathed.

My jaw clenched, stretched until I could no longer feel my lips, and I breathed.

Thousands of needles jammed into my skin, making my eyes water, and still I breathed.

Despite the moon giving off ample light, colors disappeared from view. Yellows blurred into greens, orange into reds, and my field of vision broadened. Most pronounced were the grays. Each helm of grass, each line of a tree's bark, came into focus. Then, finally, the pain subsided.

"There you go. You've done it." Drake kneeled before me, in all his naked glory, and ruffled my neck. "And you're such a beautiful wolf."

I was a wolf.

Shit.

I was an actual wolf.

I lifted my hand, covered in brown and white fur, then placed it back down. I shifted my weight from left to right, testing out the pads underneath.

Springy.

I did a combination of left hand, right hand. *'See that?'* I yapped.

Drake laughed. "You're getting the hang of it already."

A song drifted from deeper inside the woods, a siren's call, luring me. I'd heard it first when I was a toddler playing in the forest with imaginary fairies and nymphs, and I'd put it down to an overactive imagination. But maybe this song was part of being a werewolf.

I stared into the gray of the first line of trees, then into the black beyond.

"Go on." He shooed. "Run free."

I swiveled back to my mate, his voice no less enticing than the music tickling the leaves.

"I'll be right behind you."

My thank you became a happy bark. Not speaking was going to be a downside. That much I could tell already.

I kinked my head at the man I loved. Of course, I didn't need vocal chords to communicate how I felt about him.

"What's wrong? Don't you want to?"

I lapped my long tongue across his face, slobber and all. Then I turned and ran, driven by my mate's soft laughter and pulled in by the trees' melody.

My toes spread out, my feet bounced off the ground, and I leaped across a branch. Skidded. Ran on. A log stretched across my path up ahead. I took aim. Timed my jump. And cleared it with bags to spare.

A shadow moved to my right. I tumbled to a stop. A small creature, a rabbit maybe, or a squirrel. I sniffed the air.

Gamey.

Delicious.

I stalked toward the bush where it had disappeared. Disturbed the leaves with my nose.

The damn thing broke away, zigging here, zigging there. I chased after it, across rockier terrain, tongue out, doing everything a wolf should do.

The distance between us grew. My lungs pumped hard, but my legs didn't tire. If only I could run a little faster, get a little closer.

Drake's wolf cut off its escape route. The squirrel zigged when it should have zagged. I snapped at it, caught its tail.

Full force, I smashed it against the ground. Repositioned it in my mouth. Clamped my teeth shut and crushed its tiny body in my jaws until it stopped jerking and its blood ran down my throat.

Heart pounding, I stood, waiting for my mate to approach. He stepped up and licked my face. *'Well done.'*

I placed the corpse onto the ground and stared at it. What now? I was hungry. I'd caught food. The one thing missing was the connection from one to the other.

Drake nudged closer.

I snapped my head up. *'My kill. Back off.'*

He took a step back and pounded with his front legs on the ground.

His communication skills were the worst. Was he doing a happy dance? Did he have a splinter in his paw?

He fixed one end of a branch to the ground with his feet, and yanked on the other end with his teeth.

Got it.

I placed my front paw on the creature's body and pulled at it until its delicate body split. My stomach growled, and I finally gave into my hunger.

The animal tasted like it had smelled, but its bony frame didn't yield much meat. When only its cracked skeleton was left, I licked my lips and stepped aside.

Drake approached cautiously. He nuzzled under my jaw, and I could feel my ears pricking sideways. So weird.

I lifted my head to give him better access, and he rubbed his throat against mine. If I could purr, I would, but the sound I made was best described as a content growl.

My insides cramped, and I jerked away from Drake.

Shit. Maybe I should have stuck to rabbit. Or chocolate. Squirrel would challenge anyone's stomach.

Another sharp ache raced across my body. My arms, legs, mouth twisted as something ripped me into every which direction. Why was this happening? If I'd taken my time. Eased myself into being a wolf. Because this—

I curled up on the ground, weak, trembling with pain. Drake had got it wrong. Something inside me was skewed, something so hideously defective, I couldn't hold my animal form.

"It's okay." Drake's voice soothed me through the fits. He'd pulled me onto his lap and stroked my head with even movements.

Invisible bullets bounced through my drained body, but I was too wiped to even react to the pain.

"What's wrong with me?" I wiped a tear from my cheek.

"Nothing's wrong with you. The first time is painful and short. It gets easier, I promise."

The moonlight illuminated Drake's smooth chest, made his tattoos curl like ropes and chains across his bicep. With his help, I tilted his head down so I could kiss him, just for a second. A glorious second.

Squirrel-taste and all.

"Was it like that for you?" I asked. "Painful?"

"Yes and no. My change didn't hurt that much, but then I come from a long line of late-generation werewolves. Your genes belong at least fifty percent to the past, when shifting was still a new experience for human bodies." He guided me up until I sat on his lap. "But I didn't hold my animal shape longer than you did first time around."

"Do you think my mom's changes were even worse?"

He slid his hand up my bare leg and thigh, brushing off dirt and plant matter where he found it. "Possibly."

I wrapped my arms around his neck and breathed him in. It would never have occurred to me that, one day, I'd find a scent homier than that of the woods, but here it was, clinging to every one of his pores.

"Are you going to be in trouble for not letting Jonah in on your plan for the Moon Promise?"

"No. Love isn't something an alpha can rule over." He swept my hair aside, and stroked my shoulder. "A father on the other hand…"

"I told you I should have called him." I grinned into his neck. "Worried my dad is going to tar and feather you for defiling his only daughter?"

"Worried? No. Terrified? Absolutely. Your father commands an army. I command a four-slice toaster."

"Guess we'll see."

"Not sure I care for your casual attitude toward my life."

I lifted my head and locked onto his gaze. "I'll protect you."

"Phew."

"Besides, the Moon Promise comes without a return policy, so your life is very important to me. I only hope my dad feels the same way."

"Aaand the terror is back."

"He'll love you. How can he not? You're adorable." I giggled and smooshed his cheeks between my fingers. "Besides, he's been after me for getting a mate. Once or twice he even mentioned how much he'd like a moon son. I always thought he was a romantic, when all along he'd known I needed to take the Moon Promise."

"Okay. But do me a favor."

"What?"

"Don't tell him I'm adorable."

"Deal. And you'll tell your brother about the mating tomorrow?"

"Um, sure."

"What, you don't want to?" I gave him my most badass stare. "Ashamed of me already?"

"He kind of already knows. Once I heard the cops were looking for me, I went by his place. We talked and your name came up."

"I still don't get—"

"He asked me if, once my name had been cleared, I'd track you down in Chicago. I said I'd make you mine the minute I was a free man." He held my chin firmly in his hand and smiled like an Olympic medalist.

"You decided my future without asking?" I narrowed my eyes, then slapped his shoulder for good measure. "You didn't think I should get a say in this?"

"Of course I was going to ask you."

"What if I'd said no?"

"I'd have compelled you with my dominance."

I slapped him again, harder. "Watch it."

"I'm kidding." He laughed. "Hell, of course I'm kidding."

"You'd better be."

"Look at that." He winced. "You've found *your* dominance."

I nearly fell off his lap, but he caught me in time. Wow, he was right. The hole he'd previously filled with his own power brimmed with familiar strength. It was a solid force, and I flexed it like a muscle.

Drake grimaced again.

How much could he take without unleashing his own power?

"Don't push it." Drake lifted my chin toward him. "Don't push *me*."

"All this, it's new." I stowed it away, folded it like a blanket, then I curled up tight in his lap. "Sorry."

"It's okay. In a weird S&M way, it's quite pleasant." He wrapped me into his arms to share his warmth with me.

"I have a better idea." I slipped off his lap, got up, and quickly took two steps away from him. "Aren't you curious?"

He got on all fours, and even in his human form, the wolf in him was all too evident.

I beckoned with my finger over my shoulder and strode, hurried, then ran toward the house.

He chased me for a while, even though he could have so easily caught me.

The black of the forest morphed into grays as I exited into the clearing within the circle of trees. The blanket lay crumpled on the ground. Still running, I swerved left, but Drake snaked his arm around my waist and yanked me back.

"I think I know what you had in mind." He turned me in his arms and moved his face close to mine, gaze fixed on my lips.

"Took you long enough." I smiled and leaned in for the kiss.

He softly pulled me down onto the blanket and covered me with his weight.

I had been so wrong about so many things. I wasn't a dud. Drake wasn't a bully. And the Moon Promise wasn't an inevitable end, but only the beginning.

THE END

About The Author

USA Today Bestselling author Carmen Fox lives in the south of England with her beloved tea maker and a stuffed sheep called Fergus. She's an award-winning writer of urban fantasy with heart and sassitude, and loves meeting her readers.

Read More from Carmen Fox

http://www.carmen-fox.com

Guarded – The Silverton Chronicles, Bk. 1

July 2015
Sexy Urban Fantasy Mystery

When everyone's existence depends on the lies they tell, trust doesn't come easy.

Ivy's neighbors have a secret. They aren't human. But Ivy has a secret, too. She knows. As long as everyone keeps quiet, she's happy working as a P.I. by day and chillaxing with her BFF Florian, a vampire, by night. When a routine pickup drops her in the middle of a murder, her two worlds collide.

While Florian knows how to throw a punch, deep down he's a softie. His idea of scary? Running out of hair product. It's time Ivy faced facts. Even with a vampire on stand-by, one gal can only kick so many asses.

For help, she must put her faith in others. A human, who might just be the one. A demon, who will, for a price, open the doors to her heritage. And a werewolf, who wants to protect her from herself.

Torn between these men, Ivy must tread carefully, because one wants her heart, one wants her body, and one wants her dead.

Divide And Conquer – Champions Of Elcnia, Bk. 1

November 2018
Urban Fantasy

Prophecies suck. Catapulted into a do-or-die fight to save a magical kingdom, Lea Daniels would give her comic book collection for a step-by-step survival guide. Instead, the physicist must entrust her future to Nieve, a woman with kick-ass powers that seem to defy the laws of nature.

Jaded warrior Nieve isn't thrilled either about her new role as a mentor to a "chosen one" who can't tell a sword from a hairbrush.

Together, the mismatched duo must protect the world from the conquering ambitions of a cut-throat king. The good news is they're not alone. The bad news is that, as former foes assemble to take a stand by their side, it soon becomes clear everyone has an agenda.